DEEP IN THE SLAVE-DENS

"You're a magician!" Lothar gasped.

The Mooncrow smiled. His psithe-sword gleamed whitely as he melted the shackles on Lothar's wrist. "Quickly!" he urged.

The two men raced through the tunnel. They passed a guard and before he could raise the alarm Lothar lifted him...

"It's been too long since last I slew a Moldorn," the redbeard grunted with pleasure as he dashed the guard's skull against the tunnel wall.

"Strike a bargain with me," the Mooncrow laughed, "and you'll have the chance to slay many!"

The all-new heroic adventure
in the great CONAN tradition!

MOONCROW
JACK MASSA

A BERKLEY BOOK
published by
BERKLEY PUBLISHING CORPORATION

MOONCROW

A Berkley Book / published by arrangement with
the author

PRINTING HISTORY
Berkley edition / December 1979

For information address: Berkley Publishing Corporation,
200 Madison Avenue, New York, New York 10016.

ISBN: 0-425-04287-1

A BERKLEY BOOK® TM 757,375

PRINTED IN THE UNITED STATES OF AMERICA

To M.
For making
the future
desirable.

Chapter 1.
WARSHIPS IN THE CLOUDS

And the children of Ibor did traffic with the Evil One and learned the secrets of his power. And they built upon the Earth fortresses tall as mountains and ships that sailed the air and rained brimstone on their enemies.

> —Brother Kuthemes,
> Chronicles of Tann and Ibor
> 107 New Calendar
> (Norrling Year 8182)

The evidence is irrefutable: at the very height of the Glacial Ages, while the rest of the Earth wallowed in barbarism and superstition, the peoples of the Iboran Continent rediscovered ancient science, and developed a technology capable of producing both incendiary weapons and a form of dirigible aircraft.

> —Ivann Demmering,
> Anomalies of History
> 1370 New Calendar

AT THE HOUR when the airships first appeared over Telyrra, the Grand Duke and his court were watching the performance of a magician. The magician called himself Teron the Mysterious, although in his own country, where wizards bore the names of birds, he was known by the less distinguished title of Teron the Magpie.

Teron performed beneath a canopy of leaves and roses, in an unwalled roof garden near the top of the Grand Duke's palace. Tall and slender, he stood before an oaken table, clad in tunic and scarlet cape, black hair confined by a jeweled headband. Typically for his race, Teron's face was long and thin, eyes metallic gray, skin a swarthy gray color. Teron's people were the Ombernorrs, a mutant race inhabiting the remote north.

Nearby a blond, bearded minstrel named Topiedeon strummed chords on an ivory-worked mandolin. To this accompaniment Teron's long, deft fingers manipulated a

1

sphere of energy—which he called a *psithe*—transmuting its formlessness into various shapes: a wand the size of a quarterstaff that floated in the air, a silver cup full of water, a sword with a bluish moonlight glow.

Recumbent on cushioned benches in the shade of pines and flowered trellises, the Telyrran nobles displayed their approval with languid applause. Bedecked in loose robes of silks and brocades, they tasted sherbets, sipped iced wines, and enjoyed the balmy summer breeze that blew in from the sea.

The magician stood at the garden's edge, and behind him a bank of lofty clouds hovered over the city's blue harbor. The harbor was crowded with ships—triremes and caravels, galleons and zebecs—for the Isle of Telyrra was a rich and prosperous trading center, the crossroads of three continents. And yet Teron, whose bleak homeland lay at the very edge of a northern glacier, felt strangely at home in the cosmopolitan atmosphere of the island.

He made the psithe into a large silver disk that appeared to be stamped in the image of anyone who looked on it. He showed the disk to the white-haired Grand Duke, saying it bore the visage of the world's most noble ruler.

Duke Kenerese chuckled. "You've been in my house only a month, magician, and already you flatter like the most accomplished of courtiers."

Teron smiled. "We of the bitter north must of necessity learn things quickly, my lord." He bowed and turned to Adria, the daughter of the Duke and the heiress to his throne. "But look, lady, the disk has changed. From the image of the most noble ruler to that of the most lovely woman."

Adria, her pale hair crowned by a chaplet of lilacs, smiled and took the disk from Teron's fingers. "May I keep it, magician?"

The smile froze on the Magpie's lips. To give away the disk was to give away the psithe—and the psithe, the life-essence of an actual magpie, was the source of his magic.

Teron was discomfitted only a moment though and

then he bowed graciously. "Regretfully, lady, if kept long from my hands the disk would revert to a formless condition. But if you permit I shall make a disk of gold that will hold your image and not dissolve."

The magician walked back to his table. "I shall make the disk from a rose," he said, and plucked a bloom from the trellis.

Topiedeon the minstrel caught the heightened mood and strummed faster, producing an eerie tune.

Teron laid the rose on the table and held the psithe-disk over it with both hands. He closed his eyes and uttered an incantation several times in an ancient, magical tongue.

"Behold!" he said, and a beam of light lanced from the psithe and fell on the rose, transforming it—or so it appeared—into a golden disk. "And behold." He held the gold disk aloft, showing that it bore the image of the Duke's daughter.

Enthusiastic applause started, but ended almost at once as Count Colpern, the Grand Duke's chief advisor, jumped to his feet and pointed at the sky.

"Look there!"

Teron whirled around as cries of astonishment rang through the garden. Emerging from the tall bank of clouds above the harbor were five black-hulled ships, floating hundreds of feet in the air.

For several moments no one spoke in the garden. Wars had raged intermittently on the Iboran continent to the south for more than a century. And lately the Telyrrans had heard reports of fabulous new weapons developed by the Empire of Moldorn—even to the creation of ships that sailed the sky. But that five such ships should be here, hundreds of sea miles from the nearest warring coast, came as an utter, devastating surprise.

Duke Kenerese conferred in hushed whispers with Count Colpern. The court was dismissed, except for the Duke's councillors who were to meet downstairs at once. Palace guards in chain mail hastened up to fill the battlements below the roof garden and the three watchtowers above. The Duke and his retinue hurried off down a balustraded marble staircase and beneath an arch. Most of the courtiers remained in the garden, eyes fixed on the airships, which had come to a stop hovering over the harbor.

Teron stood at the edge of the promontory, one sandaled foot resting on a half-buried merlon which dated from ancient days when the garden was walled with parapets. Between his gray fingers the disk glittered, silvery in the sunlight.

"Teron." Adria stood beside him.

Rumors concerning her relationship with the itinerant magician had been whispered about the court for a fortnight. But all attention now was settled on the airships, and no eyes noticed that she took his hand.

"Incredible," she murmured. "I wonder how it must feel to fly . . . I don't know whether to be afraid or just excited."

The Magpie's expression was gloomy. Months ago, aboardship, he'd heard a seaman describe an air attack on an Iboran harbor town. Metal-encased missles had dropped from the ships, bursting into gouts of fire tall as galleons. The town had fallen in less than a day—half its population burned to death and the rest herded off in chains.

"I wouldn't be just excited," he muttered.

Adria objected. "But why should we assume the worst about the Moldorns? Any race that can create a ship that flies must surely be more than the cold-hearted pirates all the stories make them." She stared at the precisely aligned row of airships. "Besides, why would they attack Telyrra?"

"Why would they bring five warships on an unannounced social visit?"

"Now you have me worried," Adria said. "Let's go and hear the council."

Teron took a last glance at the warships, and had an impulse to make the psithe into its sword shape. But, turning away, he changed his mind and slipped the silver disk into a pocket of his tunic.

As they walked down the stairs Adria apologized for asking to keep the disk. "Though it's partly your fault," she said, "If you weren't so secretive about your magic I might have known better."

"But, dear lady," Teron replied, "mystery is the soul of my trade."

He wondered if she could detect the note of strain in his voice. Teron had resided in several great houses in his two years since leaving the north, but had found no court he liked so well as Kenerese's, and no country so genial to his spirit as Telyrra. The idea that the island might now be enslaved, the city destroyed, filled the magician's soul with apprehension and anger.

The seashell-encrusted council chamber was thronged with nobles and town officials, ambassadors from nearby islands, military men in chain mail and helms. The Grand Duke sat in a carved teak chair set upon a low, carpeted dais. The bronze doors were left open and Teron and Adria passed down the center aisle drawing only brief, distracted glances.

They sat in a corner beside an elaborately chiseled marble hearth. On the opposite wall a broad casement gave a clear view of the harbor, and Teron saw that one of the airships had detached itself from the file and was gliding toward the palace. He conferred with the man next to him, an orderly to one of the Telyrran admirals, and learned that the Moldorns had signaled by semaphore their commander's request for an audience with the Grand Duke. The commander, it turned out, was the Veglane Altazar, chief warlord of the Moldorn Empire.

The general of Telyrra's army, a black-bearded mercenary from the south named Pontes, was reporting on the state of the city's defenses. The land army was small, for Telyrra had always been a naval power; a strong fleet had always protected the island from invasion. But war galleys, of course, were of no use against ships that could fly.

Pontes noted that certain Tuvarian cities had staved off air attack by the use of giant crossbows. Unfortunately, there wasn't a single such weapon on the island, and the few catapults available lacked the range to even reach a flying ship.

Impatient, the Duke asked the general if the city could withstand an attack by the five Moldorn vessels. Pontes snorted and said that if the Moldorns had come fully armed, they could level the city by nightfall.

Teron sat scowling amid the clamor of voices that ensued. Beside him Adria maintained a mien of regal calm, but the magician could sense an agony of fear underneath.

Kenerese ordered that the chamber be cleared of all but a few advisors and guards. Adria insisted on staying. She was, after all, heiress to the throne. She insisted too that Teron be allowed to remain, claiming him as an advisor and personal friend. The Duke frowned at the magician, but allowed him to stay.

Meantime the single airship had glided closer, growing until its bulk nearly filled the casement. In size and shape it was like a large trireme, but instead of sails its hull was topped by an oblong bubble coated in gray metal, and instead of oars there was a tall tailpiece with three whirling propellers. A huge winged reptile was carved on the prow, and serpents painted along the three-tiered gunwales.

Then the airship passed out of view from the window to the palace roof, where the Moldorn emissaries would disembark. The council chamber was still, and Teron could hear the fanfare of a trumpet—which must have come from the Moldorns—as well as the clattering of chains which indicated the lowering of a gangplank from ship to parapet.

Moments later, three Moldorn officers were announced and marched with resounding bootsteps into the chamber. Tall, black-haired, mustached, they wore light-golden plate armor and dark blue capes. Elegant baldrics supporting sabers were slung over their shoulders, and each carried a pointed, plumed helmet beneath his left arm.

They approached the foot of the Duke's dais and all three drew their swords in a motion so quick and smooth that, though it was meant as a salute, several of the councillors flinched and a half-dozen guards leapt forward with halberds at the ready.

The Duke waved them back with an irritated gesture. The Moldorns sheathed their weapons in another fluid movement and then the man in the center stepped forward and made a deep bow.

"I am the Veglane Altazar." He spoke Tuvarian, the shared harbor tongue of the Capdian Sea region. "I assume it is my honor to address the Grand Duke Kenerese, Lord of Telyrra?"

"Correct." The Duke answered. "But I beg that we dispense with diplomatic niceties and speak plainly. You've led five warships into my realm, armed and ready for battle, or so I must assume. I want, first of all, to know your intentions, so I may know whether to greet you as a friend or foe."

The Veglane smiled. "I appreciate your bluntness, my lord, since my mission is also rather blunt. Whether we come as friends or foes depends entirely upon your ability to face the reality of your situation. For centuries your island has remained aloof from continental wars, protected by the sea. But that time is ended. The Empire of Moldorn has need of this island. Whether you join us as wealthy allies or conquered slaves means nothing to us..."

He was pacing back and forth, his gaze traveling about the room so as to confront all present. "You are correct in assuming that our airships are fully armed. Should we decide to attack, your city would be rubble and ashes in a matter of hours. Your sole alternative is to accept our terms of alliance. We are willing to allow your lordship to remain the sovereign of this island, but only on several conditions."

"I can see that tales of Moldorn arrogance are not exaggerated," the Duke said between his teeth.

The Veglane stepped toward the ducal chair. "We are the finest warriors in the world, and the most advanced civilization. We have a right to our arrogance. The conditions are as follows: First, you are to garrison three imperial legions and provide a suitable base for our air fleet. Second, you are to transfer to us the command of your armed forces and the disposition of your treasury."

"How dare you?" the Duke growled, pounding the arm of his chair. "Your terms are an insult."

The Veglane eyed him sourly. "I see that you need to be convinced of the desperateness of your situation.

Lieutenant." He gestured to one of his aides who stepped to the casement and, drawing a small flag from his baldric, signaled toward the airships floating above the harbor.

"Observe," Altazar said. "A small sample of our weaponry."

A projectile dropped from the underbelly of one of the airships. Falling, it made a brief whistling sound, then burst aflame on the deck of an anchored carrack. In a moment the ship was a mass of fires and roiling black smoke.

"The final condition," the Veglane announced, "is meant to insure the stable future of our alliance. The Grand Duke's heir"—he bowed to Adria—"who I assume to be this young lady, must become the legal consort of His Imperial Highness, the Crown Prince Ebbel Therion."

Adria turned pale, the corners of her mouth drawn back. The Duke trembled, face reddening with anger. But he glimpsed the burning carrack and squeezed his lips shut.

Teron the Magpie stared balefully at the Veglane. His impulse was to make the psithe a sword and to rush forward and bury it in the Moldorn's chest. But he checked himself. Such an attempt could not save Telyrra—and would probably cost his own life, since Altazar was reputed the greatest swordsman in Ibor.

The Veglane continued: "Those, Lord Duke, are our terms. You shall have until dawn tomorrow to think them over. After that we shall consider that a state of war exists between our two nations, and shall launch an attack more devastating than you can imagine."

The Veglane paused to allow his words to sink in, then bowed in unison with his officers. General Pontes took a step toward the Duke and Altazar, who had half-turned away, pointed at him sharply.

"That man, who I take it is a high-ranking military strategist to this court, is, I would guess, about to suggest that you take myself and my officers prisoner."

The general lowered his head, frowning angrily, and Altazar laughed. "I shall not insult your lordship's honor by implying that you might have considered the idea. But I shall inform you nonetheless that my ships have orders to raze the city and slaughter every soul in it should we fail to return within the hour. Good afternoon."

The Moldorns pivoted and marched from the room, leaving utter quiet in their wake. Adria rose and walked unsteadily to her father's chair. She spoke too softly for Teron to hear. The Duke sighed and shook his head woefully.

Teron, who had stood as Adria left him, sank down on the bench again. Intuitions told him there must be a way of saving Teryrra.

Or were they true intuitions and not mere wishes? Had he advanced higher in the 640-stage avian ranks of the Norrling wizards, Teron doubtless would have been able to tell. But being a Magpie, a mere fledgling, he was as helpless as anyone, and could discover no reason for hope.

Chapter 2.
THE FALL OF TELYRRA

Having promised the Telyrrans till dawn to
consider, I then ordered their city bombed during
the night. My aim was to impress upon the
neighboring islands that the Empire was not to be
trifled with. The tactic proved effective, for within
three days the eight remaining governments of the
Telyrran League all capitulated.
> —The Veglane Altazar
> War Commentaries
> 125 Imperial Calendar
> (Norrling Year 6227)

THAT EVENING Teron lay in bed with the psithe in his
hand. The disk was smooth like a mirror, but its surface
cast no reflection. Instead Teron's eyes, wide and
brooding, stared into silvery depths that swam with trails
of crimson and violet.

The room was a spacious guest chamber in a lower
story of the palace. Teron's bed, along with another like it,
stood on a low dais hung with tapestries. Beyond the dais
lay a flagstone floor scattered with throw rugs, a divan, a
table and chairs.

On the opposite wall a round-arched door opened to
admit Topiedeon the minstrel. Topiedeon crossed the
chamber, soft boots making no noise. He wore a patched
cloak over his broad shoulders, and a black seaman's cap
confining his yellow locks. He paused on the dais, looking
down at Teron, who still gazed with fixity into the psithe.

"That frosty Norrling stare," the minstrel grumbled.
"Like cat-whiskers tickling the spine."

Teron glanced up at his roommate. "Where have you
been?"

"At the harbor. While you were dallying with your lady
I was finding us a ship."

Topiedeon began gathering up his clothing, which lay scattered about his side of the dais. "Every private-owned ship in port is sailing on the late tide. Still it took five hours and cost half my purse to book us passage. Everyone's trying to leave Telyrra. Not that I blame them."

Teron and Topiedeon had traveled together since first meeting in the minstrel's native city of Peltaine several months before. The magician was not surprised, therefore, that Topiedeon had booked passage for them both. Nevertheless, Teron made no move to rise.

The minstrel paused in the act of stuffing a silk shirt into his sack. "Well don't just lie there. The docks were mobbed when I left. And our captain's a Zythinian I don't trust. He's liable to resell our passage if we don't get down there quickly."

Teron sighed and swung his legs off the bed. "I hate to leave, Topiedeon. I like Telyrra."

"Well, so do I," the minstrel said. "But not enough to die here."

"There'll be no attack," Teron said. "Kenerese decided on submission. The council broke up an hour ago. They're going to signal the airships at dawn."

The minstrel continued packing. "That's no reason not to get out while we can. The Moldorns are famous for their treachery. Likely as not they'll break their word and ship the whole population to Ibor in chains."

The idea made Teron wince. "I keep thinking of Adria."

"Ah!" Topiedeon rolled his eyes. "Of course. I should have guessed. It's the lady you can't bear to leave. Well, she's a pretty one, I must admit. But there are plenty of women in the world, Teron—and only one of you to enjoy them."

The Magpie shook his head. "I feel sorry for her."

"I know," Topiedeon was suddenly grave. "I feel sorry for the whole miserable island. But there's nothing we can do, Teron. It's not the business of entertainers to die in wars."

While the minstrel finished packing, Teron stared

down at the disk in his hand. Finally he closed his fist
around it.

"Perhaps there is."

"Is what?"

"Something we can do. For Adria at least, if not for
Telyrra. We can take her with us."

Topiedeon laughed. "You expect the Grand Duke's
daughter to sail off with a wandering conjurer?"

Teron was on his feet. "I think she'll prefer me to the
Moldorns. Anyway, I can give her the choice. What's the
name of the ship you've put us on?"

"The *Claramus*, moored at the Silktraders' Quay."

Teron tossed a pouch full of coins to the minstrel. "Go
down there and buy one more passage. And pay the
captain whatever you must to see that he saves our places.
The tide's not due till past midnight?"

"An hour past."

"Good. I'll have to wait till the folk upstairs retire. But
there ought to be plenty of time to get to the harbor."

"I don't see your plan," Topiedeon said. "There are
men-at-arms patroling every hall and stair. Even if they
let you in to see the Duke's daughter—which seems
unlikely—how do you expect to sneak her from the
palace?"

With a sudden spreading of his hands Teron changed
the disk to a wand. "Don't worry, Topiedeon. There are
more ways in and out of a bedchamber than even you
have discovered."

The moon and the five airships floated in a cloudy sky,
as Teron slowly scaled the precipitous outer wall of the
Grand Duke's palace. The Magpie wore dark velvet
trousers and shirt. The scarlet cape was knotted around
the psithe, which bore the form of a wooden wand, and
which buoyed Teron up in the air as an ordinary staff
thrice its size would have buoyed him up in water.

Far below, the white towers and red-tiled roofs of the
town glistened faintly in the moonlight. Above, a broad
vertical plane of stones stretched toward the sky—a
flatness broken only by a few balconies and projecting
windows.

Of necessity, Teron's first attention was fixed on the psithe, feeding it energy through his mind. Still, he had to grip the spaces between the stones with fingers and bare toes as he climbed, so that a steady squeezing pain throbbed in his wrists and insteps.

From above came the sound of a folding door opening, then Adria appeared on her balcony. She wore a loose nightgown of yellow silk, and her hair hung unbound to her waist. She stood beneath the stars and stared at the row of airships.

Pouring his will into the psithe, Teron scrambled up the last few yards and hauled himself over the balustrade. He stood holding the rail for balance, head swimming— an after-effect of psithic strain.

Adria gaped at him, glanced down from the balcony. "Teron. How did you...? You climbed the wall?"

The Magpie blinked. "Of course, dear lady. Did you think a few guards would keep me away?"

"A few dozen." Adria hugged him. "I'm glad you're here, Teron."

The magician held her while his breathing slowed and his mind settled. Then he moved her gently to arm's length. "Listen, Adria. I'm leaving Telyrra on the next tide, Topiedeon and I. Do you want to come with us?"

"Where are you going?"

"I don't know. Somewhere away from the Moldorns."

After a moment she shook her head. "I'd do the same in your place, Teron. But I can't leave."

"Why not?"

"Because I'm the Duke's daughter. It's my duty to stay."

The Magpie did not understand. "Think of what you're saying. You might have a duty to Telyrra, but after tomorrow there'll be no more Telyrra, only a Moldorn outpost."

"Don't say that! My father still rules this island." She lowered her eyes, continued in a soft, desolate voice. "He's accepted the Moldorns' terms. I must do the same."

"I am baffled by your sense of duty," Teron said.

"I have to stay. Don't make it harder for me!"

The magician clenched his lips. "I'm sorry, Adria. I

thought I should at least offer."

Tears glistened in her eyes. "I know. And I'm thankful, Teron."

She moved close to him, wrapped her smooth arms around his neck and kissed him.

Teron felt her body press enticingly against his. Her hair smelled of lilacs. The magician's mind grew hazy with passion.

"Do you have time to come inside?" she whispered, when the long kiss ended.

Teron swallowed, nodded.

Adria smiled and led him by the hand into her chamber. Teron paused at the threshold to yank off his cape—in which the psithe-wand remained tangled.

A blue lamp glowed beside the bed where they stood and removed each other's clothing. They made love slowly. For Teron it was a pageant of sensual delights and sweet emotions, but underneath his heart ached. When it was over, Adria lay in his arms, weeping quietly.

Then off in the night a whistling sounded—followed by a thunderous roar that vibrated the palace walls. Adria jerked up on the bed, wild-eyed and shivering with fright. Teron's stomach cringed and knotted. The appalling roar continued.

The Magpie scrambled from the bed and rushed to the balcony. Four of the Moldorn ships rolled above the town, sowing trails of bursting flame and smoke. Directly overhead, Teron glimpsed the tail of the fifth airship, swooping down on the palace roof.

The magician scooped up his wand and cape and stumbled back into the room. Adria gazed past him at the burning town.

"Get dressed," he yelled. "Hurry."

But she did not move.

Teron grabbed her shoulder and spun her around. "Hurry. We'll burn to death if we don't get out."

Adria nodded, went to her closet.

While Teron pulled on his clothes the bombs continued to fall on the city, but no direct explosions rocked the palace. Instead from the roof came the blare of trumpets, the tramping of many feet, the clash of weapons. The magician tossed aside his cape and changed the wand to a sword.

Adria had donned an embroidered robe, but left it unfastened. She stared at Teron blankly, like one in a trance.

"Adria!"

She shook her head. "We can't escape, Teron. The city's all on fire."

"We'll go inland. Hurry."

The clamor of battle was drawing near.

Adria clutched the hair at her temples. "Go if you want. I can't. There's no point." She covered her face and stood shuddering.

Teron's eyes blazed as he grabbed her wrist. "Listen to me! I won't leave you here to burn."

Feet trampled in the corridor outside. Then the round-arched chamber door burst inward.

The Veglane Altazar appeared, leading a squadron of Moldorns bristling with steel. Adria gave a shrill, hopeless cry. Teron stepped in front of her and held out his sword, straining his will to stop the hand from shaking.

Armor and blade splattered with blood, Altazar crossed the threshold and signaled with his hand. The Moldorns entered and, eyes locked on Teron, spread slowly around the edges of the chamber.

Altazar removed his helmet and bowed. "So, the young Duchess does not sleep alone. My apologies for interrupting your pleasures. But my time is short."

The Moldorns continued to surround Teron, who pointed his sword first one way, then the other. In cold fury the magician decided that when the soldiers rushed him he would spring at Altazar and try to split his skull.

"Your palace will soon be firebombed," the Veglane said. "We only landed to take a few prisoners: yourself, lady, and the ambassadors of the Telyrran League."

"My father?" Adria cried.

Altazar shrugged. "As a soldier of Moldorn I am not concerned with his fate. Only you are important, lady, as a symbol of our conquest. Take her," he ordered his men, who now had Teron fully outflanked.

Despairing, the magician leapt at the Veglane, swinging his sword in a two-handed downward arc.

For an instant it seemed his blow had caught Altazar off guard and would cleave him. But the Veglane's reflexes surprised even his own men. Altazar merely leaned forward and to the side, avoiding the bright flash of metal.

Off-balance, Teron stumbled over Altazar's extended leg. That same instant the Veglane retaliated, smashing his spiked sword-pummel against the back of Teron's skull.

The magician landed sprawling near the door and lay still, a small puddle of blood spreading out from his head. Adria screamed his name as she was caught up by two Moldorns, who carried her struggling from the chamber.

The Moldorns returned to their ship, dragging a handful of captives. The vessel glided into the air, then turned and made a pass over the palace roof—letting fall a half-dozen firebombs.

The flames spread swiftly over the ancient palace of Telyrra. The Veglane had elected to destroy nearly the entire city. He spared only the harbor section, which would serve later to garrison Moldorn troops, and the ships in the harbor, which would help transport those troops to other conquests.

Teron lay on the floor of Adria's chamber, taking short, ragged breaths. Only the life-control training of the Norrling wizards kept his spirit from fleeing his body. Gradually, painfully, the magician strained his way back to consciousness.

Abruptly he sat up, amid smoke and dancing flames. His eyes squinted to focus. The air scalded his lungs. Gray fingers sought the back of his head. With a sickening sensation he touched the place where the Veglane's pummel had torn his flesh and cracked the bone beneath. Teron kept awake only by a desperate exertion of will. But he was growing weaker. Soon his concentration would falter, and he would sink under again, this time to die.

For a moment death tempted him with its dark

oblivion. But the Magpie shook his head in anger. An unfamiliar passion impelled him to act—a pure, gnawing hate of the Moldorns.

There was one gamble he could play. Teron struggled to hands and knees, found the psithe-sword lying on the floor. With a mental command he transformed the sword into a fist-sized sphere of light. He held the sphere in his palms, gazed at it intently. His hope lay in invoking the *quinteer*, the fifth, quintessential power of the psithe. Norrling law forbade its invocation by any save adepts and masters, for only they had sufficient control to assure their minds would not be annihilated in the process of binding. Of course, in the present case, the Magpie had nothing to lose.

His lips parted and he mouthed the incantation in the ancient magical language: "Nyr solelleum quinteer, nie te porm."

In his hands the sphere of light pulsed, expanded. Teron repeated the incantation again and again. The psithe threw off sparks of ruby and sapphire, then burst in a blinding flash of multicolored light. That instant Teron felt his sense of form slip away. Mystic energies singed his nerves. The burst of light shrank and vanished—leaving a magpie flapping black wings in the place where Teron had knelt.

With a high-pitched cry the Magpie darted across the chamber and through the balcony door. Escaping the palace, the bird soared into the smoking night, between the moon and the blazing city.

For a time he flew in loops and circles, all thoughts lost in the wild thrill of flight. But finally Teron recalled himself, and remembered in what state he had left his mortal form. He set off toward the northwest then, flapping his wings steadily.

As the moon sank toward a bed of clouds the Magpie crossed the fields and meadows and woods of the island. After three hours he reached a barren, rocky shore. Without pausing Teron flew on, straight out to sea. Behind him the orange holocaust on the horizon began to fade into the first dim pink of sunrise.

Chapter 3.
WIZARDS OF PTOLLODEN

The mutant powers of the Grays, powers of
telepathy and psychokinesis, can wreak grave
destruction if not rigidly controlled. To gain
absolute mastery of ourselves is thus the primary
goal of the Psithic Art.

> —Clement Rhundacey
> The Book of Psithic Magic
> (also called The White
> Book and The Founder's
> Book) *Norrling Year 12*

The 640 stages are subdivided into eight classes of
eighty ranks each, known as octodens. The
octodens are called: 1 fledgling, 2 apprentice, 3
tyro, 4 journeyman, 5 adept, 6 master, 7 high
master, and 8 vanishing master. The last-named are
believed to be immortal.
. . . So great is the power of these wizards that if
they wished they could master the southern nations
with ease. Instead they seek to disengage themselves
from the world, by matching their natures to
those of the birds.

> —Spirus Spiracius
> A Voyage to the North of
> Llorland *Norrling Year 5436*

TERON'S DESTINATION was his homeland, Ombernorr. The reason was simple. His badly damaged human form could not contain his life unless it was healed. The only place Teron knew where such healing could be done was among the Norrling wizards.

So he flew northwest, passing several tiny islands belonging to the long chain of which Telyrra was the easternmost link. The man-spirit gave the body of the bird enormous stamina and strength. Teron did not stop to rest until dusk, when he perched himself on the yardarm of a tall-masted galleon. Within the hour he had taken flight again, beating wings as he climbled the huge, darkening sky.

In this manner, resting one hour out of twenty, the Magpie passed the larger islands and sighted the rugged cliffs of the mainland of Tann. He followed the coast of a bleak, rocky peninsula known as the Arm of Arabhedden. Three days more brought him to fertile farm country, more populous and civilized, where feudal lords dwelt in halls of stone and burgeoning harbor towns carried on a busy summer commerce.

But even in summer the nights in these northern latitudes were very cold. Freezing winds often forced the Magpie to take shelter in a tree or behind a boulder. Continuing up the coastline he passed the green, hilly country of Llorland and penetrated the immense forests of Bhakthorn.

By now Teron's head whirled from hunger and thirst—needs he dared not satisfy for fear of binding his soul forever in the bird-form. Strange, appalling visions loomed before his eyes. Having gone so long without physical nourishment, his presence of mind began to falter. There followed lapses of consciousness, blank interludes in which Teron was submerged and the bird's mind was conscious. Still the magician managed to stay on course, dominating the psithe by some unyielding core of will.

Then, a dozen hours after entering the great forest, the Magpie lighted on a tall jutting stone beside a twilit sea. He rested there on one clawed foot, keeping one eye open. In his thoughts he repeated Norrling litanies designed to strengthen the will. After several minutes his awareness was invaded by a shadow and a scream.

The Magpie leapt from his perch and twisted in the air to avoid grasping talons. A large blue oceanhawk, thrashing the air with his wings, shrieked at the prey's escape and darted for him again. The hawk's fishing luck had been poor that day, but this small black-feathered creature at least promised a meal—if it could be caught.

Beating his wings furiously the Magpie swept in a long downward arc across the black sand beach toward the shelter of the trees. The oceanhawk gave chase, and the two birds weaved in and out among the thorny pines. Teron changed directions, dipped and looped, but the blue hawk pursued relentlessly, whipping about on broad, black-tipped wings.

Exhausted, Teron tried to save himself by slipping into the hollow of a fallen log. But the oceanhawk landed with a cry. Since it could not quite reach the prey, the hawk began to enlarge the opening by pecking away chips of the rotted wood.

The tiny bird-heart fluttered in the Magpie's breast. He realized that his sole chance lay in abandoning the quinteer. He would have to gamble that his human form could contain his life long enough for him to rout the hawk and then bond himself again to the psithe.

Teron waited, catching his breath, until the oceanhawk nearly had him. Then he darted past the snapping beak and, at the same instant, inwardly chanted the counter-spell. His senses shuddered as the two energies slid apart.

Then he was in human form, rolling amid pine needles beneath the flapping wings of the bewildered hawk. The large bird hovered, uncertain whether to attack this new, larger prey.

Teron flicked the psithe into a sword and swiped angrily at the oceanhawk. The bird rose with a furious cawing and reluctantly headed back toward the beach.

Using the sword as a crutch Teron started to his feet, then rested on one knee. His memory lay in broken fragments. He glanced around with a puzzled, disoriented face. A wilderness of trees and darkness met his eyes. A faint roar of surf in his ears, and the rustle of wind in the pine boughs. A splitting pain in the back of his head. He touched the spot and his fingers came away moist and sticky. A black numbing cold pounded into his brain.

The magician collapsed on the forest floor and lay still, eyes open and unfocused. The psithe-sword lay at his hand, glowing with a pale yellow light that faded as the hours passed and the moaning wind continued to blow.

The Sanctuary of Ptolloden stood perched on a long craggy hill—the easternmost of a chain of hills that formed a stable, centuries-old barrier against the Ice. To the south lay the rolling tundra where the people of Ombernorr dwelt in clustered, hive-like houses. To the east was the sea—cold, deep blue, churning. And in the north the limitless jagged plain of the glacier stretched away to the top of the world.

The Ombernorrs said that the wizards used their power to keep the Ice from advancing further. It was even believed that the Norrlings had formed the chain of hills—raising them from the earth with the same magical techniques that had been used to build Ptolloden.

The Sanctuary itself was a colossal, rambling edifice constructed of hundreds of kinds of stone. A forest of turrets and spires sprouted from the many roofs, interspersed with numerous crystal domes. At the very center rose a gigantic dome, ringed with eight squat towers. This central dome's surface was a mirror, reflecting the blue and white daytime skies and the star-speckled skies of night.

Inside, Ptolloden was a self-contained world with endless tall-arched corridors, twisting spiral stairs and vast lofty chambers that glistened with icicle-like ornamentation.

In one such chamber Teron awoke, lying flat on his back in a huge bed. He recognized the ceiling at once as belonging in Ptolloden, but tried in vain to recall his arrival there. The last he remembered was fleeing the oceanhawk—a memory that chilled him.

Abruptly Teron realized he was not alone. He swiveled his head on the pillow and regarded a short, slender figure standing at his bedside, poised motionless on one foot. The figure wore a yellow-feathered smock and a Norrling bird mask that Teron, searching his memory, recognized as that of a Scissortail. The Scissortail's skin, visible on the lower face, had the unmistakable gray tint of the Ombernorr people.

"Greetings, fellow initiate." Teron spoke the formal words, surprised at the weakness of his voice. "Can you tell—"

The Scissortail gestured with his fingers, signaling Teron to be still and wait. The Magpie gathered that the

Scissortail was observing the rite of silence. He signaled back his apologies for breaking the quiet. The Scissortail nodded, turned and marched noiselessly across the room, exiting through a distant door.

Left alone, the Magpie raised himself to a sitting position and surveyed the chamber. Typically for Ptolloden, the room gave a sense of vast, airy spaciousness, with curving lines in walls and doorways. The floor was shiny blue stone, dotted with white rugs of polar bear and snow lion. A few pieces of furniture: chairs, a nightstand, a large desk, and the huge high-posted bed in which Teron lay. On the left-hand wall a round-mouthed fireplace glowed with crackling flames.

An orange-billed toucan flapped across the room to Teron's bed. Just before it lighted, however, a pinpoint of radiance burst from the creature's breast. The next instant the bird had vanished and in its place stood a tall, feather-robed wizard with twinkling gray eyes and a pointy black and silver beard reaching to his belt.

"Master," Teron cried.

"Greetings, Magpie," Cordavius the Toucan said. "Welcome back to the mortal plane. I trust you're feeling as well as can be expected."

Teron gingerly touched the back of his head, found it bandaged and very sore. "Being alive is more than I expected, good master."

The Toucan nodded. "More than you had any right to expect."

The Scissortail reappeared at the far door and walked forward with hands in sleeves. Cordavius tilted his head in that direction, and cast his thoughts into Teron's mind:

Since your nurse is observing the rite of silence, Magpie, let us communicate without sound.

Teron nodded. Telepathy was a common practice in Ptolloden, and a high master like Cordavius could form the mental bond with anyone he chose.

The Scissortail took his position again at the bedside, balanced on one foot.

Teron looked at Cordavius. *Master, how did I come here?*

I brought you, Magpie. I had an intuition that a

life-soul familiar to me was in peril of imminent death. I left Ptolloden to search out the source of that intuition, and found it four hundred leagues south of here: You, Teron, lying on the forest floor—along with a psithe whose light was almost completely extinguished.

Teron winced. *What became of my psithe?*

It survived, Magpie. I returned it to its life-form and set it free in the Birdhouse.

Teron breathed with relief. He might be accused of misusing the psithe, but at least he had not destroyed it.

Cordavius stared at him, letting the obvious question hang in the air.

Teron decided it would be best to confess at once. *The psithe was nearly burned out because I invoked the quinteer, master.*

A notable achievement for a fledgling. But it was audacious of you to try.

I had no choice. It was life or death.

Relax, Magpie. Both you and the bird have survived.

Yes, good master. But will I be allowed to take a new psithe?

Cordavius eyed him keenly. *Do you mean you wish to be readmitted as a student in the Sanctuary?*

Teron frowned and seemed to search himself with a brief inward glance. *I mean, good master, that I wish to claim a new psithe and return to the Warmlands as soon as possible.*

That *will be difficult*, the Toucan declared. *Your departure from Ombernorr caused quite a scandal here, Magpie. Many of my colleagues in the higher ranks reproached me for allowing you to leave Ptolloden in the first place. They called you an impudent renegade, and me a fool. Now you've returned from the Warmlands barely alive and with a badly damaged psithe—fulfilling, as it were, their worst expectations. And you intend to petition the Gathering of Eight for a new psithe, so that you may return south yet again?* Cordavius ended, shaking his head dubiously.

I'll have to find a way to convince them, Teron thought.

Cordavius laughed, heartily and silently.

The Magpie grinned. *You always did find me a comic fellow, master.*

Yes. You were one of my most gifted pupils. Also one of the most unruly. You possess the inborn talent to attain the highest mysteries, but you were always too attached to the sensual world. "More concerned with the reflected lights of the Terrestrial Plane than with the spiritual source of all illumination."

Teron recognized the lines from *The Golden Book*. He replied with a quote from *The Green Book*, one of the older but more tolerant Norrling scriptures:

"Complete disengagement is not the course ordained for every soul." That's why I left Ptolloden three years ago, to try and discover my own course.

That's why I allowed you to leave, Magpie. But I never expected you would cross the boundary of our realm.

Nor did I, Teron answered. *But when I had dwelt a while on the lower tundra and listened to the fur traders describing the Warmlands, the lure became irresistible. I was certain my ordained course lay in that direction—and I still am.*

Are you sure you're not just seeking freedom or pleasure in that direction, Teron?

The Magpie shrugged. *Perhaps seeking freedom and pleasure is my ordained course, master.*

Cordavius smiled—the infinitely amused smile of a high master. *You'll have a hard time convincing the Gathering of Eight to sanction such a course, Magpie.*

Teron nodded soberly. *I know.*

But we shall see, Cordavius added. *Meantime, stay in bed until your wound is well-healed.* The Toucan produced a gold-covered book from within his robes— *Master Aswel's Book of Rules and Meditations*—and handed it to Teron. *I recommend that you use your free time to meditate—on "The True Hideous Face of the Desire-Nature," for instance, or "The Folly of Enslavement to the Senses." I chose as your nurse a brother observing the rite of silence in order to facilitate such meditations.*

The Magpie smiled wryly. *Thanks, most thoughtful master.*

Cordavius winked, changed himself into a toucan and flew from the chamber. Teron sighed and glanced briefly at his nurse. The Scissortail retained his ritual one-footed pose—still as a figure of ice.

When Teron had recovered sufficiently to leave his bed he took to wandering the corridors and giant courts of the Sanctuary, meeting old friends and fellow students, observing classes and psithic practice sessions, taking his meals in a common dining hall. Life at Ptolloden, as he recalled, had a tone and atmosphere all its own—mysterious, serene, unchanging. The very architecture, pristine and majestic, seemed ready to enfold him. Teron remembered his early days in the Sanctuary.

He was fourteen then, had just begun to show signs of the power. The long-bearded wizards had come to his village, tested him and taken him back to their Sanctuary—as they took all the young ones chosen by birth to be wielders of magic. The breeding of wizards was strictly controlled—so that the Ombernorrs would remain a unified people and no elite caste of magicians could arise. Members of the Norrling order, male and female, were permitted to mate only on ritual occasions, and then only with those who did not possess the power. All children were reared in the villages. Only at puberty were the magic-wielders taken by the Norrlings—the boys to Ptolloden, the girls to a similar High Sanctuary in the northwest corner of Ombernorr.

At first Teron was enraptured with Ptolloden, with the life of a fledgling wizard. He took keen delight in wielding a psithe, in feeling the power within him grow, become concentrated and pure. But always there was the other side, the prime Norrling command, implicit in every lesson—to disengage the mind from the world. The magician was meant to be aloof, austere and ascetic. But some deep core in Teron's being ran counter to that ideal. By the time he was eighteen he wanted more of the world, not less.

So he asked Cordavius for the leave of absence and traveled about the country, observing the roles the wizards played in the life of the villages. Hunters, judges, healers, teachers, the Norrlings were servants to the common folk, and yet always apart from them. Teron found the prospect of such a life unbearably dull. Then, at the height of his restlessness, he listened to the fur traders speaking of the Warmlands.

Now, a fortnight after his return to the Sanctuary, the same restlessness was on him again, but stronger. Now he had reasons for wanting to return to the south—to free Adria if he could, to find Topiedeon, to wreak vegeance on the Moldorns. But the masters of Ptolloden would consider all of these motives vain and unworthy. Somehow, Teron had to convince them to let him go back.

Brooding on these things, the Magpie paid a visit on an old friend named Fystus. Fystus had entered the Sanctuary the same year as Teron but, owing to his diligence, had risen much higher in the ranks. Now he bore the psithe of a Grackle, 175 places above the Magpie.

Fystus worked in the vast Library and Hall of Records, which lay beneath one of the great domes of Ptolloden. The chamber was not a circle but a colossal polygon with 640 sides. The floor measured eight hundred feet across, covered with bookshelves, couches and elaborately carved stone tables. The bookcases rose to a level of thirty feet. Above that point were other shelves containing encoded crystals decipherable only by members of the higher octodens. No ladder or stairs reached to those heights, for any Norrling capable of reading the crystals was capable of reaching them by levitation.

Teron found the Grackle seated on a tall stool behind a high, white-marble podium. Behind him, thick dusty tomes filled the shelves. Tall and rotund, Fystus hopped from his stool and circled the podium to clasp Teron's hand.

"Greetings, Magpie. I heard you'd returned."

"Hello, Grackle."

Fystus gestured him to a nearby couch. "You must tell me all about the Warmlands. I'm the librarian for the History and World Affairs section now."

"So I've heard," Teron said. "My congratulations on your advancement. But I doubt that I could tell you any more than you already know. In fact, I've come here partly to profit by your knowledge of the south."

"Then by all means we must compare notes." Fystus produced a pipe and a match from a fold in his iridescent, black-feathered robe. Like many Norrlings, the Grackle smoked a certain tundra herb that soothed the mind and helped it maintain a dispassionate perspective.

"All our information comes, as you probably know, through the Birdhouse," Fystus said. "Birds from all over the globe wander in and out and we decipher and record all the sense impressions held in their brains. So we get an enormous amount of raw information, but there are many gaps, much that we can't interpret. That's why I'm interested in hearing your impressions."

Teron smiled. "They're probably as muddled as any bird's. The Warmlands are sunny, pleasant, rich. At first I wondered how I would get along with the people, but I found I was highly prized as an entertainer. A few tricks with the psithe earned me food and drink and shelter, gifts of clothing, even the attentions of lovely women. Ah, Fystus, the women. Slender and full-bosomed, red-haired, yellow-haired, gold-haired . . ."

"I'm aware of the varieties of hair coloring among the Warmlanders," Fystus said dryly. "What about their commerce, social classes, political institutions?"

"Most of the lands I visited were ruled by fat lords who surrounded themselves with flatterers and guards," Teron said. "There are soldiers in all the halls of all the castles. They seem to fight wars incessantly."

Fystus puffed green smoke. "Has something to do with the warm climate. Excess energies of the lower sort needing an outlet."

Teron seized the opportunity. "What do you know of the Moldorns?"

"Ah," Fystus nodded. "A distinct racial type, bred in the mountains of western Ibor. Tall and muscular, but quick and agile. Sturdy specimens, very fierce . . ."

"I mean their Empire."

"What do you know of them, Teron?"

A malign expression darkened the Magpie's face. "They're mad. They want to burn the world so they can own it."

Fystus nodded contemplatively. "They lived in the

mountains in a primitive tribal state, perpetually at war among themselves, until the start of the last century. Then they were united by a strong warchief. Since then they've carved out the largest single empire seen on this planet for over five thousand years."

"And still growing," Teron muttered.

"And at a remarkable rate. Until five years ago there were strong alliances among the Tuvar and Barrandan peoples that kept the Moldorns from overrunning eastern Ibor. But then they perfected the airship, and they've been unstoppable ever since."

"The airships," Teron said. "They're mysterious, Fystus. I could sense no mind behind their power."

"There is none. It's a fundamentally different kind of power from our own."

"In what way?"

Fystus shifted his weight. "The Elder Races recognized two distinct systems of knowledge and power, Teron, which went in and out of repute with the flux of their history. One system they called 'magic' and the other 'science.' The former involved the manifestation of invisible energies on the Terrestrial Plane through the focus of the mind. Essentially it's the same system we use, though of course we're much better at it, owing to certain evolutionary improvements. Still, the Norrling founders were indebted to some of the ancient authorities on magic: Pythagoras, Agrippa, Crowley..." The Grackle waved his pipe at the rows of dusty books.

"The other system?" Teron reminded him.

"Oh yes. It involved, on the contrary, the harnessing of forces that are purely earthly in nature. And make no mistake, Teron, when the techniques of that system are sophisticated enough the potential is every bit as limitless."

"So the airships operate without any power of mind at all?"

"Precisely. Just as a sail harnesses the wind. The techniques are more complex, but the principle is the same. We know a fair amount about the airships. The birds, you see, are always running into them. The Iborans have been playing around with flying devices for over a hundred years—mainly bags filled with hot air or a light gas. But it was the Moldorns who found a way to make rigid, maneuverable ships. Turning the toy into a weapon, you see? They worry me."

"Why? You don't expect they'll threaten Ombernorr someday?"

Fystus laughed. "Not likely. A bit too chilly for them here I would think."

"Then why are you worried?"

"Because, Teron, science of itself is inherently dangerous. The Norrling art—or any other magical system—purifies and toughens the mind so that one can wield power without doing harm. But science has no such intrinsic safeguards. Earthly forces are blind, mindless. Once unleashed they can destroy an entire world. The science of the Elder Races helped bring about their downfall—and almost laid waste to the globe as well. It could happen again."

Teron frowned, recalling what history he knew of the collapse of the ancient world: Lethal radiations, from earthly sources and from space. Chaotic changes wrought among the species of living things. Then the earth's climate had begun to change, growing colder so that the ice advanced...

"But wouldn't the high masters stop the Moldorns before it went so far?"

The Grackle shrugged. "One would hope so. And yet..."

"What?"

"Well, one of the things that makes a high master is his degree of detachment from the world. They simply may not realize the danger in time. Then, too, there's the problem of getting them all to agree on a course of action. We have a three-thousand-year tradition of noninvolvement with the rest of the world. Of course in the earliest days of Ptolloden it was different: journeymen and adepts often sojourned among the Warmlanders as part of their training."

"I didn't know that," Teron said.

"History yields many surprises," Fystus replied. "At the moment though, full isolationism is very popular among the higher echelons. Every year some masters propose that this whole section of the library be shut down. They can see no purpose for studying the Warmlands, or even the history of our own people." The Grackle finished on a bitter note.

Teron was deep in thought. "Then we might suppose that there are some among the high octodens who would like to see the Moldorns stopped, but who do nothing because their colleagues will allow no breach of tradition."

Fystus nodded. "Any meddling in outworld affairs would set a precedent. And to make war on a whole empire would necessitate an unqualified sanction, since it would require a huge commitment of power."

"Perhaps not," Teron said after a moment. "Perhaps a single magician could wage an effective war."

Chapter 4.
INTO THE BIRDHOUSE

Motion is all that exists. Motion bound in a pattern is matter. Motion flowing through a recurring pattern is life. A life-entity is a recurring pattern; it functions to bring motion into the world. If one can seize a pattern and arrest its motion for even an instant, one can alter the pattern, and hence alter the motion it brings into the world. This is the basic principle of the psithic art.

> —Clement Rhundacey
> The Book of Psithic Magic.

The Attributes are best viewed as symbol-shapes that focus the wizard's mind-force at a given level of vibration. The level dictates the path through which the psithic power enters the world.... The Attributes, with their correspondence to the alchemical elements, also help deepen the sympathetic bond between the wizard's mind and Nature—the bond generated by the bird-soul which becomes the psithe.

> —Initiate Boomler's Treatise
> On Magical Theory (also called
> The Silver Book)
> Norrling Year 342

AT THE START of the next lunar month, Teron appeared before the Gathering of Eight, the supreme governing council of Ptolloden. The Gathering was made up exclusively of high masters, who rotated their chairs every month so that all twenty-two high masters presently in Ptolloden had their turns to sit in council. Teron had waited until now on the advice of Cordavius, who was himself taking a seat this month. The Magpie had spent the interim in the library, studying countless books and conferring hours on end with Fystus—preparing his case, the rhetoric and performance he would present to the high masters.

The Gathering of Eight convened in a round, marble-walled chamber high in one of the eight broad towers that ringed the central dome of Ptolloden. Teron stood in the middle of the floor, facing a half-circle of high masters seated behind tall podiums of white onyx. The wizards wore glittering, variegated rainments of feathers and precious metals, along with illusory masks generated by their psithes. The masks identified the species: Toucan, Pelican, Marabou, Dogbird, Pheasant, Flamingohawk, Limpkin and Shoebill. All were birds of the second highest Norrling level, which held mastery over Ptolloden's affairs. For although the Sanctuary housed a few wizards who had advanced to the eighth and highest octoden, these took no interest in worldly matters, having thoroughly transcended their bondage to matter.

The floor on which Teron stood had a smoky gray surface continuously disturbed by pulsing, jagged lines of white energy. A complex, moving mandala, the floor reflected the shifting currents of thought and mood among the eight masters. Like the bird-headed masks the wizards appeared to be wearing, the mandala was a figment of their psithes—a needed outlet for the vast amounts of power concentrated in this single room.

Teron gazed down at the flowing patterns and tried to conceive some measure for that power. His speculations were interrupted by a loud, imperative voice.

"What matter do you bring before this mystical gathering?"

The question was ritual. The masters already knew what the Magpie wanted. Teron raised his eyes and confronted the questioner: the Dogbird, who sat at the central podium reserved for the council's chairman.

"I come to petition the Gathering," Teron said. "I wish to enter the Birdhouse and claim a replacement for my psithe, which was damaged and had to be returned to its life-form."

"How did this psithe come to be damaged?" asked a voice deep and resonant as a tuba. It belonged to the Shoebill, who sat with his enormous beak propped by hands in white-feathered gloves.

Cordavius had warned Teron about the Shoebill. "Its energy limits were strained," Teron replied, "by my invocation of the fifth attribute."

The Shoebill's head tilted as though with surprise. "And what was your rank when you invoked this quinteer?"

Teron bowed. "I'm a Magpie, honored master."

"You mean you *were* a Magpie," the Limpkin retorted. "Whether you are anything now is for us to decide."

Cordavius had warned Teron about the Limpkin too. But before he could frame an answer the Pelican broke in:

"You must have known the quinteer would burn out your psithe."

"And probably burn out your mind as well," the Dogbird added.

"Indeed, masters, but I had no other choice. My human form was too badly damaged to sustain me."

"You decided that on your own?" the Shoebill asked.

"Regrettably there were no high masters present to consult."

"Yes!" the Flamingohawk arched his scarlet-plumed neck. "Now we come to the crux of the matter. There were no superiors to help you because you had left Ombernorr for the Warmlands."

Jabbing white lines raced and collided at Teron's feet. A downward glance made the Magpie queasy.

The Limpkin said, "You crossed the ancient border without permission, without even consulting your superiors. What explanation can you offer, fledgling?"

Teron forced his eyes to leave the floor, reminding himself that an unruffled air was crucial to his performance. "I struggled many nights against the temptation, good master. But at last I decided that journeying south was the course ordained for me to follow."

"For a fledgling you take a great many decisions on yourself," the Shoebill muttered.

Teron smiled somewhat pensively. "Perhaps, noble master. Yet who can hope to alter what is ordained by fate?"

"What made you so sure this was your fate?" the Pelican asked.

"At first only the insistent strength of the desire I felt. But lately I've become more convinced than ever. For the fate that tempted me south has brought me back to Ptolloden with a clear sense of my life-duty in this crucial moment of world history."

The masters looked from one to another. The patterns on the floor eddied and swirled. The Dogbird asked:

"In what sense, fledgling, is this moment of history crucial?"

"Then it's as I feared," Teron said. "Imagine, if I, a mere fledgling, had not been driven to travel south, the masters of Ombernorr might never have suspected."

"Suspected what?" the Flamingohawk demanded.

"That a warlike southern nation is learning to unleash the forces of Nature, forces that may one day wreck the entire world. I speak of the Empire of Moldorn."

"We know about the Moldorns," the Dogbird assured him.

Conflicting lines through the mandala showed Teron it was a subject of discord. "Then, wise masters, you must surely recognize the danger."

"Yes, we do," said the Marabou, who till now had said nothing.

"We recognize no such thing," said the Shoebill.

"Brothers." The Dogbird slapped his podium for silence. "We are wandering from the topic." He eyed Teron keenly. "You speak of having a sense of a life-duty, fledgling. What exactly do you mean?"

"That I would return to the south and overthrow the Moldorns," Teron answered. "Dismantle their Empire and destroy their power. I wish the Gathering to confer this task upon me as a Deputation."

"Sounds like a rather tall order for a fledgling who can't even hold on to his psithe," the Limpkin remarked.

"How did you arrive at the conclusion that this is your life-duty?" the Pheasant demanded.

"By a process of reasoning," Teron said. "None of the Warmland peoples have the power to handle the Moldorn threat. The wizards of Ombernorr have the power, but are detached from the south and therefore lack the inclination. If a benevolent fate were to provide an agent for ridding the world of this danger, surely it would be a Norrling wizard who was not detached, but passionately involved. And believe me, honored masters, I bear a passionate hatred of the Moldorns. It was one of their lords who cracked open my head."

"Your request is ridiculous," the Shoebill said. "You ask us to depart from a stalwart tradition of noble isolation just to satisfy a fledgling's egotistical sense of his destiny."

Teron lowered his eyes. "Besides satisfying my sense of destiny, cautious master, you will also have probed at the Moldorns, taken measure of their strength. Besides, I do not require an official Deputation if you would rather not bestow one. Just grant me a psithe. Then if I fail you will have lost nothing. And if I succeed you need never worry about the Moldorns again."

"You make it sound almost tempting," the Pheasant said. "But the fact remains that by granting you a psithe this Gathering would be giving tacit approval to your whole scheme."

"Perhaps," the Magpie replied. "But allowing one magician passage to the Warmlands would not be so dangerous a precedent of interference as an all-out war between the forces of Moldorn and those of Ombernorr."

"The idea of such a war is preposterous," the Flamingohawk declared.

"Such a war may one day be needed," Teron said, "to preserve the Earth from destruction."

There was silence for several moments and then the Dogbird spoke.

"If there are no other questions,"—the masters offered none—"then I suppose we have heard enough to consider your petition, fledgling. If you would be so kind as to fix your eyes on my psithe."

The Dogbird held up a gleaming ruby disk. Teron looked at it and instantly entered a peculiar state of trance. His eyes filled with stars and multicolored dust, his ears with soft, easeful music. The Magpie found these sensations irritating, for he knew the masters were discussing him right there in the room where his body stood.

With the fledgling's awareness of the chamber shut off, the wizards relaxed. The illusory bird masks faded away, revealing the human faces. Several beautifully ornamented pipes appeared. The Dogbird, a florid, balding old master with broad jowls, turned puzzled eyes on Cordavius.

"Well, he's your boy, Toucan. You were awfully quiet while he spoke."

Cordavius lit his pipe with a blue flame from his psithe. "I wanted to see how he would act without my encouragement. And I must tell you, brothers, I was impressed. I've never seen the Magpie in such earnest."

"He seemed rather glib to me," the Pelican said.

"And to me," the Pheasant agreed.

Cordavius chuckled. "You don't know him. Believe me, I've never seen him less glib."

"And a lightheaded fellow like that," the Flamingo-hawk said, "who has already burned out one psithe, asks for a Deputation to wage a one-man war against a foreign country..."

"The idea is absurd," the Shoebill declared.

"I think the idea has merit," the Marabou said. "It provides a convenient compromise between those of us who want to stop the Moldorns, and those who'd rather bury their heads and do nothing."

He ended staring pointedly at the Shoebill, who glowered back and retorted: "The inhabitants of the outworld do not concern us. To meddle in their affairs would be a degradation of our power."

"I'm not so sure they don't concern us," Cordavius said. "We do have to share the same planet, and as Teron pointed out, the Moldorns have already resurrected war secrets developed by ancient science."

"What is that to us?" the Flamingohawk asked.

"It will be a great deal to us," the Marabou answered, "when they finally uncover the one secret that should never be uncovered again—the one that ravaged the Earth six thousand years ago and buried the ancient world."

The eight high masters argued back and forth for some

time. The Dogbird began to lean with Cordavius and the Marabou, but the Flamingohawk, Shoebill and Limpkin remained adamant. Finally the Pelican offered a compromise which satisfied both himself and the Pheasant.

"I like the idea of at least probing the Moldorns," he said. "But not with an irresponsible fledgling. I say we let him into the Birdhouse and agree to his proposed Deputation, but only on the condition that he stay at Ptolloden and study until he attains the rank of adept."

"He'll never make adept," the Limpkin said.

"In that case he'll cause us no further concern," the Pelican said. "But if he does by chance make it to the fifth octoden, in twenty or thirty years, he'll have grown older and wiser in the process—become mature enough to see through this 'life-duty' if it's a delusion, and powerful enough to perhaps succeed if it's genuine."

"I agree with your idea in principle," Cordavius said. "But the fifth octoden is very far from Teron's present rank. Why not lower the requirement one class to journeyman? The fourth octoden will not seem nearly so inaccessible as the fifth."

The Pelican shrugged. "I might make the case that the goal should be made inaccessible. But he's your protégé, Toucan. I have no objection to lowering the requirement one class if you think it's best."

The Pheasant also agreed and so the motion passed five votes to three. The Flamingohawk, Limpkin and Shoebill insisted that the record show their voices to be the dissenting ones. The high masters then resumed their psithic masks and the Dogbird brought Teron's mind back to the Gathering.

"Fourth octoden!" Teron exclaimed on hearing their decision. "But good masters, that could take me twenty years."

"If you make it at all," the Pelican said.

"But surely attaining the second octoden would be enough to test and train me."

"The point is not debatable," the Dogbird replied.

"The *third* octoden perhaps?"

"Our decision has been rendered, fledgling. Take it or not."

Teron wore an indecisive grimace. To wait twenty

years was beyond his comprehension. Yet without a psithe there could be no hope of defeating the Moldorns.

"We require your answer now," the Dogbird said.

"I accept your terms," Teron answered.

"I sense that you harbor reservations, fledgling," the Dogbird said. "Do not try to deceive us."

"No reservations, master," Teron said glumly. "Only the fervent hope that I may gain the fourth octoden with unprecedented swiftness, or that some future Gathering may be convinced to lower the requirement."

"Both hopes are without foundation," the Shoebill declared.

In the black hour before dawn the next morning Teron faced two doors of silver eight yards tall. Upon the doors were carved, in zig-zagging ranks, 640 bird-figures representing the Norrling hierarchy.

Teron was flanked by eight wizards, robed and hooded in white plumage. Their psithes were carried as glowing wands eighty inches long. Their faces were pallid gray in the psithe-light.

Two-by-two the wizards stepped forward and aimed their wands at the bird-figures which corresponded to their ranks. Each figure worked as a lever, and when all ten had been raised by the levitating power of the wands the tall silver doors swung inward—revealing an inky blackness.

After bowing to the eight wizards, Teron marched into the chamber. The massive doors clanged shut behind him, but the noise was muffled and absorbed at once—leaving a silence so perfect that the basic vibrant hum of the Universe could clearly be discerned.

The architecture of the Birdhouse was so designed as to block out all but a selected few vibrations. This near-perfect screening of energies altered the modality of space—a process Teron only dimly understood—making the chamber beneath the great dome an area of utter stillness and spacelessness. The few beams of vibrations that were allowed to penetrate created, by their carefully arranged intersections, the many doorways that led to Ptolloden and also numerous inter-spatial "windows" that opened out on various spots around the world—spots chosen because they were habitats of the 640 species of Norrling birds.

Several paces into the chamber Teron stopped, his awareness of space smothered by the mystical stillness of the dome. The initiate only needed to wait. The forces at work in the Birdhouse would probe his spirit and select the matching psithe.

Teron felt the energies passing through him and his brain seemed to lighten. Presently he experienced a renewed sense of space, and streams of warm air rushing past him. The darkness did not dissipate, but Teron caught the scent of tropical flowers and heard the rapid flutter of wings.

A bird circled above him, confused by the dark and stillness of the dome. Teron held out his hands and called soothingly. The bird flew down and perched on the magician's arm.

"My friend, you're a tiny one," Teron whispered. "And the task before us is huge."

His fingertips stroked the feathered body, felt the fluttering life-force there. Aided by the stillness of the dome, Teron slowed the life-force vibrations. A tiny point of light appeared, grew larger as the bird began to vanish. Teron glimpsed the bird's face before the light engulfed it—the bright scarlet face of a hummingbird.

"Three places lower than magpie," he muttered. "An inauspicious beginning."

But holding his new psithe in its energy form, Teron the Hummingbird smiled, reveling in a feeling of supernal potency known only to wielders of magic.

Moments later the silver doors swung open and Teron emerged from the Birdhouse carrying a wand. The eight wizards had noted which of the bird-figures on the doors tilted up when Teron opened them from the inside. Thus they greeted him as "Brother Hummingbird."

That very hour Teron embarked on a rigorous course of training and discipline. Norrling law allowed a wizard to claim a new psithe only once a year. Teron had decided to put all his mind and heart into his studies for that length of time. At the end of the year he would measure his progress and decide if it was worth it to continue—or if some other solution had to be found.

Teron submitted his will entirely to that of his trainer, a dour, grizzled magician named Zimian the Woodpecker. Zimian led Teron to a wide northern porch facing the white cliffs of the glacier. Teron was made to strip off his feathered garments and sit naked on the ice-covered stone. The cold nibbled his flesh and made him shiver despite the efforts of his will. Zimian instructed him to meditate on the psithe for the rest of the day and then to chant incantations and litanies through the night—and to continue alternating these two disciplines until he, Zimian, returned. Teron knew the ordeal would be measured as some function of the mystic number eight. He expected it to last eight days at the most. But Zimian left him on the porch three times eight days.

The warmth Teron generated with his psithe was all that kept him alive. Such was the purpose of the ordeal, to stimulate the initiate's mental powers by making his life depend on them. Thus the body and mind were purged of weakness and other obstacles to the power's flow.

After the ordeal Teron was obliged to spend every eighth hour in meditation and chanting, and to fast every eighth day. Meantime he began to practice with the psithe. Zimian made a point of explaining the psithe's attributes in detail, as though Teron were a new initiate.

"This," he said, brandishing the wand, "is the first attribute, in the magical tongue called *honeer*, the wing of the Bird."

"I know that," Teron said, but the Woodpecker ignored him.

"Its power affects the earth's pull upon matter. Your fledgling's wand can affect only itself, rising in the air or falling with greater speed than normal. In the upper ranks the psithe-wand is potent enough to levitate other objects, including the wizard's own body."

Teron stayed silent, having realized that Zimian's aim was to deflate his pride, to give him a lesson in humility.

With a flicker of gnarled fingers the Woodpecker changed his wand to a cup. "*Duod*, the second attribute. In the body of the Cosmic Bird it is the tongue; on this plane its element is water. The cup distills water from the air. To this water the magician learns to add powders and essences, to create medicines, potions and poisons. Masters and some adepts are able to generate these various liquids directly from the air. You, Hummingbird, need not worry about rising to such levels of skill."

Teron smiled crookedly at the jibe. Zimian made his psithe into a long dagger.

"*Treel*, the Bird's claw, the third attribute. Its element is fire, its earthly shape the knife or sword. Its power brings forth heat and other radiations. But the wizard must also learn to employ the knife and sword in combat. His body must become a weapon, to defend himself and others from the hazards of the physical world."

Next Zimian produced a shiny blue disk. "*Qorm*, the eye of the Bird. It corresponds to earth, its shape is as you see. The power of the fourth attribute is a power over the mind. It enables the wizard to entrance himself and others for long periods or short. More, the magician can feed to the disk images from his mind, and the psithe can then project these as illusions to the minds of others.

"Such are the four psithic attributes, fledgling. The first and second dealing with matter, the third with energy, the fourth with mind."

"But most excellent of teachers," Teron said. "Have you not forgotten the last, quintessential attribute?"

The Woodpecker narrowed his gaze. "No, most impudent of pupils, I have not forgotten it. But the fifth attribute involves the power of life-essence, a power reserved for masters and adepts. Do not think of it again."

"Very well, teacher," Teron shrugged. "But suppose *I* become an adept?"

"Judging by your record, Hummingbird, I will feel I have accomplished much if you remain a fledgling."

But in the following months Teron proved he was no longer to be judged by his former record. He poured himself into his studies, and practiced incessantly with the psithe. He worked alone for hours at night, building his concentration by keeping the wand motionless in the air. In seminars with other fledglings he studied theory and applications of the disk—entrancing minds and filling them with illusions. In a laboratory course he learned the exact formulas of complicated tonics and drugs. In a large class taught by a Bluejay, he trained in Norrling combat—a ritualized system involving both the wand and the sword.

The power grew in him, quickening his limbs, deepening his will, strengthening the invisible tendrils of his life-force. With the power grew his passion for wielding it, for casting energies into the world. This pleasure alone compensated for the aches and dizzyness that inevitably followed long sessions of psithic exercise.

At year's end Teron entered the Birdhouse and found he'd become a Mockingbird—gaining thirty places and crossing into the second octoden. His progress surprised all who heard of it, except Teron himself. He was certain by now that he would attain the rank of journeyman in far less than twenty years. The growth of the power in him seemed to verify that he really was fated to receive the Deputation, to wield his magic against the Empire of Moldorn. In the serenity of Ptolloden his hate of the Moldorns had not vanished but had cooled, becoming hard like iron.

The next year Teron jumped 53 places, and the third year 78. The rate of this advancement amazed the masters of Ptolloden. Teron's name and tale were known to every wizard in Ombernorr. He was now well into the third octoden, a mere 31 places short of his goal.

In his fourth year Teron studied all the Norrlings knew of the Moldorns, and formulated numerous plans for his mission, fully certain that the fourth octoden lay within his grasp.

But when he emerged from the Birdhouse at year's end Teron had amazed even himself. He had advanced 123 places, surpassing the journeyman's octoden and entering that of adept.

The psithe he now bore was of a species rarely obtained in the six-thousand-year history of the Norrlings—a small omniverous bird native to the islands of the southern oceans. Nocturnal, black with yellow bill and crest, it was named mooncrow.

"A singularly cunning and aggressive species," Cordavius noted, having read crystals on the bird that day. "You'd probably have trouble with it even if you were prepared for the power-level of an adept."

Teron regarded the Toucan from beneath a mooncrow mask pushed up on his forehead. "But master, what makes you think I'm not prepared?"

Cordavius glanced at the mask face and the gray human face, and frowned. Master and pupil sat on cushions before a fireplace of multicolored crystal. The Toucan's study was a round, vaulted chamber cluttered with books and magic artifacts. It was evening; Cordavius had invited Teron here to counsel him.

"I'm not saying your spirit is unprepared. The Birdhouse does not err in reading the soul of an initiate. And you have certainly proven your mettle these past few years. But your training is scarcely that of a tyro. Your skill is no match for your spirit."

"I appreciate your concern, master," the Mooncrow said. "But I practiced with the new psithe this afternoon. I found its level very high, but not beyond my control."

The Toucan sighed. "Nonetheless, I feel obliged to give you this advice: Stay at Ptolloden and train another year. It will take at least that long to learn the pitfalls of the adept level regardless of where you are. I think it unwise to try to master a new psithe and topple an earthly empire at the same time."

The Mooncrow half-smiled but shook his head. "I thank you for the advice, good master. But I feel overtrained already. I'm leaving for the Warmlands tomorrow at dawn."

"You're that anxious to fulfill your Deputation?"

"I am. I feel serious about it as I've never felt about anything else. I've kept close watch on the Moldorns these past years. Their empire has continued to expand. The sooner I start, the better."

"You're a puzzle to me, Teron," Cordavius said. "All the regimens of Norrling magic are designed to disengage the initiate from the world by making him a vessel of unworldly power. But the more the power grows in you, the more it seems to sharpen your worldly interests."

Staring at the hearth fire, Teron smiled. "I find the course of disengagement beguiling for a time, master. But in the end part of me rebels. There is just too much of the world I find pleasing. Perhaps that's my main motive for undertaking the Deputation. The Moldorns are destroying all that is pleasant about the Warmlands. I want them stopped."

Cordavius pursed his thin lips. "Since your mind is made up, Mooncrow, let me give you one more piece of advice: Stay away from the quinteer. It will tempt you, but the result could be disaster."

Teron nodded soberly. "I shall avoid it. And I don't expect the temptation to be strong. None of my plans include the quinteer—except perhaps as a last resort."

"You seem to place a great deal of faith in these plans of yours," Cordavius remarked.

Teron grinned. "I've had much time to lay them out."

The Toucan chuckled.

"What is funny, master?"

"Nothing, former Magpie. I only hope your fate is polite enough to correspond with your plans."

Chapter 5.
THE TOWERS OF PONNTHERION

*Yea, and in the land of Moldorn proud kings
raised upon the earth an abominable city.*
　　　　　　　—*Brother Kuthemes*
　　　　　　　Chronicles of Tann and Ibor

PONNTHERION, imperial capital of Moldorn, loomed
above the morning mist. The city was built in a steep
canyon, where a wide plain gave way to a vast range of
bleak mountains—the ancient domain of the Moldorns.
Part of the city stood on the canyon floor, part on a
winding craggy slope that climbed up to a ridge of cliffs,
and part far above the canyon—an impregnable citadel
built atop giant pillars.

The Pillars were square but with rounded corners, built
of stone and mortar, around a frame of some steel alloy
known only to the metalsmiths of Moldorn. The Pillars
were threescore in number, all of them four hundred feet
high. They stood in precise ranks near the cliff-edge, to
which they were linked by a huge cantilever drawbridge.
Beyond the bridge the Citadel jutted up in an overwhelming display of silvers and blacks—ramparts and turrets
hung with banners, spans and iron-railed catwalks,
bartizans and spires, jagged steep-sloping roofs and lush,
verdant hanging gardens. More than forty thousand
people dwelt atop the Pillars.

At the center of the Citadel, in one of the uppermost
towers, Bortoom Therion, "Lord of the Earth," sat upon
an iron and ruby throne. The Emperor of Moldorn was
large in all proportions—broad-headed, thick-shoul-
dered, with an enormous girth of belly beneath his fine
black and gold rainments. Below the knee his flabby legs
were bare, huge feet immersed in a basin of warm, milky
liquid.

"Damn your guts, physician," he grumbled. "How long before these treatments cure me?"

"Your imperial Highness suffers from a number of severe maladies," the physician said. "Even my supreme skill cannot effect a cure overnight." Clad in white robes and skullcap, he knelt before the monarch. His sleeves were rolled up and his hands, which massaged the Emperor's feet, were covered by translucent gloves of sheep membrane. "We must learn to be patient, Highness."

The Emperor snorted and shifted his weight in the great chair. The round antechamber was full of attendants, servant girls and guards. A lone noble, short and compact of build, stood beside the Emperor's chair, dressed in tunic and cape and trousers all of royal blue. Bortoom Therion spoke to him:

"What were we saying, Gildaro?"

"We had just finished discussing preparations for the official welcome of the Veglane Altazar twelve days from now."

"Ah, yes. The campaign has been damned costly. It will be a pleasure to celebrate the victory at last." He lifted a jeweled goblet to his lips.

The silver-haired Prince Gildaro frowned for the two seconds the Emperor's eyes were off him, then resumed his neutral expression. "Unfortunately, Highness, not everyone shares in your pleasant anticipation of—"

"Ow!" The Emperor jerked his foot, splashing the physician. "Careful, you skinny dog. That foot is tender."

"A thousand pardons, Highness." Gingerly, the physician returned to work.

Bortoom glowered at him, then gestured to a girl who brought him a golden bowl of fruit. He selected an orange and began to rip away the rind.

"What were you saying, Gildaro?"

The nobleman sighed. "I was reminding Your Highness that not everyone at court will be pleased to see the Veglane come home."

"Bah. Why must you always remind me of the dissidents?"

"Because, Highness, their numbers are growing in both

houses of the Council. The merchants and other Guildsmen are tired of paying for the Veglane's wars, and many of the Pallantines are wary of his ambition."

"The Pallantines are jealous," Bortoom replied. "And the Guildsmen are only peasants who happen to have money. Besides, all great men have their enemies. But Luiz Altazar will not suffer at their hands, Gildaro. Not while he has the army on his side—and all the generals are loyal to him."

"Only because he's slain all who dared oppose his policies."

"In honorable and codified combat," the Emperor answered. "That is the tradition of our race, Gildaro. We have always been a warrior people—even though soft conditions have caused some of the present generation to forget it . . . Ow!" he yelled. "Damn you, physician! Damn your incompetence." He flung the orange at the head of the physician, who threw up his arms and begged for pardon.

"Perhaps I may be of some assistance."

Gildaro and the Emperor turned abruptly as a slender figure stepped from behind a velvet curtain. He wore green robes and a white turban set with a ruby. His black-bearded face was long and thin, his skin dark brown, his narrow eyes pale gray. He approached the Emperor's chair and bowed.

Then the sentries, who had been taken aback by the stranger's abrupt entrance, finally reacted—placing themselves and their spears between the intruder and the Lord of the Earth.

"Who the devil are you?" Bortoom roared.

"I am Aurik Ib Bhendi of distant Indus," Teron answered, rising from his bow. "Pardon my unannounced entrance, Highness, but I have been trying to see you for nearly a week."

"How did you get in here?" the Emperor demanded.

Teron shrugged. "Your underlings gave me promises but no assistance. I could not wait forever, Highness."

The Emperor bolted to his feet. "But only one corridor leads to this chamber. How did you get past my soldiers?"

"Ah, forgive me, Highness. I did not mean to startle

you. One with my, eh...training is capable of moving about virtually unnoticed."

"Watch him closely," the Emperor advised his guards.

"What do you want?" Gildaro asked.

The magician gave a glance of amiable greeting to the Moldorn prince, then returned his eyes to the Emperor. "I have a mission, a duty to perform. I am to devote myself to the service of Your Highness."

"Why? Who sent you?" Bortoom asked.

"I am of a clan of scholars and philosophers. Part of our philosophy states that all living beings have a life-duty to fulfill. My duty, so I have learned, is to serve your Highness—the most powerful ruler on earth."

The Emperor sat back on his throne. "How can you serve me?"

"As a counselor and a scholar," Teron answered. "A master of the known and a student of the unknown."

"You're talking gibberish."

"Perhaps a tangible demonstration, Highness. I noted on my entrance that you are being tended without great success by this venerable physician. Perhaps I can help."

"You're a healer then? Why didn't you say so?"

"I am a student of the medical art among many other things, Highness. What is your affliction?"

"Pain! I have cramps that shoot from my feet to my belly and back again. Bad digestion, tightness in the chest..."

"His Highness suffers from a number of dreadful maladies," the imperial physician said.

"Quiet, fool," Bortoom grunted. "Get away from me."

The healer scuttled off to the side and the Emperor looked challengingly at Teron. "I've had physicians from every part of Ibor and Tann. None could cure me. What makes you think you can?"

"The fact, Highness, that the healing arts of my country are old as time itself. The cult of which I am a member was old when the world of the ancients reached its height and collapsed six thousand years ago."

"I've heard bravado before. I want results."

Teron bowed. "I shall do my best, Highness, if I may request that your sentries lower their spears."

"Let him pass," the Emperor said. "But watch him."

Teron approached a teakwood table near the throne. From the folds of his robe he produced a golden cup and a set of tiny vials. He filled the cup with water from a silver ewer and then tapped a few grains of powder from each vial into the cup. As he worked he explained:

"In my country is a sacred river which, from the time men first learned to name things has been called Ganges. Its waters have the power to effect many cures. The secret of these cures lies at the Ganges' source, where the crystal-formed stones contain magical properties. These powders are ground from various stones of that region."

In the psithe-cup Teron concocted a simple pain-relieving potion such as he had learned to make as a fledgling. He offered the cup to the Emperor, thankful that the Norrling healing art was superior to that of the Warmlanders.

"Your Highness has only to drink this."

"Guards," the Emperor said, and once more the spear points pressed close to Teron's robes.

Bortoom smiled shrewdly. "You drink it."

"But Highness, it will be wasted on me."

"Drink it!"

Shrugging his shoulders, Teron complied. He quaffed the liquid without hesitation, then inverted the cup to show it was empty.

The Lord of the Earth settled back in his chair. "Very well. Refill it now and I shall drink."

This time the Emperor and Gildaro took careful note of the vials and amounts the magician used. But once again Teron was forced to drain the cup himself. Ten minutes later he showed no ill effects.

"Very well," Bortoom said. "Mix the thing again."

Teron smiled thinly. "As you wish, Highness. But if this is to go on indefinitely I'll run out of powders and will need to send for my baggage."

"Just do as you're told."

The third time the Emperor drank the potion, downing it in a single gulp. He lowered the cup, brow furrowed and eyes blank.

The chamber was hushed. After a moment the

Emperor stood and beneath his great belly stretched each leg in turn.

"The stiffness is gone," he exclaimed. "I'm cured!"

"I'm afraid not, Highness," Teron said. "The potion is but a palliative. A complete cure, if I'm able—"

"Don't contradict me, idiot. No other healer has produced such results no matter how long they worked." He looked hard and shrewd at Teron. "You are a most welcome gift of fortune, young man. I think I shall appoint you my personal physician."

Teron presented a hearty, guileless smile. "Your Highness is very kind. But I do not seek official titles."

"I don't care a damn what you seek," the Emperor retorted. "I thought it was your mission to serve."

"Yes, Highness. But I hoped to live at court as a guest, that I might serve you according to my station. You see, in my country I am a noble, a son of the Brahmin caste."

Bortoom glowered, stretching his legs. "Nevertheless, I choose to make you my physician, and so you shall be—if you wish to remain alive."

Teron caught his breath. "In that case, Highness, I shall be honored to serve as your physician."

"Then it's settled. But since you're a nobleman, I see no reason why you can't have a nobleman's place in the court. Attend me at lunch in the north garden this afternoon and we shall discuss what other ways you might serve me."

Teron bowed, touching his fingers before his face.

The Emperor eyed the white-robed physician who had just been replaced. "So, I am finally rid of your incompetence." He crooked a finger, summoning the man to stand before him.

The physician obeyed, moving with anxiety. Bortoom ordered the man to hold up his thumb and then wrapped a huge hand around the thumb and pulled it back. With a choking sound the physician crumpled to his knees.

"Small repayment for the pains I've suffered at *your* hands," the Emperor grunted. He released the man after a final twist. "Now begone from my city. If you're seen again within its walls you'll hang by your toes for the condors."

Clutching his injured hand, the quivering physician left the chamber hurriedly, backing away and bowing at each step.

Bortoom glanced at Teron, who met his eyes meekly.

"Take warning, my new physician: I'd hang you for the condors just as willingly if you ever gave me reason."

"Be assured, Highness, I shall do my utmost to please you in all things."

"Good."

The Emperor instructed a steward to give Aurik Ib Bhendi quarters in a wing of the palace reserved for guests. Prince Gildaro begged permission to personally accompany the visitor to his rooms. The two men took leave of the Emperor and stepped into a narrow but immensely high corridor.

"You're the first nobleman of the far east ever to visit this court," Gildaro said. "I expect you'll be assailed with endless questions."

Teron glanced at him sidewise. "I shall take pleasure in telling all about my country."

"I among others will enjoy listening. For although we get a trickle of trade from the Orient, we know mostly legends about that part of the world. But tell me, how are you impressed so far with my country?"

"I am awed by it," Teron answered. "Its wealth and grandeur surpass all I've seen in the east. Your Emperor rules the greatest of nations and is rightly titled Lord of the Earth. I hope I may prove worthy of his service."

"You seem far more competent than the previous imperial physicians," Gildaro remarked. "And other than incompetence I can think of only one way you might fail to please the Emperor."

"And what is that, my lord?"

"By having other motives than you say. Were it to be learned, for instance, that you are here to spy, or to betray His Highness in some way, then nothing could save you from his revenge, which might be hideous indeed. I hope for your sake, Prince Bhendi, that you are only what you claim to be."

"And I rejoice for my sake that I am neither more nor less."

They traversed a long gallery in which one wall was all of steel-framed glass. Through the glass the gray and black towers of the Citadel could be appreciated in all their mass and splendor against a background of blue mountains.

"In truth your city is magnificent," Teron said.

"Yes. It took a half-million men forty years to construct the Citadel. It was begun in the days of Guntar Therion, the first Emperor of Moldorn, the great-grandfather of our present Emperor. The name of the city, PonnTherion, means simply 'the Keep of Therion.'"

The quarters provided for the Emperor's new physician consisted of a large antechamber and bedroom. Both rooms were amply furnished in a lavish, imposing style typical of the whole palace. Giant frescoes adorned the walls; tables, chests and doorways were inlaid with ivory and gemstones, silver and gold. The windows of the antechamber faced out on a terrace garden two stories down.

"I'll leave you to get settled," Gildaro said. "A manservant will be along soon. Until later."

Teron thanked him and bade him good-morning. Left alone, he heaved a sigh of relief and pulled off the turban, massaging his forehead with slender fingers. When the manservant arrived Teron sent him downstairs to the palace entrance, to fetch the baggage Teron had left there with the gatekeeper.

Then the magician withdrew to his bedchamber and bolted the door. He noted that the windows here faced only the buildings perched on the next giant Pillar. In between gaped empty air—and the cobbled street far below.

Sitting cross-legged on the low, wide bed, Teron changed the psithe into its disk shape and entered a mild, contemplative trance. So far the Mooncrow psithe was performing faultlessly, despite the Toucan's apprehensions.

Teron had practically fled from Ptolloden—fearful that some high master might find an excuse for revoking his Deputation. He had journeyed by dogsled across the tundras of Ombernorr, and on foot through the desolate, wolf-haunted forests of Bhakthorn. He took ship south from a Llorland harbor town, and eventually arrived in a port city on the north coast of Ibor. There he spent three months, mastering the language and studying the customs of the Moldorn Empire, solidifying his plans and practicing with the Mooncrow psithe. Then he traveled on by public coach, crossing the plains and forests of Ibor and coming at last to the imperial capital.

His plan to gain admittance to the Moldorn court had succeeded with relative ease. Still, the gloomy air of suspicion that surrounded the throne had Teron's nerves on edge. He would have to tread with extreme caution, at least until Aurik Ib Bhendi had become familiar about the court and had gained the Emperor's full confidence. Meantime, Teron planned to learn all he could about the Lords of Moldorn and their Citadel.

And he would look for Adria. He would have liked to search for his old partner Topiedeon as well, but he had no clues as to the minstrel's fate. He knew, on the other hand, that Adria had been carried off four years ago to serve as consort to the Emperor's son, the Crown Prince. If she was still in PonnTherion the Mooncrow was determined to find her—and to contrive some means of setting her free.

Chapter 6.
LUNCH AND DINNER
WITH THE LORD OF THE EARTH

THE CLOCK in the palace bell-tower struck the seventh hour of the day—one hour past noon—as Teron descended a flight of marble steps to the north garden. Rimmed with arcades, the garden measured twenty yards wide and twice again as long, but these dimensions were dwarfed by the towering gray walls that rose up canyon-like on three sides. The fourth side, Teron noted, bordered on an esplanade that overlooked the vast Citadel.

Moving with a deliberate, light-footed gait, the magician wove through the crowd of Moldorn courtiers who conversed among the hedges and palm trees and feasted from silver platters and gemmed cups. Teron attracted a multitude of glances that were bemused, scornful, suspicious, hostile. He kept his face impassive and in his turn scrutinized the courtiers: Pallantine lords clad in velvet costumes with mantelet capes, extravagant armor, plumed helms and long sabers. The ladies of the court were bedecked in thin gowns of silk and lace, and wore such jewelry as might have purchased whole cities. Many of the women were blonde, but Teron saw that Adria was not among them.

He approached a line of white-clothed tables set in the shade of the garden's single large tree, a great knotted oak. The tables were piled with food, and next to one table stood the Emperor with a small circle of courtiers.

Teron strode up before the monarch and bowed, touching his fingertips together before his beard. "Greetings to Your Highness."

"Here's the one I told you of," Bortoom grunted, his mouth full of meat. "The miracle worker, the Indusian prince who is also my new physician. I trust your rooms were suitable."

"As excellent, Highness, as one would expect in the house of the Lord of the Earth."

"Ha! An oily-tongued fellow, isn't he?" The Emperor took another bite of his capon leg, leaving Prince Gildaro to make the introductions.

"Prince Bhendi, may I present Her Highness Unez Modesta Gildaro Therion, Empress of Moldorn and, by the way, my sister."

"You are most welcome here, Prince Bhendi," the silver-haired lady said. "We are all in your debt for the relief your skill has provided the Emperor."

"I am his servant, Highness, and yours."

The Empress had a round and mild face, but her mouth was cunning and her eyes shrewd. She seemed to Teron much the feminine counterpart of her brother.

Gildaro introduced the others, an elderly Pallantine and his wife, richly dressed and with faces thickly coated with cosmetic powders, and a tall, fierce-looking nobleman of about thirty-five named Count Bartuzzi. Bartuzzi wore a corselet and a great purple cloak. At his side hung a gold-hilted example of the sleek, slightly curved Moldorn dueling saber.

At the Emperor's command Teron received a plate loaded with meat and a wine cup filled to the brim. He sipped and nibbled through the ensuing conversation.

"Well, then," the Emperor said. "You've proved a competent healer. What other talents can you put at my disposal?"

Teron's bland smile did not waver. "I think Your Highness will find that I possess all the common virtues of a good advisor, plus certain other abilities."

"Such as?"

"My country is ancient, Highness. Its temples and monasteries hold the secrets of many lost arts. In my short life I have mastered much of this arcane knowledge. Through training I've learned to discern and read the invisible influences that continuously pervade the Universe. As a result I can give counsel as to the most auspicious time for decisive action, decipher the underlying mood of a given day, or room, or person, at times foretell events before they transpire."

'"Hah, a neat set of talents if it's true," the elderly Pallantine said.

"Yes," Bortoom frowned. "We shall see."

He had finished his third platterful of sausage and fowl, and now ambled off to a separate table crowded with candies, cakes and honeyed wines. The white-haired Pallantine and his wife followed.

"I am anxious to hear about your country," the Empress Unez said to Teron. "We know so little of that part of the world."

"An interest I too have expressed," Gildaro said.

Over the next several minutes Unez and her brother inquired into the life history of Aurik Ib Bhendi. Their questions were casual but subtly interconnected, so that Teron's whole story was drawn out and could be examined for any trace of inconsistency or artifice.

But the Mooncrow lied fluidly, relying on all he had learned of the Orient from the library of Ptolloden and embellishing it with tales he'd picked up from sailors and wandering entertainers. He spoke of vast rain forests and exotic isles fragrant with spice, of holy men fasting for dozens of years and fakirs walking on burning coals. The Orient, as he described it, teemed with magic and mystery. Mad shamans wielded power over the rains and winds, mortal sorcerers grappled with demons and many-handed demigods.

"Mortals in equal struggle with immortals?" Gildaro laughed. "The western mind rebels at the idea."

"True," Unez agreed, "for the mortal must always be vanquished in the end, by death."

"At death," Teron admitted, "many sorcerers cause themselves to be consumed by fire. Otherwise their immortal enemies might seize their remains and thereby hold and torment their souls for eternity."

Unez and Gildaro exchanged looks of amused skepticism.

The Mooncrow's description of Aurik Ib Bhendi's life bore several similarities to his own true tale. "I wandered far and wide in the East and studied many arts," he said. "But I could find no duty in life that suited me. Finally I visited a blind sage, a famous oracle who dwells in the Mountains of Jarru. He decreed I was destined to serve the earth's mightiest lord."

There was a pause and Count Bartuzzi, who all the while had listened with folded arms, threw in a few questions of his own.

"How would you describe the armies of the East? How large are they commonly? What sort of weapons and tactics do they use?"

"Count Bartuzzi is a member of the Imperial War Table," Gildaro explained. "In fact he heads the Table in the absence of his cousin, the Veglane Altazar."

Teron's eyes flickered at the name. "I have heard of this Veglane, a great general I am told. He is not presently in the city?"

"No. He is away in the north," Bartuzzi answered, "finishing a campaign against the mountain dwellers of Khesperia. But you haven't answered my question."

Teron shrugged. "I fear I know little of armies and weapons, dear count. War is blessedly rare in my country, and men of my calling have no occasion to witness battle."

Bartuzzi gave a short, derisive laugh. "Luckily, in this part of the world war is not so blessedly rare." He bowed to the Empress, turned his back on Teron and marched off.

Unez smiled. "I'm afraid the count did not take much of a liking to you, Prince Bhendi."

Before Teron could respond to this the air was rent by loud barking and a whimpered cry of terror. At the end of the table two huge black hunting dogs had knocked down an old noblewoman. She cringed on the grass while the two beasts growled and snapped their jaws, restrained by leashes held by a tall, ungainly youth dressed in hunting leathers.

"My nephew, Ebbel Therion, Crown Prince of Moldorn," Gildaro told Teron amid the din of voices that arose. "He's brought his dogs to the garden, I fear, solely to aggravate his father."

Next moment Bortoom pushed his bulk through the small crowd that had formed and grabbed hold of his son's curly hair.

"How often must I tell you to keep your dogs in the kennel?" he yelled.

The Emperor launched a series of frenzied blows at the

Crown Prince's face. Ebbel snarled and blocked the blows with his arms. The dogs yowled and leapt at the Emperor, who caught one of them in the belly with a brutal kick.

"Get out!" Bortoom growled, throwing his son to the ground. "Go!"

Glaring at his father and muttering curses, Ebbel gathered up the leashes of his dogs. The crowd parted hastily to let him pass.

"And don't come to dinner either," the Emperor called. "I forbid it."

Gildaro sighed. "In a day or two the Emperor will grow moody and order his son back to table. After which Ebbel will contrive another means of enraging his father. I fear it's a cycle."

The Emperor's giant form quivered from exertion and he waved for attendants to support him until a chair could be brought.

"The whelp thinks I'm too old to beat him, but I showed him...Ohh, my stomach blazes with pain. Where's that Indusian healer?"

Calmly, Teron went to the aid of the Lord of the Earth.

The Great Hall of the palace glowed that evening in the light of uncounted candelabra. The masonry walls of the chamber leapt upward five stories and more before being lost in immense reaches of shadow beneath the unseen ceiling. About these walls at varied heights were balconies and galleries, from which depended hundreds of bright pennons and banners—flags of the Moldorn legions, and of the kingdoms and free cities they had subjugated.

The wide floor was set with oaken tables and chairs, places enough for over a hundred courtiers, and most of them were filled. Teron sat at the head table. The Empress herself had seen to his being placed there.

The Mooncrow wore a placid expression as he gazed out over the hall. A host of waiters moved about the tables, carrying platters of bread and pitchers of wine and beer. Jugglers, minstrels and acrobats performed in the open spaces on the floor, drawing irregular applause from the glittering nobles.

"We needn't worry about our being disturbed tonight by that ruffian son of mine," the Emperor informed the company. "I've ordered him locked in his apartments as punishment. The Imperial Guards sometimes find it difficult to obey me against the threats of my heir—but this time I've commanded their obedience on pain of castration. Now if that other royal child of mine would hurry we could begin a pleasant and peaceful meal."

The courtiers had been nibbling bread and cheese for the past quarter hour, but the meat had yet to be served. Custom dictated they await the arrival of the Emperor's daughter.

Teron knew almost nothing about the Infanta, as she was called, so he inquired of Gildaro, who sat on his left. A broad smile, both of fondness and amusement, stretched the prince's lips.

"Ah, my friend, having seen the Crown Prince you've seen only half the madness of this house. The Infanta is an amazing creature. She can shoot a crossbow, ride a horse and throw a knife with any man, and I know of none her age who can match her learning or wit. But don't get the idea that Rania is unfeminine. On the contrary she possesses a striking beauty, and a female charm so beguiling that ... that even I, her own uncle and too old for such nonsense, find myself speaking of her as though I were a moonstruck boy."

Another several minutes passed and the Infanta still did not appear. The Emperor was growing impatient. "Where is that daughter of yours, Unez? Our meat will be ashes by the time she arrives."

"Have patience, my lord," she said.

"I've run out of patience!"

Bortoom seemed on the point of ordering that the meat be served when a footman who stood atop a broad stair at one end of the hall blew a flourish on a golden trumpet.

"Her Highness the Infanta Rania Modesta Gildaro Therion," he announced.

The courtiers stood as a slender young girl in a maroon velvet gown descended the stairs at a near run. Her hair was long and black, and she wore no jewelry but a pair of large gold earrings. As she neared the head table, Teron noticed that her feet were bare. She took a chair across the table from her mother, who sat two seats up from Teron.

"I beg your indulgence for being late," she said,

glancing about the table. "I was observing certain stars that are only visible on the horizon this time of year."

"You were gazing at stars while the whole court sat here starving?" her father bellowed.

Undismayed, Rania poured herself a goblet of wine. "Please, father. Your overgrown son is absent this evening and we have a chance to dine in peace. Don't spoil it."

The Emperor's face contorted. Glancing about for a place to vent his wrath, Bortoom spotted the chief steward standing before the table.

"Well what are you waiting for?" he thundered. "Serve the meat."

The steward rushed off to obey and less than a minute later a train of servants marched in from the kitchen bearing huge trenchers of steaming victuals. Beef and mutton, stuffed fowl and wild boars cooked whole, sausages and vegetables and soups—all were laid before the hungry Moldorns.

Conversation at the head table lapsed as the courtiers fell to eating. Teron only picked at his food. After a while he lifted his eyes and noticed the Infanta gazing at him.

"You must be the Oriental savant, the prince from Indus," she said. "I've heard wonderful stories about you."

"What stories, Highness?" Teron inquired.

Rania grinned. "Oh, that you're a healer of extraordinary skill, a scholar of extraordinary knowledge, and a man with an extraordinary pair of gray eyes."

"Rania," her mother scolded. The girl laughed.

Teron smiled with surprise, then caught himself and resumed the bland, detached expression of Aurik Ib Bhendi. Gildaro had not exaggerated Rania's charm: She was capable of disarming even a Norrling adept.

"And what do you say to these stories?" she asked him.

"That the first and second are fully true, and that the last I must leave to your own opinion, Highness."

Laughter rose about the table. "Careful, Rania," Gildaro said. "Bhendi's not as sluggish as he looks."

The Infanta too was smiling. "I shall think it over, Prince Bhendi, and let you know what I decide."

Chapter 7.
SEARCH FOR ADRIA

It is likely therefore that the Ice Age Iborans possessed steam power. We know for a fact that the varieties of functional alloys they produced have not been equalled in sophistication until our own century."

—Ivann Demmering,
The Ancient Technicians
1368 New Calendar

PAST MIDNIGHT, when the courtiers had all retired and most of the lanterns about the palace had been extinguished, Teron bolted the door of his chamber and threw off his robes and turban. He stripped off the artificial beard and wiped the brown cosmetic film from his face and arms.

Then with ritual movements he donned the Norrling costume of the Mooncrow: woven of black feathers, snug and elastic, with soft leather boots and a huge cloak with hidden pockets and a hood. He added the bird mask, a gold-beaked headpiece with red eyescreens completely opaque from outside—the latter the mark of an adept.

The Mooncrow studied his image in the full-length, gold-crusted mirror. Then he made the psithe a wand, pushed open the casement of his bedchamber, and stepped out onto the ledge. He crouched there, an inch away from a drop of over four hundred feet.

The magician focused his mind and cast its force into the psithe-wand. Tingling in his palms, the wand made his body rise. Feet scrambling over stones, Teron scaled to the upper roof of the palace.

There a vast and baffling view confronted him. Illuminated by a three-quarter moon, the Citadel of PonnTherion was a panorama of tumbling rooflines, steep battlements and crenelated towers. All the Pillars

were interconnected by bridgeways, some as wide as
streets. Higher up, many of the separate towers were
linked by narrow catwalks or even narrower cable bridges
suspended against the stars. Teron had walked the
mystically structured halls of Ptolloden. Still this
Moldorn architecture dazzled him with its height and
scale.

And where, if anywhere, in this many-leveled maze of
stone and glass and metal, would he find Adria? Had
Teron taken the Toucan's advice and studied another year
at Ptolloden, he might perhaps have mastered a
non-physical method of searching for her, of probing the
ether with his mind until discovering Adria's particular
life-vibrations. Many adepts were capable of such
techniques. But Teron had only his mortal eyes and ears
with which to search, and his mortal form to carry them
about.

The magician began running along the roof, leaping
over gables, displaying an agility that reflected years of
regimens with the wand and the sword. He came to the
roof's edge and leapt a gap of forty feet—the psithe-wand
carrying him across in a perfect arc.

Teron landed noiselessly and paused, considering. As
well begin searching this place as any, he decided, since he
did not know where in the Citadel Ebbel Therion's
women were quartered. He started peering into darkened
chambers, his mutant eyes allowing some measure of
vision, which Norrling training had taught him to
magnify.

Over the next three hours Teron spied scores of
sleepers, their physical forms barely perceptible in the dim
glow of their auras. An overweight diplomat snored in a
canopied bed beneath a high-vaulted ceiling; a young
nobleman nestled with a black-haired slave girl; a
high-ranking lady dozed behind gossamer curtains and
strings of pearls.

When Teron had searched more than half of the vast
palace he found the seaglio of Ebbel Therion. Through
beaded curtains he observed the Crown Prince, stretched
out in a huge ivory and mahogany bed. Four naked
women slept curled about him. Adria was not among
them.

Teron began to inspect the adjacent row of windows. He discovered a series of luxurious chambers with gemmed tapestries and wide, fur-covered beds. Five more women slept in those beds, but again no sign of Adria. Then Teron's search was interrupted.

He was standing upon the last window ledge when a sentry came pacing along a battlement nearby. Previously the magician had avoided the numerous palace guards by keeping to the ample darkness—and by leaping from their paths on hearing the approaching footsteps. This time he was caught in the open.

"Name yourself," the sentry called, taken aback.

Teron gritted his teeth and leapt for the roof, commanding the psithe to lift him with all its power. For a second he hung in the air. Then with a burst of psithic energy stronger than he'd ever felt the wand swept him up four stories, like a leaf borne on a gust of wind.

The magician landed in a crouch on the edge of the palace's upper roof. Five stories below the sentry gazed up into the darkness, dumbfounded. He raised an alarm horn to his lips and Teron grimaced. But the guard hesitated, and lowered the horn. No one would likely believe what the man had seen; he was probably no longer sure of seeing it himself. And to sound an unwarranted alarm, Teron imagined, would be punishable by demotion, even flogging. The sentry put away his horn, turned and continued on his rounds. The Mooncrow let out his breath.

Teron searched the remainder of the imperial palace that night. The next six nights he searched the rest of the Citadel, including the numerous smaller castles belonging to the Pallantines. He thought perhaps Ebbel Therion kept another apartment of concubines outside his father's walls, or perhaps Adria had been married off, or traded to some other Moldorn prince. But all these suppositions, like all the Mooncrow's searching, yielded no trace of the lady of Telyrra. Teron's mind began to be troubled by other, sinister guesses as to Adria's fate.

Meantime, in the guise of Aurik Ib Bhendi, the Mooncrow continued to wangle the confidence of the Lord of the Earth. At least twice a day he treated the Emperor for cramps and other, miscellaneous complaints. The treatments were simple but potent—potions to relieve pain and aid digestion, tonics to stimulate the life-force, herbal preparations to calm the nerves. Teron presented them all with a blithe self-assurance that comforted the Emperor's mind. Bortoom became attached to the young physician, as to his favorite dog, his chief cook, and his wife. He would permit no other healer near his royal person.

And as Teron became a familiar figure in the Emperor's entourage, the courtiers' initial suspicions of him faded. Aurik Ib Bhendi was regarded still as alien and bizarre, but his strangeness now was considered harmless, laughable perhaps, but not a threat.

Prince Gildaro in particular was warmed by Teron's guileless air. The magician had been at court less than a week when Gildaro conducted him on a tour of the Pillars. They strolled over parapets and bridgeways that afforded steep, eye-boggling views of the city, the plain, the mountains. Gildaro named several of the Pallantine families and pointed out their houses.

"The Pallantines are descendants of the warchiefs who once ruled the tribes of Moldorn," he explained. "Even today their power is to be reckoned with."

Later they paused at the Citadel gate to view the imperial hill, which twisted up from the canyon floor to the wide cliff. The hill was crowded with tile-roofed houses of stone, larger ones near the summit.

"Before the completion of the Pillars the hill was the home of the Pallantines," Gildaro said, "and the cliff of the Emperor. Now the houses belong to the wealthiest Guildsmen and petty nobles."

Next he directed Teron's attention to the broad cantilever drawbridge which spanned the distance between the escarpment and the giant Pillar on which they stood. "When the gate is closed the bridge slides away, leaving a chasm sixty yards wide. The Citadel thus becomes an invulnerable fortress."

"A marvelous piece of engineering," Teron observed. "But does the Emperor never fear that this fortress might become a trap?"

"How do you mean?"

"I am unschooled in military matters, prince, but it seems to me that the true master of the Citadel is not he who commands the imperial palace—which must be nearly a half-mile from here—but he who controls this gatehouse and the bridge."

"A valid insight," Gildaro replied. "In fact the bridge mechanism is extremely complex. Somewhere in the palace there is a set of controls that overrides those here in the gatehouse. The location of those controls, along with the master code that operates them, is a secret passed down the imperial line from father to son. What's more, that same master code can work the controls here in the gatehouse. So whether he is here or in his palace the Emperor of Moldorn maintains final control over the Citadel's defenses."

Gildaro led Teron back toward the central Pillar. "So far you have seen the outer surface of the Citadel. I'm sure you'll find the internal portion equally impressive, though probably not so pleasing to the eye."

The two men entered the imperial palace and descended past the levels of the servants' quarters, storage cellars, and dungeons. They approached a pair of spiked iron doors guarded by two brawny spearmen in black and silver armor. At Gildaro's order the doors were swung open, revealing the top landing of a zigzagging stair. Teron looked over the iron rail and saw that the stair descended countless stories—deeper, it seemed, than the level of the street. The drone of machinery wafted up from the depths. Gildaro and Teron descended the stairs side by side.

Down the first forty flights they met with nothing save an increase in the volume of noise. Then they reached a wide landing where another pair of spearmen guarded another spiked door. Through the door they entered an enormous, dim chamber filled with steam engines and pipes clustered like arrows in a quiver—though each was thick as a pine tree.

"A machinery room," Gildaro said. "The power generated here is used to raise ore from the mines beneath the city."

They circled above the chamber on the uppermost of

four walkways, descended two more flights of steps, and passed through a long, metal-walled corridor lit by yellow lamps.

"We're leaving the central Pillar now," Gildaro told Teron, "and entering the one next to it on the north side."

For as Teron soon discovered, the lower levels of all the Pillars were hollow and linked together by enclosed bridgeways. From outside these bridgeways appeared to be architectural supports, bracing the Pillars some two hundred feet above street level. All together the hollow Pillars made up a vast chemical and metal works which, Gildaro explained, guaranteed that the Empire's weapon-making facilities would never fall into enemy hands, so long as the Citadel itself remained unconquered.

The two men toured huge foundry rooms where sweating laborers stoked the furnaces and skilled metalsmiths concocted the secret Moldorn alloys. They passed through long smoky halls where vats of sulfer chemicals bubbled, to lofty chambers where the gleaming hulls of airships were painstakingly assembled by armies of craftsmen.

Finally they returned to the central Pillar and walked down the stairs once more. Three stories above street level Gildaro pointed to a slab of steel ten inches thick which was raised on hinges above the stairwell.

"In a time of siege, hatches like that one are closed down over all the stairways—sealing the Pillars against attack from the lower city. The hatches are anchored to the steel frames of the Pillars so they can't be forced open. They're controlled from guard rooms in the individual Pillars, and also of course from the Emperor's master control mechanism."

"Remarkable," Teron said. "I can see that the Citadel was designed with every conceivable defense-work."

"Downstairs again," Gildaro said.

Thirty-five stories below the street the iron stairs ended in an enormous cavern lit by furnace glow and vibrating with the roar of smelting machinery. From this chamber, Gildaro remarked, tunnels and mineshafts ran off to the north, west and south, extending for miles beneath the mountains. The whole mining complex was patrolled by armored men with swords, pikes and whips. The work was done by teeming multitudes of gaunt, naked slaves.

Teron stared at the long files of mineslaves wheeling forward carts of ore to feed the giant furnaces.

"They're war captives mostly," Gildaro said. "I warned you it was not a pleasant sight. Few of the Pallantines ever venture down here. But I wanted you to see that the power and splendor of the Citadel rests finally upon this."

Teron eyed the prince gravely. Was this a simple test of his loyalty to the Emperor, or something more subtle? "Unhappily," he said, "the power of all princes is based upon the toil and suffering of others."

Gildaro nodded. "You are like me, Bhendi, I think. We both gaze without illusions on the evils of the world, and try to do what small good we can, performing our services, striving to save what reason and order we can find. I believe we can be allies."

"We serve the same lord; are we not allies already?"

"There are many factions, Bhendi: the merchants, the Pallantines, the War Table worst of all. They pull the government in different directions and would tear it apart if not held in check. You can serve the Emperor best by confiding only in him, and in myself, and in my sister. You should trust no one else, Bhendi. No one. Do you understand?"

"I do, my lord."

"Good." Gildaro sighed. "Come, there is one more set of chambers to show you."

They returned upstairs into the central Pillar, to a complex of chambers devoted to research. There white-robed men of the Technicians Guild pursued experiments and worked at deciphering ancient texts.

"Most of our scientific knowledge derives from the days of the ancients," Gildaro said. "The basic princples of the airship, many of the metal alloys, even the formula for the 'Moldorn fire,'—all were discovered in excavations of buried cities. Ahead is the hall of artifacts."

They passed under a metal archway into a long shadowy chamber filled with row on row of glass cases. The cases contained the numerous excavated objects whose secrets the Moldorns had yet to unlock. The artifacts were of varied shapes and sizes, some complete and some in fragments. They were constructed of wire, glass, wood, metal and other materials now unknown to the world.

At the end of the chamber Teron paused before an eight-foot-tall humanlike figure, blue-skinned and inanimate, which lay inside a tilted glass and metal tube.

"An artificial man," Gildaro said. "Thousands of years old, but the airless tube keeps it from decay. Pieces of others were found, but this is the only complete one."

"Was it actually meant to come to life?" Teron asked incredulously.

"Apparently so. The way it's been explained to me the ancients found a way to imprint human characteristics on a substance they made from petroleum, which in those days was plentiful. Then the artificial men were *grown* in that substance."

Teron shook his head and said nothing.

"Our technicians hope one day to rediscover the process," Gildaro added with some irony. "They dream of constructing whole armies of artificial men."

"I'd sleep little with such dreams," Teron said. "Your technicians have my sympathy."

Following this tour of the Pillars, Teron was regarded with complete trust by Prince Gildaro and his sister. At Unez's command the magician joined a select group of princes and advisors who were always welcome at the imperial family's own table.

Teron took full advantage of this privilege, since mealtimes afforded his sole opportunity to observe the Crown Prince at close range. Except for dinners and certain luncheons which he was compelled to attend, Ebbel Therion avoided his father's company. The Emperor's son spent most of his time pursuing amusement with a band of young companions, most of them sons of Pallantines. According to rumor the princelings' diversions included sharing each other's concubines. Teron paid close attention whenever Ebbel was present at table, hoping to pick up some clue as to Adria's whereabouts. But the Crown Prince was either sullenly quiet during meals, or else involved in boisterous, violent quarrels with his father.

The Emperor's daughter was different. She conversed a great deal at table, and often directed her remarks to Teron. The Infanta proved as perceptive and clever as she was charming. Teron began to worry that she might see beneath his disguise and discern the enemy of Moldorn who lurked within. He attempted to avoid her scrutiny.

But his reticence only piqued Rania's curiosity. One evening at dinner she invited him to view the stars through her telescope. Teron could see that the Empress was displeased by her daughter's boldness. Still, it was clear that a refusal could only be read as an insult, and so he accepted with a show of gratitude and humility.

Rania's observatory was in a high tower overlooking the central portion of the palace. Teron followed the Infanta there, along with attendants and two unspeaking imperial guards. On a balcony of the tower stood the telescope, a yard long and flawlessly made, set on a tripod of black steel and silver.

The early evening sky was a deep blue, and the cool mountain air so clear that myriads of stars were already visible. The rising moon, pale orange, floated over PonnTherion's numerous towers.

Teron squinted at the moon through the telescope. He turned to the Infanta with genuine admiration. "A wonderful device."

Rania grinned. "There's a larger one in the hall of the imperial astronomers. I'll show it to you sometime."

"I would be honored."

Rania took a turn at the eyepiece. "Do they study the stars in the Orient?"

"Some do," he replied. "But mainly to record and analyze the influence of celestial configurations on the affairs of the mortal plane."

She looked at him brightly. "Many philosophers in Ibor argue that the stars have no influence on earthly affairs, that such belief is superstition."

Perhaps she sought debate, but Teron turned the question around. "What does Your Highness think?"

"I'm not sure," Rania said. "The arguments of the

disbelievers seem more cogent. But we know almost nothing about the stars, so how can we dismiss any notions?"

"Indeed." Teron was impressed by her attitude. She combined keen intelligence with a vivid, open-minded curiosity—a rare combination in his experience. Her lips spread into a smile, and Teron realized abruptly that he was already smiling at her.

The magician looked down at the telescope. Not since his fledgling days had the desire-nature caught him so by surprise. He insulated himself from the aroused emotion with a wizardly effort of will. He could hardly risk entangling himself with a female at this point—especially not the Emperor of Moldorn's daughter.

Rania started to say something when the quiet was interrupted by a burst of laughing voices and lively mandolin notes. Teron and Rania both glanced down to a granite terrace some distance away. There, emerging from a bright room was a party of gayly dressed young people—three men and a larger number of women.

Abruptly, Teron swung the telescope around and peered down at the terrace, which he had recognized as belonging to Ebbel Therion.

"Just some of my brother's acquaintances," Rania said.

But Teron seemed not to hear. There were eight women, wearing satin dresses and jewels, their faces powdered various pastels. The telescope showed beyond doubt that one of the women, her face powdered a lavender shade, was Adria. Teron's throat constricted.

"Bhendi," Rania said. "It's considered incourteous to stare through a telescope at other people's balconies."

"Forgive me, Highness. I was so taken with the device. I wished to note its effects at closer range."

"Well, there are other subjects besides my brother's concubines."

"Indeed. Please forgive me." A sharpness had seeped into Teron's voice despite his efforts at control.

Rania peered at him in puzzlement, then shrugged. "I'm sorry, Bhendi. I didn't mean to scold you. It's my brother who makes me angry; the way he treats his consorts is detestable. They are all daughters of noble houses and supposed to have privileged status. Ebbel himself is not supposed to touch them unless they wish it. Instead he treats them worse than slaves, and my father permits it. Today some of Ebbel's consorts arrived from his castle in the country. He has friends in the Veglane's army who are returning this week. He's gathered all his women in the city to welcome the young officers."

Teron lowered his eyes. After a moment Rania shook her head and swung the telescope around.

"But I'd much rather talk about the stars."

"As would I, Highness."

Yet while discussing stars and constellations Teron continued to steal glimpses of the distant terrace. He saw Adria and another girl seated together on some young prince's lap. The prince had a brawny arm around each girl's waist, and by turn kissed them both. Anger rose in Teron. His voice faltered a bit as he explained to Rania the thirteen signs of the Indusian zodiac.

A short while later he thanked the Infanta for her generosity and begged permission to withdraw.

"But it's so early," Rania said.

"I have much studying to do, Highness. There is a great deal I must learn about the Empire's political affairs if I am to be a worthy counselor to your father."

Rania fixed him with a dark-eyed, skeptical look. "I hope I didn't offend you, Prince Bhendi, or hurt your feelings."

"No. Be assured you did not."

"But something's troubling you. I can tell."

"Only that I have much work to do, Highness." Teron bowed and left the balcony.

The sentry at the main door of Ebbel Therion's seraglio heard what sounded like a footfall. In the dim lantern glow he saw a black-clad figure move stealthily from the shadows.

But before the sentry could react he saw something else—a disk of swirling golden light. The guard's mouth fell open and his limbs relaxed. Teron walked past him and through the open doorway.

The power of the fourth attribute coursed freely through the Mooncrow psithe. The sentry, like the half-dozen others Teron had entranced, would come to his senses in a few moments—but with no recollection that the Mooncrow had passed.

Teron wore a dark outfit and a black hooded cloak. He had decided against wearing the feathered costume, for fear it would frighten Adria.

He crossed the seraglio's wide entry chamber, which was empty at this hour, save for one cushioned recess where two young concubines slept in each other's arms. The air smelled of incense, opium and perfumed oils.

Parting velvet drapes, the magician moved noiselessly down a narrow corridor, past the lavish bedchamber where the Crown Prince snored in his ivory-wrought bed. Teron peeked through the beaded curtains of several smaller rooms, until he spied Adria, sleeping alone on a low bed with silken sheets.

Entering, Teron threw off his hood and knelt at her side. The psithe-disk glimmered faintly in his hand, revealing Adria's face with its lavender hue.

"Adria."

Whispering, Teron slid a gray hand over her mouth—taking no chance that she might cry out. She awoke with a start and regarded him wild-eyed.

"Don't be afraid, lady. It's Teron, Teron the magician whom you knew in Telyrra."

She stared at him fearfully for several moments, then relaxed as recognition dawned in her eyes.

"Speak only in a whisper." Teron slipped his hand from her mouth.

"What do you want with me?" she demanded.

He smiled and threw out his hands. "I've come to set you free."

She eyed him mistrustfully for several seconds, then: "You're a fool. Go away. The Moldorns will hang you on meat hooks for the condors to pick—and me beside you."

The Mooncrow shook his head. "They won't. I'm not the same Teron you knew. I have far more power now."

"Please," she said slowly. "Go and leave me alone."

"I'm telling you, Adria, I'm more than a match for the

Moldorns now. I was sent by the masters of Ombernorr to make war on them, to bring down their Empire."

She shook her head, as though arguing with a madman. "Your people send one man—a conjurer?"

"A Norrling adept, dear lady. More than sufficient, believe me. But before I began my mission in earnest I wanted to deliver you out of the city, out of danger. That way, in the unlikely case that I should fail, I will at least have accomplished something."

Her expression softened a moment and she lowered her eyes. But when she lifted them again they glinted, cold and hard. "The only danger I'm in is from you, at this moment."

"Adria." Teron touched her arm but she yanked it away.

"No. I too have changed, Teron. I'm no longer the young girl you knew. I've spent the past four years degrading myself to suit the whims of the Crown Prince. I've adapted, learned to survive, but it's cost me. I no longer have room for tender feelings."

"What you've lost can be restored," Teron said. "Trust me."

"I trust no one. If you leave this moment I will not betray you. But if you stay I'll call the guards and take my chances. Ebbel will flog me for this, but at least I'll be alive."

Teron scowled at her darkly, then stood with a shrug. "Very well, I'm going. But be warned, Adria: when I do overthrow the Moldorns I might restore your throne, whether you want it or not."

He started to leave, then paused, catching sight of a line of colored lamps that sat unlit on the windowsill.

"In case you wish to summon me—"

"I won't."

"In case you ever do, light a pair of lamps, one red, one blue, and leave them burning in opposite ends of the same window."

Without waiting for a response the Mooncrow parted the beaded curtains and stalked soundlessly down the corridor.

•　　•　　•

Back in his own apartments Teron threw off his cloak and began pacing the floor. It had never occurred to him that Adria might not welcome the chance to escape from PonnTherion, that she might not believe in his power. He felt forlorn and vaguely angry. Inevitably, the anger turned on the Moldorns, and grew sharper the longer he pondered.

The time had come for him to act, to begin his war against the Empire. A sudden inspiration told him exactly how and when the first blow should be delivered: in four days' time, when the Veglane Altazar returned from his latest conquest.

Over the next three days Teron spent every free moment alone in his chamber, pouring mental energy into the psithe-disk—projecting there, again and again, the details of a great illusion.

Chapter 8.
THE TRIUMPH OF ALTAZAR

Having crushed the Khesperians at last, Altazar returned in triumph to Ibor. But unknown to the Veglane, his ultimate foe awaited him in PonnTherion itself. At this point the wizards of Ombernorr reenter the arena of Western History.

> —The Terrestrial Histories of
> Fystus the Grackle, *vol. 97*,
> *ch. 43* Norrling Year 6256

IN THE four and a half years since the fall of Telyrra the armies of Moldorn, commanded by the Veglane Altazar and bolstered by the matchless power of the airships, had continued to conquer the nations of the West. Employing the naval forces obtained by the surrender of the Telyrran League, Altazar blockaded the port cities of eastern Ibor. As a result, all of the southern continent fell under Moldorn domination by the end of that year—thus fulfilling the ultimate dream of Guntar Therion, first Emperor of Moldorn.

The Veglane then turned his attention northward and within two years extended the Empire's domain over all the islands of the Capdian Sea and up the rocky Arm of Arabhedden. The nations of eastern Tann prepared for war the following spring, but instead the Moldorns struck closer to home, pouring into the mountainous isthmus which joined the two continents of Tann and Ibor.

The wealthy kingdoms of Dhannia and Hystos fell that first summer, but the semi-barbarous tribesmen of Khesperia put up stiffer resistance. Led by a wily red-bearded warchief called General Lothar, the Khesperians baffled the Moldorns with guerrilla tactics perfectly suited to their country's precipitous terrain. The airships, unreliable at high altitudes anyway, proved of little use among the jagged peaks and narrow mountain passes.

Only by cunning did Altazar finally win. Using his airfleet as transports he struck unexpectedly late in the autumn, when the first snows had already blocked the mountain paths and both armies had camped for the winter. Trapped in a narrow valley, General Lothar was finally vanquished in a battle that lasted less than an hour.

By ancient tradition the people of Moldorn greeted their victorious generals with grand parades known as triumphs. It was the ninth time that Altazar had been so honored.

The Veglane rode at the head of his army, alone upon the banner-draped prow of his flagship, the *Basilisk*. He wore golden armor and a fur-trimmed cape, and did not gaze down on the populace which lined the parade route.

The *Basilisk* led a file of ten airships that sailed some thirty feet above the crowded streets. From the keel of each ship, suspended a few yards off the ground, hung a captive wrapped in chains. These were Khesperian chieftains, General Lothar himself hung from the flagship.

Below the airships marched row upon row of heavy infantry, bearing spears and high-powered crossbows. Actually, these were men of the City Legion. The armies that had conquered Khesperia remained there to watch the north border. Only the Veglane and his aeronauts had actually returned, but the infantry was considered a necessary part of the pageant and so the local troops were used. They herded more chained captives, and wheeled others in cages.

Drums beating, the parade followed a straight avenue along the base of the Pillars and ended in a broad marketplace at the bottom of the imperial hill. The airships continued up the craggy slope to the summit, but instead of turning right for the Citadel, veered off left toward a small airfield half-cut in the mountainside and fortified with battlements and turrets.

The Emperor of Moldorn, bedecked in gold and silver robes and flanked by his equally sumptuous courtiers, waited on a canopied dais to welcome the Veglane. A thousand spearmen in the black and silver armor of the imperial guard were marshalled to both sides. Behind them stood a cheering, brightly dressed crowd of nobles and wealthy commoners.

The airships glided in a low V-formation. Soldiers rushed in to release and drag off the captives, and then the ships landed, their steam engines putting to a stop. Carrying crossbows and lances the aeronauts leapt to the ground and lined up before their ships.

A row of trumpets blared and Altazar, after saluting his men, marched forward. At the same time the Emperor descended the carpeted steps of the dais and walked toward the Veglane. They met beside a large flaming brazier. Altazar dropped to one knee and presented the Lord of the Earth with the flag of conquered Khesperia. The Emperor showed it to the applauding spectators then tossed it into the brazier.

He was clasping Altazar's shoulders and raising him to his feet when an explosion shook the ground and a black cloud spouted from the brazier. Startled, the Emperor slipped and fell on the pavement, dragging the Veglane down with him. The vast crowd caught its breath.

For upon the black smoke was an image—a black bird against a crescent moon—and words printed in wavering letters of golden flame:

I BRING VEGEANCE FOR THE RUINED CITIES
AND THE PEOPLES YOU HAVE DESTROYED.
THE FIRE COMES HOME TO PONNTHERION.

MOONCROW

The words lingered perhaps a quarter minute, then they darkened and the cloud of smoke dispersed. Discussion, awed and anxious, spread across the airfield.

Back beneath the canopy Teron relaxed his intense stare and removed his fingers from the golden disk in the inner pocket of his robe. The magician had not doubted the Mooncrow psithe's capacity for projecting an illusion into so many minds, but he had been uncertain whether his mastery of the psithe was perfect enough to make the trick convincing. On consideration, Teron was satisfied, though perhaps the wording was a bit melodramatic. Still, judging from the crowd's reaction, the effect had been well-calculated.

Bortoom Therion canceled the rest of the ceremony and returned at once to his palace. Teron accompanied the Emperor, mixed a drug to calm him and a potion to relieve his stomach spasms. Lips pale and trembling, Bortoom drank from the psithe-cup. He sat in his private tower, flanked by a score of imperial guards. Still his nerves were obviously brittle.

"Who could be responsible, Gildaro? And why?"

"*How*, is the question I would like answered," Gildaro muttered.

"My lords, if we discover who is to blame, we shall learn soon enough how the trick was done," said Altazar, who approached the throne with Count Bartuzzi at his side.

"How did you gain entrance, Veglane?" Gildaro demanded. "His Highness ordered complete seclusion."

Altazar fixed the prince with an icy stare. "I assured the men on duty that such orders could not include the Veglane or his chief officer."

"Of course not," Bortoom grumbled. "I'm glad you're here, Luiz. What do you make of it?"

Teron stood with arms folded beside the throne. Altazar gave the magician a quick, scrutinizing glance, then replied to the Emperor:

"Count Bartuzzi informs me that this display of fireworks is the first anyone's heard of the so-called Mooncrow."

"Damned strange set of fireworks." Bortoom rose and began to pace, clutching his belly. "There's devil's magic at work here."

"Nonsense," Altazar said mildly. "Your Highness is overwrought. Some clever optical effects are at work, nothing more."

The Emperor sneered. "Anyone who'd dare threaten us must have more than optical effects for weapons!"

Altazar's voice stayed level. "True, Highness. Some sort of plot has obviously begun to unfold."

"But who is plotting?" Gildaro said. "And why?"

With a gesture the Veglane referred the question to

Bartuzzi, who responded at once:

"Ostensibly the Mooncrow seeks revenge for our defeated enemies. He chooses the day of Luiz's return to declare himself. Obviously the conspirators are opposed to our military policies."

The Emperor paused before a tall window. "Prince Harroman?" he wondered. "Martez?"

"Harroman's been my enemy for years," Altazar said. "But why do you name the chief of the Merchant's Guild?"

"Money," Gildaro replied. "The Khesperian Campaign was costly, Veglane. Martez leads a faction in the Lower House that fought each new expenditure."

Altazar approached the Emperor. "So the peasants grow unruly. What about the Technician's Guild?"

Bortoom gazed down at the Citadel through the paneled glass. "We still own Master Penderez, and he still controls the Technicians."

"Excellent," Altazar said softly. "So long as we are masters of the army and of that one guild, Highness, our power cannot be toppled."

"I'm glad you're so damned confident, Luiz." Bortoom turned away. "Whatever this Mooncrow business is, I want it stopped."

The Veglane moved to a nearby table, poured a tumbler of brandy. "Fear not, Highness. I intend to flush the game without delay." He gulped the liquor and set down the glass. "I shall await your Highness in the Hall of State, within the hour."

Bortoom winced. "I'm not feeling well, Luiz. I thought I'd postpone your report."

Altazar shook his head. "Not wise, Highness. The Council is unsettled. We must reassure them that the situation is under control."

The Emperor sighed, nodded wearily and called for servants to dress him in the proper robes. Altazar and Bartuzzi took their leave, hands on sabers. Bortoom ordered Teron to fix another potion.

"Terrible business, Bhendi," the Emperor mumbled. "Did you know my own grandfather was assassinated, butchered in this very tower by a pack of traitors? I tell you, the throne on which I sit is the most precarious chair on earth. You should be grateful you're not in my place, Bhendi."

Teron answered in a monotone, "In truth, Highness, I am."

The Imperial Council convened in the Hall of State, a lofty, skylighted chamber of cedarwood and marble. Teron and Gildaro stood together beside the Emperor's throne, which rested on a dais fourteen steps above the floor. Gildaro identified the two houses—the Pallantines who filled the gallery on the Emperor's right, and the Guildsmen seated on the left.

Altazar wasted no time in raising the matter of the Mooncrow. "The message claims that revenge is sought for our wars. As the lord most responsible for our military endeavors over the past ten years, I claim first right to defend them."

Applause greeted these words.

"A fair claim," Harroman the Pallantine said. "But why announce it to us?"

"Because," Altazar said, "I think it obvious we are dealing not with a single man, but with a conspiracy. And I have no doubt that some of the conspirators have seats in this chamber. Let my challenge be known: I will fight any of the traitors, or all of them, under the code, at any time they choose."

A din of voices responded, mixed with more applause and clear shouts of "Bravo Altazar!"

Gildaro chuckled mirthlessly and nudged Teron. "The Veglane has the majority of the Councilors where he wants them now, suspicious of each other and looking to him for leadership and security. The man is clever, Bhendi."

Teron nodded blandly. "I hear he's an excellent swordsman as well."

That evening after supper Altazar entered his bedchamber for a change of garment and discovered a note attached to the outside of his window:

> YOUR BLUNT CHALLENGE IS BLUNTLY AC-
> CEPTED, VEGLANE. MIDNIGHT IN THE NORTH-

TOWER GYMNASIUM OF THE PALLANTINE CLUB.

MOONCROW

Teron had composed the note in a mood of supreme confidence, certain his Norrling fencing skills would baffle even the renowned Altazar.

That evening in his locked and bolted antechamber the Mooncrow practiced positions and thrusts to limber his muscles. His psithe-sword was much like a Moldorn saber—basket-hilted, with a tapering, slightly curved blade. Teron swished the sword and grinned, keenly anticipating the combat. Slaying Altazar would make an effective beginning to his war on the Moldorns, and would satisfy an old personal hatred as well.

Near midnight, the magician donned the mask and feathered costume. Stretching the psithe into a wand he threw open the chamber windows and crept outside.

Rain was falling, whipped into sheets by a cold wind from the mountains. Buoyed by the wand, Teron clambered up the slippery facade of the palace. The guard had been increased all over the Citadel, but the Mooncrow kept to the dark, inaccessible roofways, avoiding the parapets and bridges that the sentries patrolled with their lanterns. Noiseless, wraithlike, he made his way across the Citadel, leaping from roof to roof by the magic of the wand.

The Pallantine Club was a tall, many-towered building located four Pillars south of the imperial palace. Within its walls were sleeping quarters, gaming rooms, vaulted dining halls and several broad gymnasiums where the lords of Moldorn exercised their muscles and practiced with their blades.

Teron gained the roof of the Club and scaled the Northtower. Pausing at an open skylight he peered inside. The gymnasium was a high-vaulted, oblong chamber surrounded by a spectators' gallery. Below, on a scarlet-carpeted runway, Teron spied the Veglane, naked to the waist, feinting and thrusting with mechanical precision at a swinging leather target. The magician's vigilant eyes detected no armed men lurking in the shadows. Silently, Teron slipped into the chamber and lowered himself by the skylight chain.

Altazar glanced up as the silent, fantastically clad figure descended the marble steps. With cape drawn close in front, hiding his arms, Teron crossed the lacquered floor, halted at the edge of the runway, and stared at the Veglane without a word.

Altazar burst out with a tittering laugh. "Your costume is splendid."

The Mooncrow offered no response.

"You'll have to remove it, you know. According to the code you must be naked to the belt."

"You lie, Veglane. I know the code as well as you. So long as I wear no armor and carry no weapon but a sword."

Altazar shrugged. "But how am I to know that?"

"You're not, Veglane."

The Mooncrow sprang in the air, sword leaping into view. He landed in a deep crouch, feinted and thrust.

The Veglane tensed, met the feint, deflected the thrust. "Come, before I kill you, at least tell me who you are."

"Don't fret," Teron answered. "You'll soon be beyond all curiosity."

The magician's blade wheeled and descended. Altazar jumped back, parrying nimbly. Teron pressed him, leaping and striking in a ritual Norrling attack. His movements were hawklike, dark wings and slashing talons. In seconds such an onslaught would have unmanned any but a fencing master.

But the Mooncrow's opponent was Altazar, called the greatest swordsman in Ibor. He retreated without a perceptible loss of aplomb, deflecting each thrust and managing an occasional riposte. The Veglane seemed to be biding his time, waiting for his opponent's fury to abate.

But Teron's fury was vast, the sum of his mortal hatred of the Moldorns. His whole being was fixed upon one lethal purpose. The psithe-sword crackled in the air and glittered an unearthly violet.

Altazar continued to give ground calmly. Then, backed against the wall, the Veglane made his stand.

Teron slashed and chopped in reckless abandon, but Altazar moved his saber with dazzling speed, perfectly deflecting every blow.

Beneath the bird mask beads of sweat coated Teron's forehead. The power of the psithe had hardly been tapped, but the magician's stamina was running out. Teron's arm grew heavy, his onslaught lost its murderous edge.

And Altazar pressed the attack anew. Teron was forced back, the spring gone from his legs. Altazar grinned fiercely. Teron's blade was beaten once, twice—and both times only a desperate backward leap saved the Mooncrow from being pierced.

The Veglane's third thrust caught him, a half-inch of steel plunging into Teron's belly. He lost his footing on the carpet and went down. Instantly Altazar loomed over him, saber point at the throat.

"Yield," the Veglane demanded.

For answer Teron lurched his head to one side and stabbed the Veglane's thigh. Scissoring his legs about the Veglane's calves, the Mooncrow upset his enemy and scrambled to his feet.

Holding his wound, Teron dashed up the marble steps to the gallery. Altazar hobbled after him, voice shaking with rage: "Come back, coward."

Teron paused at the top of the stairs, gripping the rail. "We shall finish another day, Veglane."

"I think not," Altazar said. "Your cowardice decides the issue. Soldiers!"

The spiked doors on the gymnasium floor and along the gallery burst open and troops of Moldorns poured in, armed with crossbows, sabers, pikes.

Teron glanced about wildly. There was no hope of escape except by the quinteer—and no time to debate the wisdom of its use.

Teron made his saber shrink into a glimmering ball of light. In his thoughts he uttered the incantation: *Nyr solelleum quinteer, nie te porm.* Instantly the radiant psithe reached out to engulf his life-force. Teron felt himself falling into the sphere of power, as into a bottomless well.

A burst of silent multicolored light dazzled the Moldorn soldiers. When the light had vanished so had Teron—leaving a black bird in the vacated space.

The Moldorns froze. "Shoot the bird," Altazar ordered.

But the Mooncrow was already rising to the darkened vault. Untouched by the hastily released bolts, he found the open skylight and flew from the tower.

Teron soared high above the pillared Citadel, and felt with exhilaration the rain upon his wings.

But presently, when he thought to return to the palace, he found he could no longer control the flight. The feathered body would not respond to his mental commands. A pang of fear seized the magician. Somehow the will of the bird had taken control. Teron recalled Cordavius' warnings against invoking the quinteer.

The bird continued to fly aimlessly through the curtains of rain, high above PonnTherion. Numbly, Teron fought to regain mastery, straining his will to tip the wings. The bird's will resisted. Teron experienced a frenzied struggle of energies in his skull, and an icy pain. The edges of his vision blackened.

Then abruptly he won. The bird's will had given way.

Mind trembling with relief, the magician steered toward the roof of the imperial palace. But as he spiraled down, the will of the bird suddenly asserted itself with one last impulse.

Caught off guard, Teron felt his life-force torn from the energy of the psithe. His human body materialized in the air, hung an instant, then crashed down on the palace roof.

Luckily he landed on an almost flat section, which kept him from falling farther. For several moments he lay half-conscious, gasping for air, pelted by the rain. Finally he roused himself, bruised and aching. He found the psithe lying nearby in its formless energy-state. The psithe offered no resistance as Teron changed it into a wand.

With the aid of the wand he returned to his quarters. There he bandaged his wound with healing salves, drank a tonic from the psithe-cup, and then sank into a deep sleep, mind and body exhausted.

Chapter 9.
THE CROW STRIKES

And on their awesome pillar-tops
The Pallantines did quake.
"The Mooncrow rules the dark night.
PonnTherion's not safe."
>   —*"The Mooncrow and the Moldorns"*
>   *Ballad attributed to Bandelion*
>   *of Peltaine,*
>   *(Norrling Year circa 6240)*

TERON WAS wakened early that morning with a summons to attend the imperial family at breakfast. He rose painfully and changed the dressings on his wound, then put on the robes and makeup of Aurik Ib Bhendi.

The meal was served on a shaded gold-marble veranda near the Emperor's apartments. Teron found Bortoom, Gildaro, the Empress and the Infanta already seated at a long ebony table. A troop of servants stood nearby, holding trays of food and baskets of fruit. Teron fixed the Emperor a tonic, then was given leave to sit.

"You're not looking well, Bhendi," Unez remarked. "You seem fatigued."

"All that studying," Rania said. "He needs more time for recreation."

"Are you ill, Bhendi?" Gildaro asked.

Teron touched his fingers to his forehead. "In fact, Prince, I spent a restless night. I was troubled by ... impressions of some ... power."

"What are you talking about?" Bortoom demanded.

"I have mentioned to your Highness that I am sometimes able to discern various invisible influences. Last night I was wakened by a definite sense of mystic energy manifesting somewhere in the Citadel. I felt the same energy once before, when the Mooncrow's message issued from the flaming brazier."

Gildaro and the Emperor exchanged frowning glances.

"Was there some new word of the Mooncrow last night?" Teron asked.

"There are rumors," Gildaro said.

"What rumors?" Rania asked.

"Why didn't you tell us of this 'feeling' before, Bhendi?" Bortoom said in irritation.

"I knew your Highness would be skeptical. And I myself was not certain."

"What precisely do you mean by 'mystic energy'?" Gildaro inquired.

"To be precise in these matters is exceedingly difficult, Prince. The nearest similar sensation I've experienced was in the presence of certain potent shamans who rule the islands southeast of Indus. The implication I draw is that the Mooncrow, whoever he is, has a large measure of unearthly power at his command."

A bleak, superstitious dread appeared in the Emperor's eyes.

"What rumors of the Mooncrow have you heard, Uncle?" Rania asked a second time.

"Wild stories," Gildaro said. "That the Mooncrow dueled the Veglane last night and wounded him... other, more incredible reports."

"Luiz is due here after breakfast," the Emperor said, "to go over some treaty renewals. We'll have the story from him then. 'Mystic energy' indeed. Sorcery you mean." Clearly the Emperor wanted the subject dropped as he returned his attention to his food.

Using Aurik Ib Bhendi to heighten fears of the Mooncrow had been part of Teron's plans from the start. He spent the rest of the meal measuring what impression he had made. Bortoom was definitely the most disturbed. Gildaro and Unez seemed calm, uncertain. Rania was more interested in the method than the disclosure. She pressed Teron to describe it further.

"The mind-art is not mysterious," he said. "It is like the sensitivity to danger of animals in the forest. Humans too have this hidden faculty, but it is generally dulled beyond usefulness by civilization."

"Then the art simply makes you conscious of

impressions which are there for all to feel," Rania said.

"Precisely."

The clock in the palace bell-tower rang the third hour of the day. The Emperor was scheduled to meet with the Veglane, and Altazar was always punctual in his appointments. The Veglane strode out onto the veranda past the guards, followed as usual by Count Bartuzzi. The Veglane wore dark-colored trousers and a plush blue coat. He moved with a limp not fully concealed.

"There you are, Luiz," the Emperor tried to strike a light note. "I hear tell you met the Mooncrow last night."

The Veglane bowed sullenly to the company, Bartuzzi moving like his shadow. Altazar's mordant eyes lingered a moment on Teron.

Then he turned to the Emperor. "Yes, Highness, I did encounter the Mooncrow last night. He accepted my challenge and I fought him under the code. With my point at his throat I offered him quarter. He responded by stabbing my leg and wriggling from my grasp. He escaped with a saber wound in the abdomen."

"But you didn't face him alone!" the Emperor cried.

"I fought him alone," the Veglane said. "I had men outside in case he broke the code."

"Then how did he get away, Luiz?"

Altazar's black eyes smoldered. "An illusion," he said. "The trick of a master conjurer. Surrounded by soldiers he somehow managed to disappear, leaving a bird in his place."

The Emperor's jaw dropped open.

"Then the rumors were true!" Gildaro exclaimed.

"Only a fool would take such rumors literally," Altazar declared.

"But this is monstrous!" the Emperor roared. "He made fools of us, Luiz. And he's still uncaptured. We must stop him somehow!"

The Veglane frowned with scarcely hidden contempt. "We shall stop him, Highness. But not by panicking."

"What do you propose to do?" Gildaro demanded.

"Kill him if he'll fight me again—which I doubt. We'll probably have to find another way to trap him. Meantime I intend to make the whole affair public. I still believe certain Pallantines are behind this plot, and we must not appear to be concealing anything from the Council. I also suggest that Your Highness declare military law, so we can patrol the Citadel with imperial troops. Enough soldiers constantly on watch will abort the most cunning conspiracy."

Gildaro shook his head. "Declare military law because of one swordsman? The Pallantines would think we invented the conspiracy just so we could move the troops in."

"I care nothing for what they think," Altazar said.

"He's right, Luiz," the Emperor groaned. "No imperial troops, at least not yet. We can't afford to antagonize the Pallantines. One crisis at a time is all my nerves can stand."

"Father, I think you should ask Bhendi's advice," Rania said. "He did predict that the Mooncrow had peculiar powers."

All eyes turned to Teron.

Bortoom said, "Well, what do you think, Bhendi? A man could not actually become a bird, could he?"

Teron gave a calculated shrug. "There are many magicians and shamans of the Orient who claim they can turn into animals and birds. Few disbelieve."

Bartuzzi snickered. "Fortunately, we live in a slightly more sophisticated country."

Teron answered in a placid tone. "When I crossed the ocean a man told me of a city built on pillars tall as the mountains. I believed him, and now I eat breakfast in that city. The Veglane claims he saw a man become a bird. I see no reason to doubt his senses simply because he does not believe them."

Rania smiled above her cup and eyed Altazar to catch his reaction.

The Veglane gave Teron a hard, mistrustful stare, then gestured with his finger. "You interest me, physician. What exactly is your opinion of the Mooncrow?"

Picking his words with care, Teron repeated what he had said concerning his perception of occult forces. The Veglane listened intently, his expression growing more and more dubious.

"You seem to know a great deal about this swordsman," he said. "Perhaps too much."

"What are you saying, Luiz?" Bortoom demanded.

"Think about it, Highness. There was no Mooncrow before this man appeared at court. He's the same height and build as the man I fought last night..."

Teron saw Bartuzzi's hand sliding to his saber-hilt. Before the magician could frame a reply the Veglane spoke again.

"But there's a quick way to prove the matter. If this man is the Mooncrow he has a half-inch-deep saber wound near the center of his belly."

Teron eyed the Emperor across the table. The psithe might save him, but he needed time.

"Well don't just sit there," the Emperor said. "Get up and open your robe."

"I..." He glanced at the Empress and Rania, who watched him and waited.

"Why do you hesitate?" Bortoom cried.

Teron bowed his head. "Forgive me, Highness. In my country it is forbidden for a man to bare his chest in the company of women."

"What a silly custom!" Rania exclaimed.

"Nevertheless," Teron rose to his feet. "If I may be permitted to turn my back on the ladies and expose my flesh only to Your Highness, or the Veglane."

"Very well," the Emperor stood.

Teron turned, maneuvering so that his back was to the table—and to the guards and servants as well. He reached into his robe to the large pocket containing the psithe-cup and with a flick of his fingers made the cup a disk. Focusing his mind, the magician projected an illusion into the disk: four times—for the Emperor and the Veglane, and for Gildaro and Bartuzzi who also approached.

Then Teron pulled open his robe and lifted his undergarment. At the same moment he inwardly chanted the spell to release the illusion, and felt its waves emanate from the disk. The four men perceived a thin brown torso, without a trace of wound or scar.

"So much for that idea," Bortoom grunted.

"Perhaps not," Altazar said. "There's something about

this man I don't trust. He may not be the one I fought, but he might still be part of the plot. I recommend that you assign a permanent guard to this man, Highness."

It was the Empress who protested. "That I will not allow, Bortoom. Prince Bhendi is your guest and personal physician. He has done nothing to warrant distrust."

"All right, Unez," the Emperor grumbled, returning to his chair. "I agree with the Empress, Luiz. I think you're just picking on Bhendi for want of any real clue."

Altazar frowned acidly. "Very well, Highness. But allow me to warn you, physician. If you are playing us false I shall find it out. And I shall show you no pity."

Altazar told the Emperor he would await his pleasure inside. He and Bartuzzi bowed curtly to the table and withdrew.

"First Count Bartuzzi and now the Veglane," Unez said to Teron. "You do seem to have a knack for making bad impressions on our soldiers, Bhendi."

Teron put on a weary, perplexed expression, at which Rania giggled.

In the following days Teron rested much in his chambers, and practiced mental and physical disciplines to aid the healing of his wound.

But the combat with Altazar had injured the Mooncrow's pride at least as much as his body. The failure stung and it inflamed his hate of the Moldorns, of the Veglane most of all. Sore and bitter, Teron raved inwardly. Still, the Norrling's impeturbable self-control allowed him to view the situation clearly, and to make decisions with a cold and dispassionate mind.

Teron dared not accept the Veglane's second public challenge. Another fight with Altazar was all too likely to be his last. He might have taken Altazar by stealth, of course, but even that was risky. The Veglane had a reputation for being a hard man to catch off guard.

Nor would Teron kill the Emperor, although it would have been easy. But Bortoom's death might allow Altazar to seize undisputed power. Besides, it seemed more desirable to let the Emperor live, since he was superstitious and a great coward too. With the influence of Aurik Ib Bhendi, Teron believed he could eventually frighten the Emperor into accepting his terms of peace.

That left the Pallantines and the Guildsmen to suffer the Mooncrow's wrath. Teron decided it was most just to attack the lords of Moldorn—particularly those of high military rank. While his wound healed he studied in the palace archives, learned the names and military exploits of the various Pallantine families, examined the architectural plans of their houses.

The Mooncrow would lay his terms before the Moldorns: the freeing of all lands conquered by the airships and the restoration of all the enslaved. And the Crow would strike and strike again until these terms were met. Long ago, in Ptolloden, Teron had promised himself to be as ruthless with his victims as the Moldorns were with theirs.

So, on a starless night two weeks after his duel with Altazar, the Mooncrow attacked. He assailed one Oban Penthez—prince of the House of Penthez and colonel in the imperial army—as he walked home from an evening of gaming at the Pallantine Club. The colonel was traversing a deserted catwalk when the feather-cloaked figure leapt from the dark to confront him.

The Pallantine's saber hissed from its sheath. The Mooncrow parted his cloak and held up a sword that glimmered and made the air waver with heat. The blades collided once, twice. Then the psithe-sword cut around the Moldorn's guard and Teron drove it through cloth and armor into the chest. The power coursed through Teron's brain and down his arm. The Moldorn screamed as his wound sizzled and smoked.

Teron drew out the blade and let the dead man fall. In the morning this note was found beside the corpse:

UNTIL THE CONQUERED LANDS ARE FREED AND THEIR PEOPLES RESTORED FROM SLAVERY, I MAKE WAR ON THE LORDS OF MOLDORN.

MOONCROW

He struck again in seven nights, the scalding sword disemboweling one of Altazar's top airship captains, the only son of a Pallantine house.

Five nights later the Crow surprised a Moldorn general who was taking a bath with a trio of maidservants. Teron tossed the naked man a saber, then ran him through on the first pass—staining the bath water crimson and causing the women to scream.

The broad roofs of the Citadel were too steep and irregular to be effectively patrolled. Airships were suggested, but they were too bulky to use among the Citadel's towers, and too slow to maneuver even if they could spot the assassin in the dark. The Pallantines doubled and tripled their household guard. All over the Citadel iron screens were installed on windows and double locks on doors. Many, including the Emperor, posted guards in their very bedrooms—though this was deemed cowardly by others, including the Veglane Altazar.

In the Council the Pallantines raged and threatened. Altazar's enemies spread the rumor that the Mooncrow was the Veglane's plot. The only solution a sullen Altazar could offer the Council was what he'd already proposed to the Emperor—to patrol the Pillars with imperial troops. The motion was voted down and Altazar was jeered in the Hall of State.

Winter had come, the rainy season in Moldorn. Though located in the warmest of latitudes, PonnTherion was high enough in the mountains for the air to take on a definite chill. Cool, hazy days alternated with periods of rain. Nights, when the Mooncrow stalked, were damp and foggy.

Only rarely did a sentry even catch a glimpse of the Crow—a distant, phantasmal figure bounding above the mist along some inaccessible wall, or leaping an impossible distance from rooftop to rooftop.

At times the fog would enclose the Pillars completely and the sentries would call out on the hour from their posts. One night two men's voices were missed at the imperial palace. The two had spotted Teron as he neared his own apartments. The magician had entranced both men before they could raise an alarm. Their bodies were found in the morning, crushed on the distant pavement of the lower city.

These were the first victims the assassin had claimed from the Emperor's own house. In a state of heightened terror Bortoom finally yielded to Altazar's arguments and declared military law. Despite strenuous protests in the Council, three thousand imperial troops marched atop the Pillars. The Citadel bristled with spears and crossbows.

But four nights later the Mooncrow visited another Moldorn general in his well-guarded tower, and burned out his heart with the psithe-sword. Teron left a note on the general's pillow:

> ALL YOUR GUARDS AND SOLDIERS CANNOT
> SAVE YOU.
>
>   MOONCROW

Chapter 10.
A NIGHT ENCOUNTER ON THE PALACE ROOF

*The periods of solitude required of the initiate
often cause loneliness and dejection. But these
emotional troubles must be endured, for the mature
wizard must finally be complete unto himself,
dependent on nothing and no one.*
> —Master Aswel's Book of
> Rules and Meditations
> (The Golden Book)
> *(Norrling Year 4263)*

TERON ESCAPED the tower of the slain general by
entrancing the guards with the disk. Using the wand he
crossed the fogbound Citadel and gained the upper roof
of the imperial palace.

There the Mooncrow moved freely, confident no
soldiers would bar his way. He circled the peak of a thick
tower, dashed up a steep incline. But he jerked to a halt at
the summit, nearly throwing himself off balance.

The Emperor's daughter sat before him, on a narrow
ledge.

Dressed in a white ermine robe, Rania sucked in her
breath when she saw the Mooncrow. She tried to rise,
slipped on the wet tiles, and skidded from the ledge with a
wordless cry.

Momentarily stunned, Teron watched as the girl slid
down the roof-slope and caught hold of the metal gutter.

Then the wand gleamed as the Mooncrow darted down
in pursuit, feet skidding lightly over the roof. He reached
the edge just as Rania's fingers let go.

Teron thrust down a hand and caught her forearm as
she fell. But he'd leaned too far and her momentum pulled
him over too.

As they dropped together Rania started to scream. Holding back panic, Teron tightened his grip on her arm and wielded the magic of the wand. It rose in his other hand and strained his muscles as it slowed their fall.

Shoulder aching, Teron steered toward a wide balcony faintly visible through a rift in the fog. Clutching his forearm, Rania gazed up at him in amazement.

"You can fly," she whispered.

Teron answered through gritted teeth. "Not quite."

They landed hard, Rania turning her ankle and Teron falling on top of her. She squealed at the pain.

Dazed from the psithic strain, Teron helped her up. "My apologies," he muttered. "But frankly you were lucky I managed to save you at all."

Round-eyed and trembling, Rania stared up at the bird mask. "I am grateful, Master Mooncrow." She glanced over the railing. "It takes only six seconds for a body to strike the street."

"Your father has timed it often, no doubt," Teron said.

"Six seconds. Hardly time enough to realize you're about to die." Rania shivered and drew the white fur closer to her throat.

She looked back at the Mooncrow, and seemed unafraid. Teron wondered why she'd been on the roof. Then he questioned his own motives: Judged in terms of his Deputation it was foolhardy to gamble his life to save that of a Moldorn princess.

"Can I repay you somehow?" Rania asked.

"Just keep off the roof," he answered gruffly.

He turned to leave the balcony, but Rania hooked a foot behind his heel and shoved him backward. Next moment Teron sprawled on his back with Rania above him—an armlock on his chin and a dagger poised to slit his throat.

The Infanta laughed gayly. "Don't tell me what to do, Master Mooncrow. I have enough of that from my parents. And I'm not afraid of you—even if you can fly or turn into a bird, or whatever else. To me you're just another fool who thinks with his sword-arm. Such a fool as to let a girl of seventeen get a blade to your throat."

"I'm fortunate the Pallantines lack your cunning,"

Teron admitted, his fingers groping for the psithe-wand.

"You are indeed." Rania kicked the wand from his reach. "But don't think you're so much brighter than they. It's only a matter of time before they catch you."

"Alas, you have caught me already."

"Yes," Rania shrugged. "But I'm letting you go."

"Why?"

"Because slaying a few Pallantines doesn't necessarily make you an enemy of mine. And because you did save my life just now—though of course it was your fault I fell in the first place."

She slid away from him. Teron got to his feet, picked up the wand and bowed soberly.

"You have my thanks, Highness."

"Just stay clear of me next time I choose to sit on the roof."

Beneath his mask Teron eyed her with respect and a certain grim amusement. "On such occasions, Highness, I shall stay clear of the roof entirely."

The magician vaulted over the railing and vanished into the fog and darkness. Rania stared after him and let out her breath. She slipped the dagger back into her robe.

Next morning Teron was roused by a page who informed him that the Infanta wished Aurik Ib Bhendi to attend her as soon as possible. Teron rose at once, dressed as Bhendi and hastened to Rania's apartments.

She received him in a plush antechamber with blue tapestries and white marble columns. Two guards were posted outside the chamber, but inside Rania was attended only by maids-in-waiting. The Infanta sat in a luxurious chair upholstered in turquoise fur. She wore a yellow silk dressing gown and golden pins in her black hair. Her left foot rested on a huge lace pillow. "I've finally found an excuse to summon you here, Bhendi," she said with a smile. "I twisted my ankle."

"I doubt my company could be worth the discomfort, Highness."

Teron knelt and removed the silken stocking she wore. "The joint is badly bruised," he remarked, prodding with his fingers.

Rania winced. "I was lucky not to be killed. I fell off the roof, you see."

Teron massaged the ankle gently. "Indeed? And what were you doing on the roof, Highness?"

Rania sighed and sank back in her chair. "I was restless last night and could not sleep. Usually I walk in the garden on such occasions. But because of the Mooncrow all the gardens are locked or else filled with imperial guards. Luckily there's a secret stairway that leads from my chambers to the roof. I went up there last night, just to be alone. Then the Mooncrow popped out of nowhere and the shock made me lose my balance."

"The assassin himself? You must have been terrified."

Rania nodded. "At first. But he saved my life, Bhendi, and after that I was hardly afraid at all. I felt almost sorry for him. He seemed lonely, a little desperate."

She regarded him with a dreamy, somber expression, and for a moment Teron wondered if she suspected his secret.

Then a lanky black-furred creature pranced stealthily across the carpet and bounded into Rania's lap. Teron recognized the animal as a klurri, an arboreal cat native to the forests of southern Ibor, a popular pet among the Empire's wealthy.

"This is Bintah," Rania said, stroking the creature behind the large pointed ears.

Teron placed the foot back on the pillow and stood. "That's the best I can do for now, Highness. I recommend you avoid walking until the swelling disappears."

"It feels much better," Rania said. "Your healing skills are everything my father claims."

"Thank you, Highness."

"Will you stay and have breakfast with me?"

Teron paused, then shook his head. "I regret not. It's nearly time for me to attend your father."

"You know, Bhendi," Rania said, "you and the Mooncrow have one thing in common: You're both always in a hurry to rush off. But I'm not letting you go so easily. If I'm unable to walk about, at least I'll have good company. I want you to attend me again tomorrow morning—*after* you've seen to my father."

Teron returned her glance a moment, then smiled and
bowed his head. "Just as you wish, Highness."

The Infanta nodded, pleased with herself. "If I'm to
have your company each morning, who knows how long
this injury may last?"

Teron returned to the Infanta's apartments the next
morning and the next six mornings. Rania soon
persuaded him to join her for breakfast on a regular basis.

At first he was suspicious, half-expecting a trap. But
the Infanta gave no further sign of suspecting a
connection between Bhendi and the Mooncrow. The talk
was of stars, geography, the oceans. Teron began to feel at
ease. Rania's company offered a pleasant change from the
tense, gloomy solitude which otherwise filled his days.

She flirted with him at times, always with subtlety—
touching his arm during conversation, allowing her foot
to nudge his beneath the table. Teron felt amused, even
flattered. He kept close check on his emotions, however,
and carefully maintained the passionless exterior of
Aurik Ib Bhendi. Rania seemed satisfied with that.
Withdrawing her hand she would smile faintly, as if
equally amused by Bhendi and herself.

For a while Teron worried that his emotions might
become entangled, jeopardizing his Deputation. But he
convinced himself it was good strategy to gain Rania's
confidence. Being of the imperial family, she might be
party to information that the Mooncrow could use.

Yet when he tried to steer the conversation toward such
matters Rania usually changed the subject. All the
magician succeeded in bringing out was the Infanta's
disdain for her countrymen's manner of ruling.

"I don't want to talk about politics," she complained.
"It's all so stupid, Bhendi. Wars abroad, rivalry and
murder on the Pillars. And it never improves, never even
changes."

"Perhaps one day you may change it, Highness."

"Not possible," Rania said. "Females are permitted no
authority in Moldorn. Even if I were the only imperial
heir I'd never rule. My father would chose me a husband
from among the Pallantines and the sovereignty would

pass to him. Can you imagine that?"

"A peculiar custom," Teron sympathized.

"Tradition," Rania pronounced the word with distaste. "It goes back to the days when our ancestors lived in the mountains and did nothing but hunt and make war—not that the present-day Pallantines do anything more worthwhile. Anyway, since I can never rule I choose to ignore political affairs and concentrate on other things."

Teron could get her to say no more. But he continued to visit her anyway—assuring himself it could do no harm so long as he remained detached.

Then, at the end of the week, the Empress Unez summoned Teron to her apartments and informed him flatly that his visits with the Infanta must cease.

"I do not accuse you of dishonorable intentions, Prince Bhendi. Nevertheless, Rania has taken too high a fancy to you. You are all she talks about, your learning and cleverness. My daughter is obliged to marry a Pallantine-son. I'll not see her spoil her chances for happiness by falling in love with a man she can never wed. You must understand, Bhendi, Rania's happiness is the most important thing in the world to me."

Teron bowed his head. "I understand, Highness. I will do whatever you command."

Next morning Teron arrived in the Infanta's chambers accompanied by the Empress. He massaged Rania's ankle carefully, then replaced the stocking.

"I am happy to say, Highness, that the injury is all but healed. It will not require further treatments."

Rania, who had looked on her mother's appearance suspiciously, suddenly comprehended. "I see. Well...I hope you will still feel free to visit my apartments at any time, Bhendi."

The Empress answered for him. "Unfortunately, daughter, that is not possible. Propriety forbids—"

"But he's my physician."

"You're not ill, daughter."

"He is also my friend," Rania answered.

"A young lady is not permitted to receive gentlemen friends in her private chambers."

"But our relationship is perfectly proper."

"That is not the point," Unez shouted. "I will hear no more."

Rania clenched her lips and glared. The Empress turned to Teron.

"I'm sorry you had to hear this, Bhendi. Were my daughter more sensitive to the feelings of others she would not have embarrassed herself and you with such behavior."

Teron said nothing. His impassive eyes met Rania's.

"I shall miss talking with you, Bhendi," she said.

"I shall miss it also, Highness."

Teron offered both women a formal bow, then turned and left the chamber.

That evening the Mooncrow's meditations were haunted by thoughts of the Infanta. He realized he'd grown accustomed to the girl's companionship. Losing it now he felt moody, disheartened.

The months of solitude and the burden of keeping up the masquerade had taken their toll on his spirits. So too had the wielding of magic to slay so many men. He didn't allow himself to doubt that his actions were justified. Still, each killing seemed to draw a bit more darkness into his soul.

Teron had begun to wonder, for the first time, if his Deputation might not ultimately fail. For all his planning and intuition he had never figured on the Moldorns being so stubborn. Already he'd killed a half-dozen Pallantines, yet none in the Citadel seemed willing to even consider his terms of peace. And Teron couldn't keep up the campaign of assassination indefinitely. Sooner or later his luck was bound to run out.

Especially if the psithe continued to trouble him. Since that night when he'd employed the quinteer, Teron had sensed that his control of the psithe was not flawless. The power it generated was still vast enough, but all of the power was not discharged at his command. Instead a small part lingered, as if the will of the bird were storing it up to use against him, though he knew such a thing was impossible.

The Mooncrow sighed amidst his meditations. Despite

all these worries his will remained fixed on accomplishing his Deputation—fixed firmly and not to be swayed. Forlorn, the magician stared at streaks of yellow in the psithe-disk, and wondered if he would live through the winter.

Chapter 11.
ARROWS IN THE GARDEN

IN A MORNING cape of scarlet and silver the Veglane Altazar paced the carpet of his study chamber. The walls were adorned with pennons and weapons—trophies taken in battle—and with maps of all the known regions of the world. Tall windows commanded a dizzying view of the Pillars, which glinted in the early light.

Altazar was alone save for a pair of giant guards posted at the door. The guards were Gashoons—fierce, hairless brutes with skin like orange leather and mutilated ears hung with golden rings. The Veglane kept a troop of Gashoons as his personal bodyguard—the only men of that mutant race who dwelt atop the pillars. They wore no armor, only scant garments of silk. Their single weapon was a long, thick-bladed scimitar.

A knock sounded on the oakwood door and Altazar ceased pacing and signaled one of the Gashoons to open it. Count Bartuzzi entered, dressed in black.

"I sent for you a half-hour ago." Altazar said, "I want the War Table to meet this afternoon. And they'd better have some new ideas on dealing with the Mooncrow."

Bartuzzi was grinning. "Luiz, I think I may have found the solution."

"What? Speak, man."

"With your permission, cousin." Bartuzzi left the chamber and returned a moment later with a slim, red-haired woman dressed in a gold satin gown.

"This is Yvonn, a young lady of Ebbel Therion's seraglio. She has a story you ought to hear, Luiz."

Altazar looked her over. Her face, dried by the frequent use of colored powders, wore a sullen expression.

"Well?" the Veglane said.

"It was nearly three months ago, milord, the week before your return. I was wakened one night by whispering and overheard a conversation between one of the Crown Prince's legal consorts and a man I did not know. The man identified himself as a magician, and said he had come to make war on the lords of Moldorn. He also described a way that the woman might summon him, should she ever wish to."

"Who is this woman?"

A crafty smile on her lips: "Oh no, milord. I am here to bargain, not give my information away."

The Veglane's eyes narrowed. "Why have you waited this long? And why come to me?"

"I didn't know the information had value, until the Mooncrow started murdering Pallantines. Then I began searching for a way to make a bargain. I'm a slave, you see. I have no personal freedom. It took me this long to find a guard who would risk conducting me from the seraglio."

"You won't be missed?" Bartuzzi asked.

She shook her head. "The prince has gone bird-gaming till this afternoon."

"Why have you come to me?" Altazar asked again.

"Because you're a powerful man who has need of my information. I in turn have need of your power."

Altazar glanced at Bartuzzi, folded his arms and leaned back against his desk. "So you're offering a means of summoning the Mooncrow, and the name of the woman you claim you overheard. What do you want in return?"

"Freedom," Yvonn answered. "Enough gold to buy myself from Ebbel Therion, and your support of my legal right to do so if the Crown Prince objects."

Altazar gestured with his head and Bartuzzi stepped behind the woman. Suddenly Yvonn was lifted off her feet and caught in a wrestling hold—arms pinned in the air, shoulders yanked back. Screaming oaths in Khesperian she kicked and writhed furiously, but could not break free. Grunting, Bartuzzi squeezed with his thick arms, tightening the pressure until the woman's mouth opened and she shrieked in agony.

"Tell me," Atlazar said calmly, "or your arms will be torn from their sockets."

Resistance shattered, Yvonn cried out what she knew in a high, hysterical voice. "To lure the Mooncrow you

must light two lamps, red and blue . . . leave them burning
in the same window . . . The woman's name is Adria, the
Duke of Telyrra's daughter—Please!"

Altazar nodded once and Bartuzzi dropped the
woman. Yvonn cringed on the floor and wept like a
beaten child. The two men watched until her sobs quieted,
then the Veglane prodded her roughly with his boot.

"If your information proves false you will suffer much
worse torture. If it proves correct you shall be rewarded."

"It's true, milord. I swear."

"If so you shall be paid half the gold you asked for. If
you bring me other information from time to time, I will
pay you according to its value. The guard who brought
you here will also be paid. I'll see to it he's promoted and
put in charge of the Crown Prince's apartments. You may
yet earn your freedom, young woman, with my help. Here
is a small amount of silver, to seal our bargain. You may
kiss my hand as a sign of your fealty."

Yvonn hesitated, face streaked with tears. Then she
accepted the small pouch of coins, lowered her head and
brushed the Veglane's fist with pale lips.

Altazar lifted her up. "Now back to the palace before
you are missed."

Yvonn wiped her eyes and took a deep breath. She
bowed to Altazar and Bartuzzi, and left the chamber with
an even gait.

The count smiled when she was gone. "Khesperian
blood, full of guile. Quite a vixen, eh? If she ever does
earn her freedom I think I'll snatch her up for my own
house."

"Never mind that. What do you think of her story?"

Bartuzzi slouched on a cloth-of-gold divan. "I feel as I
know you must, Luiz. The story is too absurd to be a
fabrication." He laughed. "But who would have guessed
the Mooncrow had a lady love?"

The Veglane nodded. "We may at last have the bait to
trap him."

"That is, if we can use it. I don't suppose we can just
take over the Crown Prince's playrooms and borrow one
of his women."

"We can at the Emperor's command. And Bortoom

will give it to me, never fear. I shall speak to him in private—and caution him to reveal the plan to no one, not Gildaro, not even his wife. There must be no chance of word leaking to the assassin."

"The Mooncrow will be difficult enough to capture, I'm sure," Bartuzzi said.

"Whether he's captured or killed makes little difference," Altazar replied. "The crucial thing is to design a trap from which there is no escape."

Pausing on a roof-edge in the misty night, the Mooncrow glanced across a garden and a granite terrace to the Crown Prince's apartments. A red lamp and a blue lamp winked inside a lower-story window.

Teron scowled and his heart quickened. He had checked the seraglio out of habit, nothing more. He had long since stopped expecting Adria to summon him.

He wondered if she might have betrayed him, perhaps under torture. On the other hand she might need his help. Teron's eyes detected no hidden soldiers in the garden—though of course any number might be concealed inside the building...The Mooncrow sighed, shaking his head. The signal had been his idea. He had no choice but to answer it.

The magician glided down from the roof and landed noiselessly on the garden lawn. He moved stealthily across the empty garden, mounted the granite steps and crossed the broad terrace, past cushioned chairs and round metal tables. The lamps burned in a paneled window beside a pair of glass-paneled doors. Teron approached the doors and peered inside.

Through gauze curtains he observed a long and narrow room dimly lit by tapers. A gallery looked down on a tiled floor, with an ebony table set against one wall. Adria sat at the table alone, dressed in a red silk gown. Her yellow hair was piled atop her head, her face and bosom powdered a pale, rosy hue.

The doors were locked but Teron used the wand to slip the bolt. He turned the handle silently and stepped into the room. Adria gave a nervous start and gazed at him open-mouthed.

Teron glanced about uneasily, then stepped quickly to the table. "You summoned me, Adria. Why?"

"I knew you would bring me trouble," she whispered.

Abruptly the room burst with light. Soldiers had appeared along the upper gallery and set torches to strips of some incandescent material that hung on the walls. Teron whirled to face the end of the chamber where a line of crossbowmen had appeared, led by the Veglane Altazar. Outside an alarm horn sounded.

Altazar called out: "I treated you as a man last time, Mooncrow—an obvious mistake. This time you will be shot from a distance, like a dangerous beast."

The Veglane and his men raised their bows and fired.

Teron dove to the side, upsetting the wooden table and dodging behind it. A flight of bolts whizzed overhead and cracked on the tabletop.

Adria cowered beside Teron, her ankle chained to the table leg. "Run or we'll both be killed," she whimpered.

But the Mooncrow had only waited for the first flight of arrows to be short. He bolted from behind the overturned table and dashed for the terrace. He guessed the door would be well-covered by arrows from the outside, so he crashed through the window instead.

Rolling amid broken glass, Teron scrambled to his feet. The terrace blazed with the same white incandescence as the chamber. In fact white flares burned all across the garden, and in their light Teron glimpsed row on row of archers. A pack of hounds barked and bayed nearby. The whiz of arrows—

Teron darted aside but one bolt pierced his calf. He knocked over a table, rolled behind it and yanked the bloody arrow loose. Shots clattered on the terrace stones. One ripped the metal near his head. Teron changed the wand to a globe of light and spoke the words to invoke the quinteer.

But the psithe fought him, refused to yield its energy. Teron's arms shuddered, holding the psithe. The will of the bird had waited until now to resist him—as though by some impossible malign intelligence. Teron chanted the words and strained his will, trying desperately to merge with the psithe. But the other will blocked him, repelling his life-force with vibrant walls of power.

The Veglane and his men were coming through the terrace doors. The pack of hounds had been released to flush the Mooncrow from cover. They loped forward, howling and snapping their jaws.

Abruptly Teron changed his mental tact, catching the will of the bird off guard. He made the psithe a wand and immediately sprang in the air. The wand yielded a burst of force, lifting him up and over the railing of a second-story gallery. The Mooncrow half-crouched and began to run toward the parapet at the garden's outer wall.

Below, alarm horns sounded and officers barked orders. Crossbowmen fired, their arrows singeing the air. But the gallery was far dimmer than the garden floor, and Teron moved with erratic, streaking bursts that made him a difficult target.

A troop of soldiers raced across the parapet to cut him off. Count Bartuzzi led the column, saber drawn.

The Mooncrow reached the end of the gallery, clambered over a section of roof and leapt to the parapet. Bartuzzi was on him, but Teron sidestepped the count's blade and shoved with his wand. Bartuzzi was knocked into the legs of another Moldorn. Both men tumbled off the parapet into the garden. The Mooncrow vaulted atop the crenellated wall.

He stood there a fraction of a second, and an arrow tore through his back. He spun around with a muffled cry, then toppled head first down into the blackness.

"The arrow passed through the center of his back," a sergeant who'd been on the wall told the Veglane moments later. "He fell stiffly, my lord, as dead men fall."

"Idiot!" Altazar replied. "The man is a master illusionist. We must have his corpse to be certain."

The Veglane ordered his lieutenants to search the lower city at once. "Take a hundred men. Descend the stairs inside this Pillar. Search until you find the assassin's body. I will accept no excuses."

The officers saluted sharply and trotted off. Altazar turned to an aide. "How's Count Bartuzzi?"

"A broken arm, my lord. It's being tended. What should we do with the Crown Prince's consort?"

"Hold her. If the Mooncrow still lives we may need her again."

Chapter 12.
THE SMILING SERPENT

THE MOLDORN sergeant's report was inaccurate. The last bolt had entered the Mooncrow's back near the shoulder and had punctured no vital organs. Teron blacked out for a moment, but regained consciousness as he fell.

He was conscious first of the pain—as though the arrow had half-ripped shoulder from torso. Cold air streamed upward, biting the wound like a frosty blade. Teron's eyes gazed past his feet at the receding Pillar-tops. Part of his mind recognized that he had less than six seconds to live.

Teron kicked over to fall feet-first, made his body limp. He clutched the wand tightly and poured in his mind-force. But the psithic power sputtered and stalled. The will of the bird was fighting him still.

The Mooncrow reached for the lowest depths of his strength and forced the psithe to obey. The wand rose in his hands, buoyant against gravity. But he was very close to the ground.

The plunge of his body slowed, but that was all his overstrained will could accomplish. Teron clung to the wand and watched the dark street rush upward. He struck the cobblestones hard, lost his mental grip on the psithe, and consciousness.

The magician lay motionless in the middle of a narrow, empty street. On both sides rose sharp-gabled tenements of two and three stories—wooden buildings typical of the lower city. Tatters of wet fog drifted along the grimy street. A watchdog barked somewhere in the night.

After several minutes two hooded figures, one bearing a torch, slipped from a dark alleyway and approached the fallen magician. The shorter of the figures knelt, examined the shoulder wound and pulled the arrow free. He rolled the body over and held the torch close to the face. The bird mask had slid up, revealing the sharp gray features.

"Glory and death," the man whispered. "I know him, Mirabelle. He's Teron the magician. The Ombernorr I've told you about."

"Is he alive?" a woman's voice asked.

"Warm and breathing. Ha! Who but Teron could have fallen from the Pillars and lived? Yet I'd never in a thousand ages have guessed he was the Mooncrow."

The woman glanced up and down the street. "We must get him away from here. They'll send down soldiers."

The man nodded.

Together they lifted Teron, slung his arms over their shoulders and carried him back to the dark alley.

The Mooncrow awoke with a stabbing pain in his shoulder, a soreness where his head had struck the street—and the smell of old wine in his nostrils. With a grimace he looked down and saw his torso bare, his shoulder bandaged.

"Good morning, Mooncrow."

Teron glanced at the speaker and his mouth dropped open: a short, square-shouldered figure with mirthful eyes and a curling blond beard.

"Topiedeon!"

"None other."

A dark-haired woman stood at Topiedeon's shoulder. Behind her a row of wine casks. Sacks of flour served as Teron's bed.

"Where are we?"

"The cellar of the Smiling Serpent, a tavern in the lower city. You fell from the Pillars, Teron."

"Yes . . . I remember." He tried to sit up, grunted at the pain and sank back.

"Don't try to rise," the woman said. "I bandaged you as best I could, but the shoulder-wound is deep. You must lie still."

The woman was tall and slim, with braided hair and green, wide-set eyes.

"This is Mirabelle, who owns the tavern," Topiedeon introduced her. "And this is Teron of Ombernorr, lately called the Mooncrow."

The magician smiled wanly. "The Crow is known in the lower city then?"

"Dear lad, the Mooncrow's known across Ibor. The mysterious assassin who changes into a bird, whose burning sword has the Pallantines cringing in their towers. Why, the Mooncrow's a legend. I've even written a few ballads about you."

"I'm honored."

"You should be. Also grateful, for that's how we came to pick you off the street. We heard the alarm horns and noticed the flare lights atop the Pillar. We thought it must be the Mooncrow and climbed up on the roof to see what we could. We caught a glimpse of you as you fell."

"I am grateful," Teron said. "I owe my life to both of you."

Topiedeon grinned. "We felt it would be a shame to let the Mooncrow perish. Any man who can make the Pallantines swallow their own medicine deserves a chance to survive."

Teron nodded soberly, thinking that if his Deputation was to survive he would have to get back upstairs.

"How many hours of darkness are left?"

Topiedeon shrugged. "Two, or a little more. You slept a while."

"Time enough." Teron struggled to a sitting position, agony warring against his will.

"You really ought to lie down," Mirabelle said.

The Mooncrow shook his head. "Did you find a wand with me?"

"Tight in your fingers," the minstrel said.

"I'll also need the feathered cloak."

Topiedeon brought him both articles. Teron shivered as he touched the wand, recalling how the psithe had fought him. But he encountered no resistance in changing the wand to a cup.

"How?" Mirabelle cried.

Topiedeon chuckled. "I never could figure it out."

From a hidden pocket in the Norrling cloak Teron took three tiny stone vials and emptied their powdered contents into the cup. He murmured an incantation and water from nowhere filled the psithe-cup. Teron stirred the mixture with an index finger, drank it down, then settled back with a soft moan. The potion would temporarily deaden the pain, and help restore his life-force.

"I have to be back on the Pillars by sunrise," he said.

"Why?" the minstrel demanded.

"Because there's another role I play besides the Mooncrow. Things came apart badly tonight, Topiedeon. My being shot was only part of it. But if I'm to salvage any hope at all of winning, I have to preserve my other identity."

"I only hope you don't kill yourself trying," Mirabelle said.

The Mooncrow sighed. "Sooner or later I probably will. But meantime I feel I must keep trying. But don't worry about these wounds," he said, feeling the potion starting to work. "I know well enough how to heal the body. You see, in my other disguise I'm a physician—the Emperor's personal physician."

"You don't mean it!" Topiedeon cried.

"In truth. But please, don't mention that in any ballad."

"Don't worry," the minstrel laughed. "I don't sing my Mooncrow songs in public. Too many soldiers in the audience. All they care to hear are blustery drinking songs and maudlin laments."

"Poor Topiedeon," Teron said. "Tell me, how did you end up in PonnTherion?"

The minstrel made a bitter face. "Like most of the poor wretches in this city I was dragged here in chains. I never made it away from Telyrra. The Moldorns bombed the first few ships and forced the rest to turn around. They collected all the passengers, along with those on land who'd survived the bombing, and put us on slave vessels bound for Ibor. Being a musician, I was spared the galleys and the mines and bought by a merchant who lives on the imperial hill. I sang in the man's house for three years. Then one night when he'd drunk too much I managed to talk him into a bargain. In exchange for my freedom I'd write a ballad cycle celebrating his family history. It was an ugly business, Teron, singing of slavers and money-lenders as if they were heroes. But a man in a cage will do almost anything to gain his liberty."

The Mooncrow nodded somberly.

Topiedeon smiled and spread his arms. "Anyway, I've lived in the lower city ever since, earning my bread by singing in taverns and public houses. Lately I've sung upstairs in Mirabelle's tavern—and also more softly in her private rooms."

He slipped an arm around her waist. Mirabelle smiled, bent and kissed him on the lips.

The throbbing pain was dulled now. Teron climbed gingerly to his feet.

"You're not leaving yet," Topiedeon exclaimed. "You haven't even told us how you came to be the Mooncrow."

"Another time." The magician slipped on his feathered shirt. "For now I must ask you to hide my cloak and mask, and to lend me a cloak to wear. I imagine the streets are full of soldiers searching for my remains?"

Mirabelle nodded. "I'll find you a cloak."

The Mooncrow pondered: If the soldiers found nothing, the Moldorns would remain uncertain as to his fate. And since they still had Adria, they would probably use her again, perhaps torture her publicly in hopes of luring the Mooncrow into the open. Plainly Teron had to make them think the Crow was finished.

"Topiedeon, I've imposed on our friendship already, I know. But I need to ask another favor."

"Whatever I can do, Teron."

"I want you to go out walking. Sing if you like, or better, pretend to be drunk. When you come upon some soldiers tell them you saw the Mooncrow fall, and that he burst into flame on hitting the ground."

"A strange story," the minstrel said. "You want them to think you're dead, I take it."

Teron nodded, and received a gray cloak from Mirabelle. "Will they believe such a story," she asked, "from a man they think is drunk?"

"Probably not," Teron said. "But finding no other clue they'll report it just the same. Once upstairs in my other disguise, I'll find a way to substantiate the tale."

"Well, I'm normally a singer, not an actor," Topiedeon said. "But I suppose I could make an exception this one time."

The magician and the minstrel departed together from

the cellar of the Smiling Serpent—Mirabelle admonishing both to be careful. In the street Topiedeon took the lead. Teron followed some distance behind, limping because of his leg wound. Topiedeon began singing in a loud, drunken voice.

Before long the minstrel turned a corner and approached a detachment of Moldorn troops. Teron ducked into an alleyway and listened. Topiedeon told his story to perfection, describing the burning of the Mooncrow in vivid, extravagant detail. The skeptical soldiers demanded to be shown where the body had fallen. The minstrel led them to a random spot a few blocks away, and seemed at a loss to explain the lack of ashes.

A sergeant suggested they hold Topiedeon, but the officer in charge cursed the minstrel for a drunken buffoon and sent him on his way with a kick in the pants.

Topiedeon staggered back up the street and winked at Teron, who hid in a darkened doorway. Then the minstrel proceeded on through the fog, singing again at the top of his voice.

While the soldiers resumed their search the Mooncrow hurried down an adjacent street. Around the corner of a building he observed the base of the central Pillar. A short flight of steps led up to a landing, an archway and an iron gate. The gate stood open since, as Teron had surmised, the soldiers had used the stairs in the Pillar to reach the lower city. Four spearmen guarded the gate.

A short time later the Mooncrow hobbled across the open space and climbed the steps to the landing. The four spearmen snapped to attention, for the magician's form was enwrapped in an illusion generated by the psithe. Teron appeared to be a lieutenant of the imperial guard, marching briskly.

Saluting the sentries the Mooncrow passed beneath the arch and climbed a narrow spiral stair. He searched along several passageways until finding the zigzagging central stair that led to the top of the Pillar. In grinding pain he climbed the endless metal steps, nodding curtly to the many guards he encountered on the way.

● ● ●

Teron was not summoned to attend the Emperor until mid-morning. The Lord of the Earth sat in his round antechamber, alone save for servant girls and a heavy guard.

"A draught to ease my stomach," Bortoom grunted. "I ate too much breakfast. Celebrating, you see."

Teron bowed and took out the cup.

"Have you heard the good news, Bhendi?" the Emperor asked. "The Mooncrow is wounded, perhaps dead."

Teron nodded over his powders. "I've heard rumors, Highness, but not the exact details. I myself sensed that the Mooncrow was abroad last night, but my perception of his power flickered out in the usual way."

"Well, he was shot from the palace wall by bowmen," Bortoom said, "and fell to the lower city."

"That is in truth good news."

"I know. But the assassin's body was not found. A drunkard reported that it burned on striking the ground, but no ashes were found either."

The magician's eyes widened as he handed the psithe-cup to the Emperor. "I may have the explanation, Highness. Perhaps I have mentioned already that in the east many wizards cast spells on their bodies to make them burst into flame at the time of death—as a protection against enemies both mortal and immortal. The flame is of a supernatural character; it burns only moments but leaves not even ashes."

Teron had marked the passage describing such a burning in one of Fystus' books on the Orient. Intuition had suggested that the idea might be useful. Now he watched the Emperor, measuring his reaction.

Bortoom had drained the cup and was staring at his physician. "Do you think the Mooncrow is dead, Bhendi? Altazar insists we can't be certain without the corpse. Gildaro too is dubious. But you say perhaps...?"

"If the Mooncrow was a powerful wizard as we must suppose, then I would think the report of his burning true. And if so, you have no need to fear the assassin ever again—unless he's capable of returning from the dead."

Bortoom scowled. "Please, Bhendi, don't make mention of that possibility again."

Chapter 13.
THE ABERRATION

The old books speak of demons and familiars
conjured up by the practice of sorcery. In Norrling
lore these phenomena are viewed as aberrations.
Formed of undischarged energy, they are given
shape and personality by unwitting projection from
the wizard's lower mind...
The aberrations are of course discouraged by all
Norrling teaching, and destroyed by wary masters
when they do occur. Most likely they will one day
be eliminated completely from the Norrling realm.

> —Initiate Boomler's Treatise
> on Magical Theory (Silver
> Book).

IN THE FOLLOWING days nothing was heard from the Mooncrow. The Lords of Moldorn began to accept the opinion that the assassin had perished. The twelve-day Festival of the Glowing Pikes arrived, which in Moldorn marked the new year. The Pallantines celebrated in a loud and jovial mood.

The Emperor in particular was jolly. Each night of the festival he downed quarts of beer toasting to the Mooncrow's demise. Bortoom seemed to emanate a rare feeling of good health. He was said to be sleeping better at night.

The Veglane Altazar, in contrast, showed little inclination to join in the festive mood. Altazar openly harbored suspicions that the Mooncrow still lived. Due to the Veglane's maneuverings the imperial troops remained to guard the Citadel a while longer.

The Crown Prince Ebbel Therion also kept aloof from the prevailing atmosphere of mirth. The Prince bitterly resented Altazar's confiscation of his legal consort, and protested so vehemently that the Emperor finally relented and ordered Adria restored to her rightful master.

Seraglio intact, the Crown Prince announced he would go hunting in the mountains. He departed in the middle of the festival, taking several of his friends and all his dogs and women.

In the entire crowded Citadel only the Emperor's daughter felt any regret at the Mooncrow's passing. And Rania expressed these feelings to no one, except the amber-eyed klurri, to whom she confided all her secrets. "I knew they would kill him in the end, Bintah. Still, it makes me sad. He seemed less an idiot than most young men."

Meantime the Mooncrow rested and gave all his energy to healing his wounds. Teron was relieved when Adria was taken from the Veglane's custody, more so when she left PonnTherion. With her out of danger for the moment, the Mooncrow could reflect, sort out his problems, and then set about solving them.

First he had to gain unchallenged mastery of the psithe. His obvious course was to confront the will of the bird and try to overpower it. So far Teron had avoided such a confrontation, partly from apprehension, partly from the faint hope that the problem might disappear by itself. But the bird had manifested itself twice now, and each time only narrowly missed causing his death. Teron was resolved to offer it no third opportunity.

So after a fortnight's rest he settled down to face the bird. He sat crosslegged on the carpet of his bedchamber. The psithe lay before him, a pulsing multicolored sphere the size of a human heart. Teron pushed his mind-force into the sphere and sought the will of the bird. But all he sensed was a vague confusion of power. Somehow the bird was hiding.

Teron was puzzled and dismayed. Once again his adversary displayed a guile and intelligence inconceivable in a mere bird. For three days and nights the Mooncrow used all his free time to probe the psithe with his mind, seeking to draw forth the bird—but in vain.

Late on the fourth night frustration and weariness compelled him to cease. Teron made the psithe a disk and placed it on his bedside table. As he drifted off to sleep he thought of Cordavius the Toucan, and of how he would welcome the high master's advice.

Then he slept, and presently began to dream.

In the dream Teron felt his mind rise from his body and stream through space with impossible speed, to Ptolloden. He entered the tower of Cordavius and found the Toucan seated before a blazing fire in his study. Cordavius glanced up from his meditation and smiled.

"Greetings, Mooncrow. How's your Deputation going?"

"I . . . master? Am I truly here or do I dream?"

Cordavius chuckled. "Both, ex-Magpie. By the power of the disk you have invoked a qorm dream—inadvertently, as I might have guessed. You have come to Ptolloden in a dream-body."

Teron glanced down at his semi-transparent hands. He tried to scratch his head but his finger passed through the scalp. "Very strange," he muttered.

"The dream-body has no substance," the Toucan explained. "It's merely an illusion your mind projects to facilitate movement and observance. We masters generally receive dream visits from our advanced pupils only when they're in need of some counsel. Is this by any chance the case, Mooncrow?"

Teron paused a moment. "Why yes, good master. As a matter of fact I could use some advice. The bird-will in my psithe opposes me. And with a diligence and cunning I find incredible."

"Describe the bird's manifestations."

Teron did so, and the Toucan's face grew solemn.

"I warned you about the quinteer, Teron."

"I know, good master. But believe me there was—"

"No choice, I'm sure," Cordavius said.

"I thought I could handle the bird," Teron said. "I had no idea it could acquire such intelligence."

The high master shook his head. "It would be more correct to say that the bird *has been acquired* by something else."

"What do you mean, master?"

"Judging by your description, Teron, I would say your psithe is possessed by a manhead."

"I don't know the term," Teron said.

"A manhead is a species of psithic aberration caused by invoking the quinteer without full mental control. Such aberrations are extremely rare in the present age, because our teaching methods have been perfected. Of course if the pupil does not take the time to learn..."

Teron bowed his head. "Your rebuke is justly deserved, master."

"In truth, Teron. Anyway, when a psithe of the higher octodens is joined in quinteer by a wizard who lacks full control, some of the power remains undischarged. Under certain conditions this residue power can gather into an entity, which takes on a character and will exactly opposite to the magician's character and will."

"Why, master?"

"Because the psithe is an instrument that focuses power. The process of focusing involves an inversion and a re-inversion. But energy that is not discharged remains inverted. So when this energy condenses to form an entity, the entity turns out to be the exact inverse of the one who uses the psithe. The entity is called a manhead, because in physical manifestation it resembles a bird with the head of a man—just as a wizard in ritual costume resembles a man with the head of a bird."

Teron wore a troubled frown. "How does one get rid of a manhead?"

"It's difficult," Cordavius said. "Once entrenched in the psithe the entity will continue to absorb energy until it feels strong enough to strike at the wizard—as yours has struck already, and will do again. My advice, Teron is that you return to Ptolloden without delay."

The Mooncrow sighed. "I can't, good master. I am entangled with the Deputation."

"You can return to it later."

"I've established an identity which must continue. Besides," Teron added grimly, "the Gathering of Eight might decide not to let me return. I've accomplished little to boast of so far, I'm afraid."

Cordavius drew in his lips. "Well, your other choice is more perilous. You can confront the manhead yourself, and try to annihilate it by the power of your mind."

"I've been attempting to force such a confrontation,"

Teron said. "But the entity hides itself."

"Driving a manhead into the open is a long and arduous task," the Toucan answered. "You must identify all within the psithe that seems alien and odious, and force it out bit by bit. After the psithe is cleansed, though, you must still be on your guard..."

Teron blinked, for the Toucan's figure was starting to dissolve. "Master—?"

"Your dream is fading, Mooncrow."

"How can I stop it from doing so?"

"You can't. Be wary, Teron. Especially after the psithe is clean."

Teron's eyes came open and the shreds of dream-color vanished—leaving the ornate ceiling of his bedroom in the Citadel of PonnTherion.

In the morning the Mooncrow was dubious about the qorm dream, uncertain whether he'd actually been in contact with the high master.

Nevertheless, at his first opportunity Teron employed the method Cordavius had suggested. In the dull, shifting cloud of power within the psithe the magician sought out all that felt abhorrent to his nature. His mind plucked at these minute threads of energy, unraveled them, cast them from the psithe.

Teron sensed that the process was working, yet progress was slow and painstaking. The Mooncrow worked day and night, pausing only to sleep one or two hours a night, and to make his appearances as Aurik Ib Bhendi.

After six days he noticed that the air in his bedchamber seemed unnaturally dense and charged—like the air before a thunderstorm. He tried several times to duplicate the qorm dream, that he might ask Cordavius specifically what to expect after cleansing the psithe. But failing to contact the high master, the Mooncrow shrugged the matter off: one problem at a time.

Finally, on the tenth night of struggle, the Mooncrow banished the last of the manhead entity from the psithe. The magician lay back on the floor and relaxed his mind, closed his aching eyes and massaged the lids with trembling, bloodless fingers.

Suddenly a freezing wind passed over him, followed by a hideous, screeching bird cry. Teron thrust himself up and caught a glimpse of a swooping black shape. Then his eyes closed by reflex as talons slashed his face.

The Mooncrow fell back and blindly flailed the air with his fists. He managed to roll over and scramble halfway to his feet before the thing descended again—raking claws across his scalp. Whining in pain Teron tore the creature off his head and flung it away.

The Mooncrow leapt up. Half-blinded by blood he saw his foe for the first time as it wheeled in the air—a black bird with a four-foot wingspan and the head of a man, the head of Teron himself but with features contorted by hate and eyes glazed with fury.

The magician staggered back, shuddering, keeping the manhead at bay with his arms and hands. He scanned the floor for the psithe, but it was gone.

Then he understood: somehow the manhead had taken it over. It was the psithe that gave the monster physical form.

Backed to the wall, Teron picked up a glass decanter and flung it. But the agile creature avoided it with ease and swooped in. Impelled by fencer's reflexes, Teron feinted one way and lunged the other. His right hand closed on the manhead's neck. Teron shivered and held on despite the thrashing of wings and the slashing talons. In a moment his other hand gripped the neck as well.

The Mooncrow sank to his knees, dragging the manhead down. He ignored the sting of his wounds, ignored the revulsion he felt at touching this creature, at staring into the hideous replica of his own face. His fingers tightened on the manhead's throat.

The manhead screeched and writhed in the magician's grip, but could not break free. A new look appeared in the bulging eyes, a look of fear. Its fear fed the rage in Teron's heart and he squeezed harder.

Suddenly the manhead's body exploded with light. Dazzled, Teron felt his hands emptied of the feathery neck. Then the magician was flung back with a strangled cry in his throat.

The manhead had abandoned the psithe and leapt upon Teron. The two life-forces had merged and the battle continued now inside the Mooncrow's body, which writhed fitfully and clawed the carpet.

In the blackness inside himself Teron perceived a continuous roar—and the manhead's grisly face at the center of a radiant circle. Spears of energy lanced out from the circle, piercing and burning Teron's mind. Infuriated, the Mooncrow fought back, thrusting his will against the manhead.

The roaring struggle continued for a time, wavering in each direction. Then the manhead's will began to crumble. The circle of his power collapsed inward and shrank.

Sensing victory, Teron pressed his will to wring all energy from the manhead's being. Losing that energy, which was its only substance, the entity grew smaller and smaller. At last it was a speck of light, lost in a vast abyssmal darkness.

The Mooncrow walked over grassy meadows, through knee-high banks of rosy mist. The sky shone with a keen gray light. A mild breeze sighed.

Teron approached a lofty rotunda with gray columns and cornices hung with icicles. He ascended sixteen steps, crossed a portico and entered a high-domed chamber. In the center of the chamber, on a blue cushion that floated above the obsidian floor, was seated Cordavius the Toucan.

"Welcome, Mooncrow. I'm glad to see you."

"Greetings, good master. I take it I am dreaming again."

"Actually, Mooncrow," Cordavius spread his arms, "it is my dream that surrounds us."

Teron glanced over the multicolored reliefs that spiraled on the chamber walls. "And a most excellent dream it is, master. I am honored to be summoned here."

Cordavius smiled. "You've been in my thoughts lately. I wondered how you made out against your manhead."

"Reasonably well, I think," Teron answered. "I

managed to cleanse the psithe of the entity, but the next thing I knew it had seized the psithe again and turned it into a physical body."

Cordavius nodded. "I didn't have time to explain: Cast out in bits from a psithe, an abberational entity is capable of collecting in the air and holding itself together for a time. What happened next?"

Teron shuddered to recall it. "I grappled with the entity on the physical plane and managed to strangle it. But at the last moment it leapt into my body and fought me there. I finally succeeded in drawing away its energy, and it seemed to grow smaller, until it became too tiny for my mind to touch. That was four days ago, master. I've tested the psithe since then and it's performed flawlessly, discharging all its power in each of the four shapes. From this I would conclude that the manhead is finished, except that when I meditate I have a vague, shadowy sense of the entity's presence, as if it were somehow still attached to me."

"Sounds like it," Cordavius said.

"What do you mean, master?"

"The proper solution is to annihilate the entity, Teron. But since you allowed it to enter your body you could not accomplish this completely—not without annihilating yourself as well. The manhead remains as a particle of sentience embedded somewhere in the fabric of your being. *The Purple Book* describes several cases of this type. The ancient magicians would say you had chained the demon but not destroyed it."

Teron frowned. "What happens now?"

"Probably nothing. Denied the nourishment of psithic energy the manhead should eventually dissolve. The one way it might threaten you again would be if it were given access to a large quantity of energy—if, for example, your entire being were to become imbued with psithic power."

"You're warning me again to avoid the quinteer, master?"

"I'm avoiding warning you to avoid it, Mooncrow. Warning you seems to have no effect."

Smiling, Teron bowed his head. "I understand, good master."

Cordavius shrugged. "Nor do I suppose it would do

any good to advise you to return to Ptolloden and have the manhead exorcised just to be certain."

"I cannot return, for the same reasons I related previously."

"After all this you still feel fated to accomplish your Deputation, Mooncrow?"

Teron's eyes narrowed to slits. "I still feel fated to try. I still hunger to see the Empire of the Moldorns broken, to see their Citadel torn down."

"Then I think you must tear it down, Mooncrow. Or else learn to live with your hunger unsatisfied."

"My feelings exactly." Teron grinned.

Cordavius waved his hand and began to vanish.

"Master . . . ?"

"I wish you good fortune, Teron. But for now you must excuse me. I have other dreams to pursue, and only an hour before I must wake."

"Farewell then, harried master. And thank you for the visit."

The Mooncrow bowed. When he rose the domed chamber had disappeared, and he stood in a dream he knew was his own.

Chapter 14.
BENEATH THE LOWER CITY

THE MAIN chamber of the Smiling Serpent was large, high-ceilinged, crowded with customers. Candles flared atop the tables, casting enough light to show faces, goblets, hands and bowls.

A log fire blazed in a wide hearth of rough-cut stones. On a stool beside the hearth Topiedeon played his mandolin. He sang of love and war and drinking.

Following his performance the minstrel bowed to a smattering of applause and left the fireside. He walked halfway along the adjacent wall before a flicker of light caught his eye. At a table near him a candle was being lit—revealing a jug of wine and a sharp gray face.

"Teron." Topiedeon whispered the name, sliding into a seat across from the black-clad Mooncrow. "It's been over a month, lad. You had us worried."

"All is well," the magician smiled. "Though I've had a few misadventures along the way."

Topiedeon glanced about, then gestured with his head. "Follow me. We'll talk in private."

Teron followed the minstrel up four flights of narrow steps. They entered a spacious chamber with slanted ceilings and a polished wooden floor. Mirabelle appeared from an adjacent room and greeted Teron warmly.

The three friends sat at a small oakwood table beside a paneled window. Topiedeon poured wine from Teron's jug into tumblers.

"All these weeks I've wondered about you," the minstrel said. "Start at the beginning: How did you fare on the night Telyrra burned?"

Teron grinned over his cup. "Would you believe I turned into a magpie and flew back to Ombernorr?"

The minstrel laughed. "Do I have a choice?"

"Well, believe at least that I returned to my own country." In a soft voice Teron told of how he'd acquired the Deputation to make war on the Moldorns, and of how the war had unfolded up until the night he fell from the Pillar-tops.

"A prodigious tale," Topiedeon exclaimed. "What's happened this past month?"

Teron shrugged. "Let's just say I've been healing myself, regaining my strength."

"You're going to attack the Pallantines again?" Mirabelle inquired.

"I can't," Teron said. "For one thing, there's a woman."

"Adria of Telyrra," Topiedeon said. "We heard rumors the Veglane used one of Ebbel Therion's consorts to trap the Mooncrow. I assumed it was she."

Teron nodded. "And they'll use her again if they need to. That's why I've stayed under cover. But I've used the time to advantage. I've reconsidered my plans, altered my tactics. I've been studying in the palace archives for a week, reading engineering charts, military reports..."

"For what purpose?"

Teron drained his cup and set it down. "The only way I can overthrow the Empire is to take the Citadel by storm. So that's what I intend to do."

Topiedeon chuckled. "A fine idea. I'd be glad to help. But, uh, where do we get the army?"

The Mooncrow grinned. "Ah, there's the beauty of my scheme. There's an army of over twenty-five thousand men, ours for the taking, beneath our feet at this very moment."

Topiedeon scowled.

"I'm speaking of the mine slaves," Teron said.

"Then you're speaking from ignorance," Topiedeon answered. "Most of those slaves starve to death after only a few months underground. They work naked, they're whipped. Even their names are taken away."

"Exactly." Teron's gray eyes glinted. "In their place wouldn't you gladly fight to get out?"

Topiedeon snorted and jarred his tumbler, setting it down. "Listen, Teron. You're an entertainer, a sleight-of-hand artist. You've made a good show as an assassin— due as much to theatrical effects as to your skill with a sword. But war is serious business. What do you know about planning battles or leading armies?"

"Nothing," the Mooncrow admitted. "We'll need another partner."

"'We'?"

Teron laughed. "You said you'd be glad to help."

"That was before I knew you were serious!"

"In any case, I know just the man: General Lothar, the Khesperian commander, the one Altazar hung from his own ship on the day of his triumph. I've been studying Lothar's tactics. He baffled the Veglane at every turn. I'm sure he'd relish another chance."

Topiedeon shook his head in amusement. "A crafty barbarian general allied to an Ombernorr wizard, both seeking revenge against the Empire. It does have poetic possibilities at least."

"Glad you like it. I'm going down tonight to see if I can find Lothar."

"Down to the mines?"

"Do you want to come?"

Topiedeon sighed. "The mines swarm with guards day and night, Teron. And they run for miles in all directions. Even if you found Lothar, how would you escape with him? No one's ever escaped from down there."

The Mooncrow stood and stretched. "Topiedeon, old friend, I appreciate your concern, but"—he held aloft the disk, dark gold—"I bear the power of a Norrling adept, more than enough to enthrall a few guards. Compared to some of the Mooncrow's exploits a descent into the mines is a child's errand. Now, do you want to come with me or not?"

The minstrel tugged his beard and seemed about to consider the notion. Then he glanced at Mirabelle, laughed and shook his head. "Not for all the salt in the sea. But I wish you luck."

Teron pursed his lips. "I fear I must ask for more than your good wishes. I need a place to hide Lothar until we're ready to strike. I was hoping I could use your cellar."

The minstrel and his lady exchanged frowning looks.

"Of course I could hide the man in the sewers," Teron said. "But he's less likely to bolt if I keep him well-fed and comfortable."

"It's no small thing you ask," Topiedeon said.

"It's no small thing I want to accomplish," Teron replied. "The Veglane's invading Tann this spring. Who's to stop him, Topiedeon, if not us?"

The minstrel pondered. "There are a few small storage rooms that are hardly used. For my part, I'd say yes. But it's your cellar, Mirabelle."

The woman fingered the rim of her wine cup, then looked at Teron. "I've helped you so far because I hate the Pallantines, like many folk of Moldorn. I've lost a husband and two brothers to the Veglane's wars, Teron. I don't know what chance you have of succeeding. But I'll do what I can to help."

Teron laid his hand on hers. "Lady, you are very kind. Also very brave. It's getting late and I should start. With luck I'll bring Lothar back by morning. If not, expect us tomorrow night, or the next."

The Mooncrow bade his friends goodnight and departed from the tavern. He traveled swiftly through the curving streets below the giant Pillars. Avoiding an occasional guardsman of the city legion he came at length to the base of the cliff, four hundred feet below the cantilever bridge.

The network of mines beneath PonnTherion had many entrances, including the main shaft that rose inside the central Pillar. But while the Mooncrow could have passed that way with ease, coming back with General Lothar would have been more difficult. So Teron had studied charts of the mines, and had chosen another way—an obsolete entry tunnel at the bottom of the escarpment.

The Crow came to the end of a narrow street and climbed a steep gravel slope. He found the tunnel's entrance boarded over, pried loose two of the planks and crawled inside. He made the psithe a wand and gave it a yellow glow to light his way.

The air was dense and moist. The tunnel throbbed with faint echoes of distant machines. After about a hundred paces Teron referred to a copied chart of the mines and turned into a side tunnel, which slanted deeper into the earth.

The magician proceeded cautiously, picking his way

through the maze of shafts and tunnels, bearing toward those areas presently being worked. The noises grew louder and more distinct—the rolling of ore carts on iron rails, the endless clink of metal tools on stone. The work in these mines continued day and night, the slaves toiling in alternating shifts twelve hours long.

Soon Teron was peering into tunnels dimly illumined by lanterns. He observed gangs of slaves, haggard and naked, laboring with pickaxes and shovels, overseen by Moldorn guards with pikes and whips. The Mooncrow kept to the shadows, of which there were ample ranges. Any guard barring his path was quickly transfixed by the disk.

There was no easy way of finding Lothar, since no records were kept of the slaves' identities. Hours wore on as Teron continued to search. He scanned numberless lines of toiling slaves, like fettered ghosts in the gloom. He crept through huge subterranean chambers where hundreds of the captives slept in exhaustion on the stony floors. There were men of all the western races—swarthy Iborans from Tuvar and Barranda, blond-haired men of the north, orange-skinned, hairless giants from the Kingdom of the Gashoons and beyond. Teron spied many redbeards among the slaves, but none proved on close inspection to be Lothar.

It was not until late on his second night of searching that the Mooncrow found the Khesperian general. Near the bottom of a deep shaft Teron gazed down a curving tunnel. At the end of a long line of slaves stood Lothar—a huge, bearish man with mountainous shoulders.

Two Moldorns guarded the tunnel, each standing beside a glowing lamp. Teron crept up behind the first man and knocked him senseless with a blow of the wand on the back of the neck, just below the helmet. The other guard failed to notice in time, and also fell victim. The few slaves who saw the guards fall stopped their work and regarded the Mooncrow in baffled silence.

Teron trotted past them, toward Lothar. The Khesperian lifted his head and a wolfish gleam flickered in his eyes.

Teron opened his mouth to speak, then lurched

backward. Quick reflexes saved him from a broken skull, for Lothar had suddenly struck with his chains.

"I thought you dogs had learned to keep out of my range," he growled in the Moldorn tongue.

The Mooncrow leaned aside to avoid the second blow. A saber suddenly flashed in his hand. With a feint and a pass Teron toppled the ankle-bound redbeard onto his back and pressed the point to his throat.

"You wrong me, General Lothar. I'm not a Moldorn. I'm here to free you."

"Why?" the Khesperian snarled. "Who are you?"

"One who needs your help. But we'll talk later. Will you wait and follow my instructions if I set you free?"

Lothar chuckled grimly. "Why not?"

"See that you keep that promise," Teron said. He knelt and tested the ankle chains with his saber.

Lothar sat up. "Don't you think I've tried that? Even a pick won't snap those links. They're Moldorn metal, forged by magic."

Teron fitted his point into a link and wielded the power. The psithe-sword gleamed whitely with heat. In a moment the chain came apart.

Lothar stared wildly. "You're a magician!"

The Mooncrow smiled. He melted the shackles of Lothar's wrists. The Khesperian stood and stretched with a hissing sigh. All the slaves were watching now. Some muttered among themselves, but none approached the magician.

"We must get out quickly," Teron said.

Lothar eyed him dubiously, seeming to weigh the promise of escape against a distrust of anything supernatural.

"Come on," Teron urged.

The general clenched his mouth and nodded. The two men moved swiftly down the tunnel past the mutely watching slaves.

One of the guards was just coming to his senses. But before the man could raise an alarm Lothar knocked off his helmet, lifted him up and dashed his skull against the tunnel wall.

The redbeard grunted with pleasure. "It's been too long

since last I slew a Moldorn."

"Strike a bargain with me," Teron said, "and you'll have the chance to slay many."

The Mooncrow led the way up through the mazy underworld. Progress was slow, for Lothar lacked the superhuman stealth of the magician. But at last they reached the surface, emerging while night yet covered the city.

One half-hour later, in the cellar of the Smiling Serpent, Lothar lowered an empty soup bowl from his face and loudly smacked his lips. He looked from Teron and Topiedeon to Mirabelle, and winked at her.

"You're a good cook. Also a fine-looking woman."

"I pay a man to do the cooking," she said. "And I have the only man I want to pay me compliments."

"Well, your cook's a good cook then," Lothar grumbled. "I never thought my belly would feel full again. You say I was only in the mines three months, magician? Believe me, it felt like thirty."

Teron nodded. "I can imagine. But you haven't said what you think of my plans."

"Aye."

"What do you mean?"

"That your plans are hopeless, magician. The Moldorns have vanquished half the world, and you would have me fight them with an army of slaves."

Teron scowled. "Even slaves will fight if they have a chance of winning. And even if only half of them fight we'll still outnumber the Moldorns by almost three to one."

"Three to one?" Lothar said. "Where do you get those numbers?"

"I told you, I've studied the problem. Altazar is planning a huge-scale invasion of Tann next summer. He hasn't announced it officially yet, but he's conferred with the Emperor in my hearing. He's taking the district armies and the city legion with him. That will leave only the imperial guard, the sentries in the mines and Pillars, and the private guards of the Pallantines, five thousand men at the most."

Lothar glowered, pondering.

"Besides," Teron said, "we'll have surprise on our side."

"Aye, at first. But suppose we broke out of the mines and took the lower city. The Pallantines could just hole up in their Citadel and wait for relief."

The magician smiled. "Not if the Mooncrow opened the iron hatches inside the Pillars."

Topiedeon objected: "I don't know if even you could manage that, Teron. The hatch mechanisms are known to be complicated, and the control will be heavily guarded at the first hint of trouble."

"True," the Crow replied. "But there's an overriding control board worked by a master combination. It's hidden in the palace. The system is designed so that the Emperor himself can never be trapped by the Pallantines."

"Are you sure you can work these controls?" Lothar demanded.

"I guarantee it."

"Well, then." A glimmer came to the general's eye, then faded. "No."

"Now what?" Teron said.

"Even if we took the Citadel and slaughtered all the Pallantines, we couldn't win. Altazar would just march his army back and either starve us out or attack the Pillars with airships."

"He has a point," Topiedeon said. "There was a rebellion of Pallantines sixty years ago. They took over the Citadel and killed the Emperor, but a loyalist faction rescued the imperial heir and later recaptured the city."

"I've thought of that also," the Mooncrow said. "We won't make the mistake of slaying the Emperor. Instead he will continue to rule, but only on our terms—which will include the liberation of all territories conquered in the last ten years."

"The Pallantines will never agree to that," Mirabelle said.

"They will if they wish to keep their heads."

"But what about Altazar?" Topiedeon asked. "He'll still have the army in the north."

"The army will be there," the Mooncrow said. "But

Altazar himself will be in the Citadel when we take it."

"And how will you arrange *that*?" Lothar demanded incredulously.

Teron smiled. "At the correct moment the Mooncrow will reappear. Out of fright the Emperor will summon Altazar back to the city."

"Are you certain?"

"I know the man. Just as I know Altazar will return alone, without a single cohort of soldiers. He'll be in the midst of invading Tann, you see, and will refuse to jeopardize the campaign by weakening his forces. So we shall have Altazar and most of the Pallantines here, while the army stands leaderless in the north. Now, can you think of any other objections, General Lothar?"

"Aye. The scheme is too complicated to work. Any of a hundred things could go wrong and wreck it." The redbeard scratched his matted hair. "Still, it's better than dying in the mines, I suppose. I like you, magician. I like your nerve. If you can accomplish half of what you say, then I guess I can turn a rabble of slaves into an army."

"Good. Then we have a bargain?"

"Aye, and woe to the Empire."

Teron clasped the Khesperian's hand, then stood. "It's nearly dawn, so I must go. Topiedeon and Mirabelle will look after your needs, General. Be sure you stay in this room. We can't risk your being recaptured."

Lothar glanced about the storage room and nodded. "I'll be content enough here, magician. Shelter, food and a bed. The only thing I'm lacking is a woman."

Chapter 15.
THE INFANTA'S BETROTHAL

*In the spring of 6229, in preparation for the
invasion of Tann, the Moldorns assembled the
largest army seen in the West since the days of the
Elder races.*

> —The Terrestrial Histories
> of Fystus the Grackle,
> vol. 97, ch. 44

COUNT BARTUZZI, arm in a sling, sat barechested in a
huge bed with curtains and coverlets of gold and purple
silk. The women of his seraglio stood in mute attendance
about the lavish chamber, holding bowls of fruit and trays
of beverages, waving plumed fans, languidly plucking
harps and lutes.

Left-handed, Bartuzzi flung darts across the room to a
small round target held at shoulder height by a quivering
slave in a loincloth.

"Hold still, damn it," the count growled. "Or I'll put
one in your throat."

The target shook more violently. Some of the women
giggled.

The Veglane Altazar strode through the doorway past
two motionless Gashoon guardsmen.

"Luiz," Bartuzzi said. "Good of you to look in on me."

"How's the arm?" Altazar asked.

Bartuzzi removed the sling and stretched the limb. "A
little stiff, otherwise fine. My pride sustained the worst
injury. I'd dearly love to get that close to the Mooncrow
again."

"So would I." Altazar poured himself a cup of wine. "I
need you at the War Table. How soon can you join us?"

Bartuzzi shrugged. "Tomorrow?"

"Make it this evening."

"What's the hurry?"

Altazar signed with his hand. The count nodded and ordered the room emptied. The loinclothed slave hastened to the door ahead of the women, who departed with skirts rustling.

"I need detailed plans for the invasion of Tann," the Veglane said when the doors were shut. "The imperial troops are withdrawing from the Citadel. The Pallantines are in the mood for reconciliation, and the Emperor remains in good spirits. The climate is favorable for pushing a campaign proposal through the Council."

Bartuzzi frowned. "Everyone's so sure the Mooncrow is dead?"

"Yes. And it rankles me, Bartuzzi. I hate leaving serious matters unresolved." Altazar set down his cup and began pacing. "On the other hand, I can't allow uncertainty about the past to delay me in the present. The proposal must be ready by the end of the week."

The count nodded. "How large a force are you planning on?"

Altazar threw out his arms. "We have the numbers, the airships and the tactical position all in our favor. There's no reason why we can't subdue Tann in a single season. I calculate we'll need about two million men."

The corners of Bartuzzi's mouth twitched. "That will leave us nearly defenseless here in Ibor, Luiz. Some of the provincial rulers will get ideas."

"I'm taking the airfleet on maneuvers next month," Altazar said. "I'll make a point of visiting all the provincial capitals and I'll make sure the ruling lords are properly impressed—impressed enough to add their personal armies to the invasion force."

"A smooth tactic if you can bring it off."

"I shall. But I'm more concerned about conspiracy here in PonnTherion. I had a talk yesterday with Yvonn, our spy in Ebbel Therion's seraglio. It seems that while the Crown Prince was away in the mountains he received a visit from Prince Harroman, and they talked at some length."

"Harroman again," Bartuzzi grunted, "trying to play Ebbel against us."

"And I'm sure he found it easy. The Crown Prince was highly indignant when I borrowed his concubine to trap the Mooncrow."

Bartuzzi weighed a dart in his hand. "Ebbel's a halfwit. Even without Harroman's influence he's going to cause us trouble once his father dies."

"One of his first acts as Emperor would probably be my replacement," Altazar said. "I've given the matter careful thought, Bartuzzi, and decided it's time to act. I must establish a base of power independent of the Crown Prince."

"Ah. But how?"

The Veglane smiled thinly. "By marrying his sister."

"You and the Infanta?" Bartuzzi laughed.

Altazar picked a dart off the bed and tested its point with his finger. "I had planned to marry the girl off to one of our nephews—just to keep her in the family. But if it becomes necessary to dispose of Ebbel Therion, things will be much more convenient if I myself am next in line for the throne."

The count grinned slyly. "A fine idea, Luiz. But will the Emperor see things your way?"

Altazar's smile became contemptuous. "I'll talk Bortoom into it, don't worry. I need only convince him that the move is wise in terms of political security. I'm going to propose it this afternoon while he and I exercise our gaming birds in the park."

"I see." Bartuzzi tossed a dart across the room. "There will be more game about than his Highness suspects."

That afternoon in the imperial park, which sprawled over four of the giant Pillars, the Emperor and the Veglane competed in an ancient sport of Moldorn lords called bird-gaming. They met on a wide, sunny lawn, flanked by rows of attendants in purple and red livery, imperial guards in black and silver, and a colorful gallery of spectators.

Two wheeled metal cages contained the hoodwinked birds: falcons, owls, deerhawks, condors. The Emperor's birds, diamond-collared, were larger and stronger-looking than Altazar's. Bird-gaming was Bortoom's favorite sport and his team was indisputably the finest in the Empire.

"Nice cage of birds you have there, Luiz," the Emperor said.

"Thank you, Highness. I only hope they may offer a slight challenge to your splendid team of champions."

The Emperor smiled.

The contest began. Each man selected a falcon and perched it upon a leather-shielded forearm. A flag was waved and at the far end of the lawn a pigeon was released. The Veglane and the Emperor unhooded their birds and flung them off. Both falcons raced for the prey. But the Emperor's bird proved swifter and returned with the feathery corpse in its talons.

"My kill," the Emperor gloated.

A crier announced the score and the gallery applauded.

As the match continued the Veglane turned the conversation to the upcoming invasion of Tann— predicting with confidence that one year hence all of the western world would be under imperial rule. Then, with a note of gloom in his voice, Altazar expressed concern that the Empire might disintegrate one day, when Bortoom's strong hand no longer held power.

Absorbed in the contest, the Emperor was reluctant to discuss politics—more so to discuss his own death. But Altazar persisted, saying he feared that once the Crown Prince sat on the throne the realm would be torn asunder by competing factions of Pallantines and provincial lords.

Bortoom bit his lip and stared into his cage. "But you're still a young man, Luiz. You'll be here to hold things together when I'm gone."

"Perhaps not, Highness. Ebbel bears me no love. I fear he'll replace me as soon as he comes to power."

The Emperor sighed. "You're probably right, Luiz. The boy's an idiot. If only there was some way we could secure your post against his tampering."

"There is, Highness. You can appoint me Veglane for life."

"What? But my appointment would not bind Ebbel."

"It would under the law, *if* I was one of your legal

heirs. The Veglaneship would then be viewed as a secondary inheritance, after the throne."

Bortoom lowered suspiciously. "Sounds like you've investigated the matter, Luiz."

"I have, Highness."

The Emperor reached into his cage and removed a huge owl. "Since you know the law so well you must also know that I can't appoint legal heirs at will."

"You need not, Highness," Altazar said. "Merely command me to wed your daughter."

"What?" Bortoom started and the owl on his forearm screeched.

"That way, Highness, I shall be permanently empowered to defend the Empire." The Veglane chose a falcon from his cage. "Moreover, with the Infanta married to me, Ebbel need never fear the ambitions of his brother-in-law, who will be next in line for the throne."

The Emperor's eyes narrowed. "But how can I be sure your ambitions will be satisfied, Luiz?"

"Is there a man among the Pallantines you would trust more?"

The Emperor snorted, petting his owl.

"I do not dissemble my selfish motives, Highness. I state them plainly. I wish to hold the Veglaneship for life. You wish your son to hold the throne, that your house might continue. Give me your daughter to marry and both our wishes will be granted."

The pigeon was released and the two lords threw off their birds. Altazar's falcon outstripped the Emperor's owl and returned with the first prize taken by the Veglane's team that day.

Bortoom sighed in irritation. "Well, I must admit your plan makes sense, Luiz. I've worried over which Pallantine house should get my daughter's hand—for fear of provoking the jealousy of the others. But why shouldn't I give the girl to you? You've surely served me better than any other prince of the realm." He laughed harshly. "Of course I doubt Rania will consider you a very romantic husband."

"Surely we can't allow the whims of a girl to interfere in matters of such importance."

"I was only joking, Luiz. All the same, I don't want my daughter informed until the last minute. The less warning she has, the less complaining I'll be forced to hear. When do you want to be married, Luiz?"

"I think it would be best to accomplish the marriage before my departure in the spring, Highness."

"Very well. I'll notify the Infanta ten days or so ahead of time. Don't mention it to anyone until then. Now let's get back to the match. I still lead four kills to one."

At the start of the following week the Veglane presented his campaign proposal to the Imperial Council. The invasion of Tann would require an exorbitant amount of money, and as a result the plan was strongly opposed by many of the Guildsmen. But the Emperor and most of the Pallantines supported Altazar fully. The proposal passed after only a half-hour debate.

During the next month the Veglane paid frequent visits to the plain before PonnTherion, where the massive army gradually assembled. Raw youths, pressed into service by force of arms, drilled with spears and swords until collapsing from exhaustion. Battalions of horsemen, infantry and archers arrived daily, summoned from distant garrisons by imperial command. Each day the sky was full of airships manned by novice crews, practicing attack formations and bombing maneuvers.

The rainy season waned. A warm east wind blew for days off the lowlands. The nights were clear and full of stars.

At month's end Altazar gathered a fleet of thirty airships—he would have eighty-five for the invasion—and toured the provincial capitals of Ibor. The Veglane inspected the local armies, then issued orders that they march at once to PonnTherion. Any governor or ally king who objected was faced with an airfleet of thirty craft—all of them armed with firebombs. The Veglane returned to PonnTherion after three weeks. He had defused the threat of the provinces, burned one city, and added 400,000 men to the imperial host.

While the army trained and fought mock battles before

the city walls, Altazar and the generals of the War Table studied maps and spy reports, constructed various strategies, and plotted timetables. The bulk of the invasion force would depart for the north on the first day of spring. The airfleet, commanded by Altazar, would leave PonnTherion two weeks later.

When the first of spring arrived the legions of Moldorn paraded through the city to the music of trumpets and drums. The Emperor and the Veglane reviewed the parade from a lofty bastion above the main gate of the imperial palace. From this point numerous columns of soldiers could be seen—marching across the Citadel and the cantilever bridge, down the imperial hill and across the lower city, through the eastern gate and out over the plain for many miles, before at last turning northward for Tann. The parade began before dawn and lasted all day, while above the city scores of airships floated in an overcast sky.

That evening Teron was summoned to the Emperor's apartments at an odd hour. The Lord of the Earth sat on a huge divan, his bare legs propped by velvet pillows. His left shin was badly bruised.

As Teron prepared a draught to ease the pain he asked how the injury had occurred.

"My daughter," Bortoom growled. "The filthy brat kicked me, Bhendi. She didn't like the man I chose for her husband."

"What man, Highness?"

"The Veglane Altazar."

The magician's pupils widened.

"But she doesn't want him, the ungrateful whelp. First she whined and stamped her feet. When that failed she wept and pleaded deplorably, as if I'd condemned her to the condors. I stayed calm and firm, Bhendi, until she lost her temper and did this to me. Then I gave her something to really cry about. I had her stripped and flogged by the guards. Twenty lashes..."

Teron's face went rigid and his eyes glared.

"Why are you staring at me like that?" Bortoom grunted.

The Mooncrow swallowed. "Your pardon, Highness. I did not mean to stare." He handed the Emperor the psithe-cup.

Outside Teron was met by a page. The Empress desired his presence at once, in the Infanta's apartments. Teron hastened down the long, lofty corridors and candle-lit stairways.

The Empress greeted him in Rania's bedchamber, flanked by two strong-looking womanservants. In the canopied bed Rania lay on her stomach, stiff and shivering. The crisscrossed marks of the whip on her back made Teron wince.

"I suppose you know how this happened," Unez whispered.

Teron nodded.

"She's wept herself into a fever, Bhendi. And she'll hardly speak to me. Please, do whatever you can."

Teron approached the Infanta's bedside and fixed a potion to cool her fever. But Rania kept her head buried in the pillow.

"Go away, Bhendi," she murmured.

"Please, child. Take your medicine," Unez said. "You'll feel better."

"I have no reason for wishing to feel better."

Teron's heart writhed in sympathy. He hesitated, then stroked the Infanta's hair—a gesture which elicited a look of surprise from Unez, a look that Teron ignored.

"Please reconsider, Highness," he said to Rania. "One cannot think clearly when the body is plagued by illness."

"There's nothing to think about, Bhendi. I've no choice at all."

"Please."

In that moment the magician sensed a deep and perfect empathy with Rania's soul, a harmony of their life-vibrations. He was sure Rania sensed it also. She rolled onto her side and gazed at him through sore, fevered eyes. After a moment her lips parted and she took the cup from his hands and drank.

Teron called for an unguent to soothe her flayed back. While he applied the unguent Unez spoke to Rania.

"Your uncle and I did our best to make your father reconsider. But you know how stubborn he is when his mind is set on something. It was all we could do to convince him to postpone the wedding six months, in accord with your legal right. He agreed to that only on condition that the engagement be formally announced before the Veglane departs for Tann."

"Is he Altazar's puppet?" Rania asked bitterly.

"I don't know, daughter." The Empress wore a dark and troubled look. "Altazar circumvented us completely in this. Bortoom gave no warning of his intentions. Gildaro and I both are worried."

The Infanta ground her teeth at the sting in her back. "My father is a rodent," she said, "intent on marrying me to a jackal."

Teron wiped his hands on a towel. Abruptly, as though afraid he was leaving, Rania turned to him.

"Bhendi, what shall I do?"

Teron glanced at Unez, then took Rania's hand. "Be calm, Highness, and take heart. Many things may change in six months, many solutions occur that you cannot now foresee."

She squeezed his hand tightly. "If only I could believe that."

The Mooncrow smiled faintly. "Believe it, Rania. I give you my word as a diviner. Besides, if I'm wrong, there'll be plenty of time to despair later."

Rania let out her breath with a grim smile. She rested her forehead on Teron's hand.

Ten days later the Infanta's betrothal was officially announced to the nobles of Moldorn. Rania attended the sumptuous reception held in the great hall of the palace. She behaved with all propriety, though her eyes remained downcast and her demeanor solemn. She wore a dark velvet gown that covered the scars on her back.

On the third morning after the reception the Veglane Altazar sailed from PonnTherion with his airfleet—to Tann and the inauguration of the great campaign. The airships of Moldorn had been developed and used exclusively by the military, and Altazar's departure now left not a single airship in all of Ibor—a factor on which the Mooncrow was counting.

Chapter 16.
THE CROW AGAIN

Then on a moonless midnight
The Crow again did stride.
Upon a stallion, raven-black
To Glaverstone he rides.
　　　　—Ballad fragment attributed to
　　　　Bandelion of Peltaine.

IN THE QUIET of a moonless night Glaverstone Castle jutted its black roofs and towers against the stars. The large, iron-framed castle loomed above the treetops, at the summit of a broad, craggy hill.

Cloaked and garbed in black, the Mooncrow approached on foot, furtively scaling the pine-covered slope, nimbly climbing over boulders. He crouched at the edge of the castle's well-trimmed lawn and scanned the fortifications—small turrets set at intervals along a twenty-foot wall.

Teron's eyes detected no sentries pacing the battlements. He had expected none. Glaverstone was Ebbel Therion's favorite hunting retreat, but at the moment the Crown Prince was in PonnTherion—sixty miles to the north and east. Half his seraglio slept in Glaverstone, however, including Adria. According to rumor she was under the personal guard of the Lieutenant of the Castle, because Ebbel feared she might be taken from him again.

She would be, the Crow had decided. Rescuing Adria was a necessary first step in his new campaign against the Empire.

Teron darted across the lawn and leapt upon the castle wall. The wand lifted him, and his soft boots clambered over the masonry. He paused at the top of the wall, glanced in both directions, then vaulted over the crenels and jumped from the parapet—drifting down slowly into a still, dark courtyard.

A lone spearman guarded the arched doors of the donjon. The Mooncrow advanced on him noiselessly. All the sentry perceived was the swirling amber glow of the disk. His mind was insensible for six seconds, in which time Teron quietly opened the door, slipped in and shut it behind him.

Inside, the Mooncrow traversed a lofty foyer and ascended a marble stair. The walls were adorned with frescoes: gigantic scenes of hunting and revelry crowded with rugged youths and plump, unclothed maidens.

Teron passed another sentry and crept down a massive corridor lit dimly by candles in niches. Silently opening and shutting doors, he searched a sequence of splendid sitting rooms and bedchambers. A few of the beds were occupied, by women with pastel faces, sleeping alone or in pairs.

Finally the Mooncrow found Adria, asleep on a wide canopied bed. A tall, swarthy Moldorn slept beside her—the Lieutenant of the Castle, judging by the plumed helmet and fine, silver-worked corselet that lay on the floor. Teron frowned and closed the door behind him.

He made the psithe into a saber and advanced on the bed.

Then he changed his mind and returned the psithe to its disk shape. He had planned to entrance Adria, but the power of an adept could lay spells of entrancement on two persons as easily as one. And the Mooncrow's rescue would be all the more mystifying to the Moldorns if the Lieutenant was left alive.

Teron stepped to the foot of the bed and lifted the glimmering disk. He chanted in his mind for several minutes, building enough energy to make the spell last three hours and more. Then he spoke the final words and cast the spell—feeling its power burst from the psithe.

The magician probed with his mind to be sure the trance had taken hold. Both Adria and the Moldorn were cut off from their senses. Teron circled to Adria's side. She wore a blank expression, her face painted silver. The Mooncrow wrapped her in the satin coverlet and hoisted her over his shoulder. He paused to leave a note on her pillow.

Carrying Adria, Teron departed the chamber through a window, crossed a section of roof and climbed up and over the outer parapet of the castle. Lightened by the wand he drifted down outside the wall, hampered slightly by his burden. He landed in a crouch and stayed low as he trotted across the lawn.

He carried Adria down the rocky hill to a small clearing. There a cavalry horse, borrowed from the stables of the imperial guard, stood tethered to a branch. Teron slung Adria's limp body over the saddle, paused to catch his breath, then mounted and set off through the forest toward the road.

Teron's experience as a horseman was slim, and this Moldorn charger high-spirited. The magician had to fight with reins and heels to keep control. His head and neck and back ached with the steady pounding of the hoofs. Still he kept the horse at a gallop, for he had to be back in the city by sunrise.

When the Mooncrow approached the western gate of PonnTherion he was clad in a black uniform with steel helmet and breastplate—all borrowed, like the horse, from the imperial guard. The sentry stationed over the gate peered down through the darkness.

"Open the gate. Quickly!" Teron yelled.

"You again, and still in a damned hurry." The Moldorn sneered as he signaled those below to raise the portcullis.

"As I told you, Sergeant," Teron answered, "when the Crown Prince orders a wench brought, it's trouble for the man who makes him wait."

The magician spurred his mount and passed beneath the portcullis and the massive, frowning arch.

A short time later, in a basement chamber of the Smiling Serpent, Teron invoked the power of the disk to wake Adria from her trance. She opened her blue eyes and glanced about in bewilderment—at Teron, Topiedeon, Mirabelle, and Lothar, who surrounded the narrow couch on which she lay.

"Where am I?"

"With friends," Teron replied.

Adria sat up and wrapped herself tighter in the

bedspread. "Why did you bring me here, Teron? I told you to leave me alone."

"Unfortunately the Moldorns took the matter out of my hands," Teron answered. "They're too willing to use you as a hostage."

"I don't care. I want you to let me go."

The Mooncrow shook his head. "I'm sorry, Adria."

"Please. Ebbel beat me last time. This time he may kill me."

"And you want to go back to him?"

Adria sucked in her breath. "You can't hold me. I'll find a way out."

Teron gripped her shoulders. "Listen to me. When this is over I intend to restore your throne, and to treat you with all the honor due your rank. But in the meantime I'll tie you to that couch if I must, to keep you out of the way."

She trembled, on the verge of tears. "How long will I be your prisoner?"

"We'll be ready to move against the Empire sometime in the next month," Teron said. "Meantime Mirabelle here will look after you, she and Topiedeon, who you should remember from Telyrra. And this"—Teron clapped the redbeard's shoulder—"is General Lothar of Khesperia, who's going to help me defeat the Pallantines."

"You've no reason for weeping," Lothar said. "You have powerful friends now. And you're a beautiful girl."

Adria stared at him with wary, hostile eyes.

"Perhaps we should leave her alone for a while," Mirabelle said. She ushered the three men out of the chamber.

"A fine-looking woman," Lothar remarked as they walked in the basement corridor. "Is she yours, magician, or can I have her?"

Teron answered in a matter-of-fact voice: "You'll leave her alone if you value your body intact, Lothar. She's been through enough already."

The redbeard muttered something under his breath, then demanded, "So what happens next? How long before we strike?"

The Mooncrow shrugged his shoulders. "It depends on

how soon the Emperor sends for Altazar. He should receive my note sometime around mid-morning."

"You told me he was dead!" Bortoom yelled, waving the Mooncrow's note at Teron. "So how do you explain this, Bhendi?"

With a puzzled face Teron received the parchment from the Emperor's hand. It was an hour before noon and the magician had been summoned to the round antechamber in the Emperor's tower. The room was occupied by Prince Gildaro, a few attendants, and twice the usual number of guards.

Teron made a show of reading the note:

> SOON ALL YOUR CAPTIVES WILL BE FREED.
> HOW MANY OF YOU WILL SURVIVE THAT TIME,
> LORDS OF MOLDORN?
>
> MOONCROW

"It seems the assassin stole the Crown Prince's consort from Glaverstone Castle during the night," Gildaro explained to Teron.

"I knew he wasn't dead." Bortoom slumped into his throne. "When there was no body I knew it. But everyone else was so sure!"

"Highness, my conclusion was based on the premise that the Mooncrow's body had burned," Teron said. "Even at that it was only a guess."

"Never mind," Bortoom grumbled. "Just fix something to calm me. My belly's a furnace and my heart feels ready to burst."

While Teron prepared a drug for the Emperor, Count Bartuzzi arrived. The count stepped up before the throne, removed his plumed helmet and saluted with an elaborate flourish of his saber.

"To hell with your swordsmanship," Bortoom yelled. "The Mooncrow has returned."

"So I've heard, Highness," Bartuzzi said. "As ranking military officer in PonnTherion I was notified of the incident at once. I also received another report of interest: Near dawn a rider dressed as an imperial guardsman entered the west gate of the city. He had a blonde-haired woman over his saddle."

"And the men at the gate let him pass?" Bortoom demanded.

Bartuzzi shrugged. "He wore the plume of a lieutenant and claimed to have the Crown Prince's orders to deliver the concubine to the palace."

"You think the Mooncrow's in PonnTherion then?" Gildaro asked.

"It seems obvious he's hidden the woman somewhere in the city," Bartuzzi said. "If we recapture her we have no worries. I recommend a building-to-building search of the lower city and the hill."

Bortoom shook his head. "We can't spare the men. I've ordered the whole imperial guard into the Citadel. And I'm writing to Altazar and ordering him back to PonnTherion with the army."

Bartuzzi's expression darkened. "I strongly advise against that, Highness. The campaign is only a week old, and the whole first month is crucial."

"I don't give a damn," Bortoom growled. "What good will the conquering of Tann be when the Mooncrow's slitting our throats?"

Teron handed the potion to the Emperor, who swallowed it down.

"Perhaps, Highness," Teron said, "my judgment was not incorrect after all."

Bortoom handed him back the cup. "Yes?"

"You'll recall, Highness, that I predicted we need not fear the Mooncrow again unless he returned from the dead. In fact, that is what may have happened. The Mooncrow may not be a wizard at all, but rather a dead soul bound to an earthly task. Such stories are told in Indus and Bolthoven. In that case it will prove impossible to slay him. Sooner or later he will again return from the grave."

"Enough," Bortoom cried, clutching his temples. "Just fix me another draught and keep quiet."

The Emperor glanced at Bartuzzi. "And I'm ordering the legions back to Ibor."

The count winced. "I advise against it, Highness."

"As do I," Gildaro said—which made Teron lift his eyebrows in surprise.

"With respect to Prince Bhendi," Gildaro continued, "there's scant evidence to support his supernatural theory. In fact, we don't even know for certain it was the Mooncrow who left the note. Besides, we have nearly three thousand imperial guards to patrol the Pillars. I think we can afford to wait, Highness, at least until we know what sort of plot is afoot."

"Prince Gildaro offers sound advice, as usual," Bartuzzi said—a hint of confused suspicion in his tone.

Teron thought he perceived Gildaro's motive: The chief minister wanted the Veglane to stay in Tann not for the sake of the invasion, but because he feared Altazar's influence on the Emperor, and wished him away from PonnTherion as long as possible.

Allies for once, Gildaro and Bartuzzi managed at length to convince the Emperor to leave the army in Tann.

"Very well." Bortoom tugged morosely on his beard. "I shall wait—for the moment."

Teron viewed this outcome as a partial success. With the imperial guard no longer patrolling the lower city, the Mooncrow could initiate the second stage of his plan. And it was obvious that one more note from the Mooncrow would be enough to make the Emperor call Altazar home.

Late that night Teron and General Lothar broke into a coalyard in the lower city and made off with two huge freight wagons and two teams of mules. They drove the wagons through winding, empty streets beneath the Pillars, arriving finally at an armory near the imperial hill.

The armory was left unguarded, and the magician melted the lock on the main gate with his sword. Over the next hour the Mooncrow and the barbarian hurried in and out of the building, loading the coal wagons with spears, swords, breastplates, crossbows and quivers of arrows.

Robbing the armory had been Lothar's idea. The redbeard said that weapons and armor would help persuade the first slaves to join the rebellion, and would boost morale in the early battles. Teron and Lothar plundered enough equipment for some four hundred mine slaves—who would serve as the first recruits of their army.

In the stillness of the night they drove the wagons around the bottom of the imperial hill and along the base of the escarpment. They maneuvered close to the gravel slope, unloaded the weapons and stashed them some distance inside the mine tunnel. After carefully replacing the wooden planks on the tunnel's entrance, they drove the wagons back to the coalyard and left them.

Lothar then returned to the cellar of the Smiling Serpent, and Teron to the imperial palace. But before seeking his bed the weary Mooncrow ran one more errand—paying a secret visit to the Emperor's tower.

When Bortoom was wakened that morning by his servants he saw a note pinned to the inner curtains of his bed:

LAST NIGHT I LOOTED THE ARMORY NEAR
THE OLD WALL. TAKE HEED, LORD OF THE
EARTH, MY LEGIONS WILL SOON CARRY YOUR
OWN STEEL AGAINST YOU.

MOONCROW

"Enough. Enough!" the Emperor cried, rolling from his bed. "I don't care what Bartuzzi says, or Gildaro. I'm ordering the legions home at once."

Within the hour six imperial couriers left PonnTherion. Changing horses at various stations along the land route, the messengers were expected to reach the Veglane's army in eight or nine days. Returning from Tann by airship would consume another five to seven days, depending on the winds. Teron would therefore start looking for Altazar's return in thirteen days.

Meantime the Mooncrow had nothing to do but wait—and hope he'd read the Veglane's character as accurately as the Emperor's. Teron had gambled everything that Altazar would return alone. If he brought even a small fraction of his army back to PonnTherion, then the rebellion would be finished before it could begin, and all the Mooncrow's planning would have gone for nothing.

Chapter 17.
UPROAR IN THE UNDERWORLD

ON AN AFTERNOON exactly two weeks after the departure of the imperial couriers, a single airship was spotted in the northern sky. As it drew near PonnTherion the craft was identified as the *Basilisk*.

At dusk the airship glided down from a gray and purple sky toward the roofs of the Citadel. The *Basilisk* did not seek the airfield on the escarpment, but settled instead atop a square tower of the imperial palace—in a wide slot between two splayed parapets. This architectural structure, unique in the Citadel, was a sky-dock capable of mooring a single craft. With the rumble of pulleys and chains the two parapets closed about the upper rails of the *Basilisk*, leaving the oblong, gas-filled bubble exposed above the roof.

Inside the port-tower the Lord of the Earth, bleary-eyed and pallid, waited to greet the Veglane. Teron stood at the Emperor's shoulder, for lately Bortoom's health had been poor and the magician was required to attend him through most of his waking hours. Prince Gildaro and Count Bartuzzi were also present, backed by a line of steel-clad guards.

Altazar descended the gangplank, a blue-plumed helmet under his arm. He wore the gold armor and dark blue cape of an aeronaut officer. He bowed to the Emperor, then saluted with his sword.

"I'm glad you're here, Luiz," the Emperor said. "When will the rest of the army arrive?"

The Veglane clenched his lips a moment. "I'm afraid they won't be arriving, Highness. I returned with only the *Basilisk* and her crew."

"But, but Luiz—"

"The war goes on in my absence, Highness, and the Tannites offer stiff resistance. I dared not spare a single legion, or even one squadron of airships."

"But Luiz, I ordered you to bring the army home."

"I had to risk disobeying that order, Highness, or else risk the certain ruin of our campaign in Tann. I chose the former alternative. There are more than enough men here already to deal with the Mooncrow."

"But he's raising an army!" Bortoom cried.

"I doubt that, Highness. Reflect a moment. Where would the assassin get an army? Can he recruit soldiers from the air?"

"Who knows?" Bortoom grumbled. "I must sit down."

Two servants emerged from behind the row of guards, carrying a folding chair which of late had become a fixture in the Emperor's entourage. Teron and Gildaro supported Bortoom's arms and helped him sit.

"Has there been any further word from the Mooncrow in the past two weeks?" Altazar asked.

"None," Bartuzzi said.

The Veglane nodded. "Has it occurred to anyone that perhaps it was never the Mooncrow at all, but only some plot by our enemies to disrupt the war in Tann?"

"It occurs to me, Veglane, that you're obscuring the issue," Gildaro replied. "The point is that you've disobeyed a direct imperial order."

Altazar stared at him acidly. "I performed my duty as best I perceived it. If His Highness wishes to relieve me of my post he has that power. You, Gildaro, do not."

Bortoom rubbed his forehead. "Of course I don't want to replace you, Luiz. It's just that I'm worried."

"I think all of us are overwrought," the Veglane said mildly. "I myself have hardly slept the past week, being airborne all the time. I suggest we get some rest tonight, and talk things over in the morning."

"Perhaps you're right," the Emperor muttered. "You're sure we have enough men to stop the Moon-crow?"

"I am positive, Highness."

The Lord of the Earth retired at once and Teron was obliged to spend the next several hours at his bedside. But finally the numerous drugs and sleeping potions took effect, and the Emperor slept.

●　　●　　●

A glowing lantern and a tall bottle of wine stood on the table in General Lothar's room. The Mooncrow leaned back in his chair and grinned across the table at Topiedeon and Mirabelle.

"The Veglane reacted just as I hoped. Couldn't spare a single legion, he said. Now he's trapped on the Pillars with the rest."

"It'll take powerful action to turn that stronghold into a trap, magician." Lothar stood across the room, fastening on a wide belt with iron spikes.

Teron glanced at the long two-handed broadsword which hung from the belt. "You'll have action soon enough, Lothar."

"Action at least," Topiedeon said. "It's hard to believe we're just going to stroll down there with our stock of weapons like three peddlers and invite the slaves to join us."

The Mooncrow lifted his shoulders. "What did you expect?"

"I don't know. That you might have contacted some of the slaves earlier perhaps, made some preparations."

"Too risky," Teron said. "The element of surprise is critical. The plan must work all at once."

"Or not at all," Lothar added, putting on a great black cape.

Mirabelle gazed anxiously at Topiedeon. "I still don't see why you have to go."

"I told you, Mirabelle, I'm a poet. If this scheme succeeds, minstrels will sing of it for hundreds of years. I must be there to watch—or I'd regret it the rest of my days."

Mirabelle looked away from him.

"Don't worry," the minstrel laughed. "I'm no soldier, lady. I'll keep well away from the fighting, I promise."

"Aye, and what good will you be then?" Lothar jested. "Carrying a mandolin instead of a spear."

Topiedeon strummed a high chord and smiled. "Don't fret, general. My music may help your soldiers learn to march."

The Khesperian produced some tumblers and opened the bottle of wine on the table. "Before battle my countrymen always drink a libation to Koliandri the Life-Goddess." He filled two of the cups, then paused. "Wait, I'll be right back."

Lothar left the chamber and returned in a few moments, leading Adria by the wrist. "We should all toast together," he said.

Adria wore one of Mirabelle's simple dresses. Her face was pale and unpowdered, her hair confined by a cloth band.

"Glad you've joined us," Teron said, as Lothar passed around the cups.

"I don't mind toasting with you," she answered. "I even wish you good luck. But that doesn't change the fact that I think you're all mad."

Topiedeon chuckled. "Who can argue with that?"

"No, I'm serious," Adria said. "You three are going to your deaths."

"All men are going to their deaths," Teron answered. "All women too. But I think we three will topple this Empire before we're finished."

"Aye." Lothar raised his tumbler. "Let us drink to that, in the name of the Goddess Koliandri."

Cloaked and cowled in black, the three men left the basement by the back stairs and emerged on a narrow alley. The alley was crowded with fifty olpondas—docile, surefooted pack animals native to the mountains of western Ibor. Topiedeon had seen to the purchase of the olpondas—buying them with a handful of gemstones the Mooncrow had pilfered from about the palace.

Teron, Topiedeon and Lothar each led a train of the mute, plodding olpondas as they marched three abreast through the winding streets of the lower city. The giant Pillars loomed above them, immense columns blotting out the stars. Teron's face was set in rigid, brooding lines. Adria's prediction gnawed at his mind as he rehearsed all the manifold plans and preparations he'd made—all of them hinging on tonight.

At the entrance to the tunnel Lothar tore off the planks and threw them aside. The olpondas proved skittish, afraid to enter the dank, murky tunnel. The Mooncrow

went first, holding high the luminous psithe-wand. Eighty
paces inside, the men stopped and loaded the pack
animals with the stolen armor and weapons.

The descent continued single file, Teron again in the
lead. He chose a path that slanted deeper and deeper into
the earth. The plan called for them to strike first in the
lowest reaches of the mines, then to work upward as the
size of their army increased.

After perhaps an hour they approached a portion of
the mines presently being worked. Leaving Topiedeon
with the olpondas, Teron and Lothar crept forward to an
outcropping of rock and peered into a lighted section of
tunnel. About fifty slaves worked the area, supervised by
three guards with short swords and pikes. Lothar signed
to Teron and drew his broadsword. The Mooncrow
nodded, and the wand he held changed to a saber.

The magician and the Khesperian charged into the
tunnel together. Lothar brought down the first two
Moldorns, cleaving both despite their armor. Racing up
the tunnel, Teron slew the third guard—running him
through the throat before he could blow the alarm horn
which already touched his lips.

Teron stared farther up the tunnel to be sure it was
empty, then returned to where Lothar faced the haggard
slaves. The men appeared to be mostly Iborans, so Teron
spoke in the Moldorn tongue:

"Listen to me. We've come to free you. With your help
we can overthrow the Moldorns."

Most of the prisoners stared at him in silence. A few
continued mindlessly to work.

"Look!" Teron held up his saber, which glimmered
with unearthly heat. "I can melt your chains with this.
Who will be first?"

But the slaves cowered, frightened by the brightness.

"I was afraid of this," Lothar grunted. "A man loses
even his memories in these mines, forgets what the world
is like. I was a slave too," he yelled. "Now I'm free. Look
at me, fools! Which do you think is better?"

Many of the slaves were scuttling off, returning to
work. Teron glanced anxiously up the tunnel, knowing
that an ore-cart or a guard might appear at any moment.

Then, abruptly, music burst from the lower end of the tunnel and Topiedeon came strolling around the outcropping, leading the olpondas by a tether rope tied in his belt—for both hands were occupied playing the mandolin. The minstrel had flung off his cloak, revealing a bright-colored costume. The mine slaves stared at him with round eyes and gaping mouths.

"Remember, you're a conjurer," Topiedeon called to Teron. "We must make these poor lads recall what it's like in the daylight."

Teron sensed that the slaves had been roused by the music, and he changed the sword to a golden disk. While Topiedeon picked out a melody, lively and sweet, the magician moved among the slaves and displayed the disk to their startled eyes. Over its surface passed images— trees and grassy meadows, beaches and starry skies, palaces, taverns, cities and ships.

"This is how the world looks, if you've forgotten," Teron cried. "We're here to help you win it back. We have weapons, plans. All we need is your help."

"Aye. And what have you to lose?" Lothar demanded.

"He's right," a slave declared. "Why not die like men at least, fighting?"

His voice was echoed by the shouts of others. A tide of indignation and hate rushed over the prisoners. Several approached the Mooncrow, held up their chains and cried out to be freed.

Teron made the sword again and smashed through the shackles. Seeing this, more of the slaves crowded the Mooncrow. With a surging thrill Teron cut them loose, while Lothar and Topiedeon started passing out the armor and weapons.

Teron had cut free a number of the captives when he spotted a Moldorn guard some distance up the tunnel. The music and shouting had been heard farther up. The Moldorn stood observing the scene for an instant, then turned and dashed in the other direction, raising an alarm horn as he ran.

The Mooncrow was about to give chase when one of the mine slaves lifted and hurled a spear—sending the point clear through the guard's body, which pitched forward and lay still on the tunnel floor.

"A good cast," Lothar declared. "What's your name, man?"

"Yargus. I was a spearman in the royal army of Dhannia."

"Well, you're in the army of General Lothar now."

Some of the slaves recognized the general's name. This, along with the fact that one of their number had slain a guard, helped dispel lingering hesitations. Some still held back, mute and fearful, but more than half of the fifty donned armor and lifted weapons and placed themselves at Lothar's command.

Soon they were moving up the tunnel two abreast, with Lothar in the lead and Teron and Topiedeon bringing up the olpondas in the rear. In a few moments they came upon another work party and overwhelmed the half-dozen guards. Convincing the second group of slaves to join them was easier, for now a tangible army existed to be joined. The Mooncrow shattered some of the chains with his blade. Others were melted by a few drops of an acid mixture which Teron had concocted and carried to the underworld in jugs packed on several of the olpondas.

The newly-freed slaves were given weapons and in their turn helped cut down the guards in adjacent tunnels. Before long the slave army had grown to hundreds. Lothar divided it into separate units. He made the best fighters lieutenants, gave them soldiers to command and separate areas to capture. Teron and Topiedeon stayed with the general, who led the massive main column up to the next level of the mines.

Gaining momentum, the rebellion spread from level to level, rising up the shafts and twisting tunnels. Alarm horns wailed in the distance, but by then Lothar's army was too huge to be contained. The Moldorns retreated at the first sight of the mutinous slaves—leaving whole trains of captives, many of them shouting and rattling their chains, anxious to greet their liberators and join them.

Within four hours the entire south and eastern portions of the underworld had fallen. Pouring out of several large tunnels the army of slaves converged on the main smelting chamber beneath the central Pillar. The chamber was empty, abandoned by the fleeing Moldorns. Teron judged that the army must now number near ten thousand. Most of the men were still naked, armed with picks, spades, lengths of chain, or with weapons stolen from the corpses of the guards.

Wasting not a moment, Lothar led the bulk of the army up the iron steps to take the lower city. Topiedeon followed the general, carefully cradling his mandolin in the surging mob on the stairs.

Meanwhile the Mooncrow took a squad of men down into the north and western sections of the mines. For the next five hours Teron labored in the underworld, freeing slaves from their chains and seeing that the few remaining guards were captured and disarmed.

The sun was already high when the magician finally emerged from the base of the central Pillar—leading a host of twelve thousand men. These joined the army which already filled the narrow, curving streets beneath the Pillars. Most were off duty, feasting on plundered food, fitting themselves with equipment looted from imperial armories, or simply sleeping in the open air. Patrols of rebel spearmen kept some measure of order. Teron saw few civilians in the streets. Most of the doors he passed were closed, the windows shuttered.

The Mooncrow proceeded to the Smiling Serpent. In the main room he found General Lothar eating breakfast with Topiedeon and a half-dozen armored men— Khesperians they were, with red beards and braided hair.

Lothar raised his goblet to the Mooncrow and laughed. "We did it, magician! Did you ever see such an army?"

"Never," Teron replied. "Did you check the iron hatches?"

"Aye. They were locked already, as we expected."

The Mooncrow took a chair across from Lothar, grateful for a moment's rest. He felt too excited to eat, but poured a cup of water.

"We captured the city walls and the armories without any trouble," Lothar reported. "But Altazar counterattacked soon after."

"He only had about two thousand men," Topiedeon said. "But they came marching down the hill like a hundred times that many."

Teron smiled crookedly. "The Veglane expected a rabble that would break before a strong attack."

"Aye, but I was ready for him," Lothar said. "I sent out long flanks to encircle him, then arranged my front line to look haphazard. I almost drew him in too. But he caught wind of it near the end and sounded the retreat."

Topiedeon grinned. "Still, it warmed the heart to see imperial troops routed on the streets of their own capital."

"We killed about ninety," Lothar added. "The rest retreated behind the old wall at the bottom of the hill. Five thousand of our men face them now across the marketplace."

Teron nodded. "If they stay there they'll be out of the way when we attack the Pillars."

"Aye. When will that be, magician?"

"Tonight," Teron said. "There'll be time for the men to rest, and for you to get them organized. Any trouble from the townspeople?"

"A few protested our looting," Lothar said, "but not with any organized force. Some have even joined us."

"Good," the magician said. "Allow any who wish to leave the city to do so. And keep a short rein on the looting, general. No reason to make more enemies than we already have."

"Aye. I've men patrolling," Lothar said.

Mirabelle and Adria came down the stairs to the main room. General Lothar greeted them with a broad smile and cleared the seat beside his own for Adria.

"I knew you'd come to see things our way," he said as she sat down.

"I still expect all of us will be doomed for this," Adria replied. "But I've decided I may as well enjoy my freedom while it lasts."

"Aye. A proper attitude," the general said.

Adria looked across the table at Teron. He returned her gaze a moment, then looked away. Anxious thoughts plagued him. Presently he rose from the table.

He descended to the basement and donned the clothes

and makeup of Aurik Ib Bhendi, which he'd carried down from the palace on the previous night.

Back upstairs, Lothar's eyes widened when Teron approached the table.

"What? Is that you, magician?"

The Mooncrow smiled thinly and bowed. "Yes, general. This is how I look in the Emperor's court. It's time I returned to the palace."

"Why?" Topiedeon demanded. "What use to keep up the masquerade now?"

Teron's face turned rueful. "I'm afraid I have no choice. I still must learn the means of opening the hatches."

"What?" Lothar slapped the table with both hands. "A damned fine time to tell us that, magician!"

"It had to be this way," Teron said, "so that the army would be ready to attack. And so the Emperor would see our power and be frightened enough to make a bargain."

"The Emperor?" Topiedeon repeated. "You expect the Emperor himself to help you?"

Lothar groaned and ran his hands through tangled red hair. "Why did I ever trust a magician?"

"Don't worry." Teron's laugh was harsh. "I know the Emperor well enough. Just have the men ready to storm the five middle Pillars; those are the ones worked by the master controls. Hopefully I'll open the hatches around midnight."

"And suppose you don't?" Lother demanded.

"I will!"

"I don't like it, magician. Who knows what sorts of weapons the Moldorns have in those Pillars? Suppose they try something in the night, with all our men herded like goats right under their stronghold?"

"You can't make war without taking risks," the Mooncrow answered. "Besides, I'll warn you in advance if they plan another attack."

Chapter 18.
THE VEGLANE'S SOLUTION

*In politics as in war, morality is properly judged
after the fact, by the victor.*
　　　　　　　—*The Veglane Altazar,
　　　　　　　　　unpublished writings*

UNDER A flag of truce, a detachment of rebel soldiers
conducted Teron to the Moldorn lines. The magician
identified himself as a prince in the Emperor's service and
demanded immediate safe conduct to the palace. The
colonel in command of the old wall recognized Teron
from the court and provided him an escort of five
spearmen.

In their company the magician climbed the silver-
railed steps which ran straight up the imperial hill—at an
angle to the zigzagging streets. The morning was
unnaturally quiet, the stone houses and tile-roofed
mansions of the hill deserted. The inhabitants had fled,
Teron was told, to the security of the Pillars.

The magician arrived at the imperial palace and found
the Emperor in an antechamber to the Hall of State.
Prince Gildaro paced the lacquered floor, before rows of
grim-faced guards. Outside, the Imperial Council was
gathering to deal with the emergency.

Slouched on a wide divan, Bortoom seemed abnormally subdued—stunned, Teron judged, by the events of
the night and the morning.

"Bhendi," he moaned. "Where have you—?"

"Highness, I bear you a message from the Mooncrow."

Gildaro ceased his pacing.

"What?" the Emperor said.

"Before dawn, Highness, I was wakened by an invisible
disturbance so strong and intensely focused that I could
actually sense the direction of its source. I followed it,

down the imperial hill to the lower city. I arrived just as the Mooncrow was leading the slaves from the mines. He'd lured me there, Highness, that I might witness his power and report it to you."

Bortoom stared at him blankly.

"Report then," Gildaro said.

"Whether the Mooncrow's a wizard or a ghost," Teron answered, "the supernatural powers I sensed in him are incredible—more than he's yet displayed in any of his known exploits. Add to that the power of an army twenty-five-thousand strong—all of them ready and eager to do his bidding."

The Emperor gave a weak groan.

"But there's good news, Highness," Teron said. "That's the message I bear: The Mooncrow offers you the same terms of peace as before. If you will free the countries conquered by the airships, and free their peoples, he will allow you to keep your throne."

"Do you think he can be trusted, Bhendi?" Gildaro asked.

"I do, my lord. I sensed honor in him."

"What are you saying, Gildaro?" Bortoom demanded. "You don't mean we should consider surrender?"

"I mean we should at least consider it. The Mooncrow has an overwhelming position to bargain from."

"I know." Bortoom shook his head dully. "But the Pallantines would never agree. Nor Altazar."

"I believe, Highness," Teron said, "that the Mooncrow has plans of his own for the Veglane."

A trumpet sounded in the Hall of State.

"The Council's seated," Gildaro said. "Not a word of your report to anyone, Bhendi. And I strongly recommend silence to you as well, Highness."

The Emperor nodded as he pulled himself erect. With a dreary sigh and a rustle of glittering robes he trudged across the chamber and through the high golden doors. Teron and Gildaro followed. Out on the dais they took their positions behind the Emperor's ruby-crusted throne.

The Hall of State was thronged and noisy. Guildsmen and their advisors overflowed the left-hand gallery and crowded along the walls and in the corners. The

Pallantines too had come in force, many carrying weapons and wearing elaborate armor. Teron noticed with surprise that Ebbel Therion was present—seated beside Altazar's old enemy, Prince Harroman.

The Veglane was the first to speak, pacing the tessellated floor with no hint of weariness or worry in his stride. In precise, confident tones he summarized the military situation. The lords of Moldorn had just under five thousand men at their command, against an army of slaves which, Altazar said, numbered no more than eighteen thousand. The *Basilisk* had been dispatched in the early morning to summon aid. In four days the Citadel would be relieved by a nine-thousand-man garrison from Ponn-Dorqual, and seven days later by another ten thousand troops from Istria and Tuvar.

"But can we hold out that long?" one guildsman asked.

Altazar half-smiled. "With four thousand men I could hold this Citadel indefinitely against all the armies on earth."

"It's not all the armies on earth we're worried about." Harroman was on his feet, speaking in plangent tones. "It's the Mooncrow."

A storm of shouts greeted these words. Altazar waited calmly for the uproar to diminish, then replied:

"The Mooncrow is an uncommon foe, I admit. But his powers have their limits. Twice I have faced him, and each time he just barely escaped with his life. Next time he'll not be so lucky."

Cheers and catcalls competed in the hall. After a moment Altazar continued:

"Without the mine slaves the Mooncrow is but one man. And I have devised a plan to destroy the slaves."

"Another attack?" Harroman yelled. "Like the one this morning that almost wasted half the imperial guard?"

"The foray this morning was meant to test the enemy," Altazar said. "And was successful as such. But this time I intend to take advantage of our superior weaponry. My plan is to station most of our soldiers at the old wall, then to firebomb the lower city."

The Veglane paused and there was utter silence.

"The slaves will be trapped by the flames," he said. "And our troops will be blocking the one easy route of escape. I will plot the bomb patterns myself, so no one need worry that the fire might spread to the imperial hill."

"But Luiz," Bortoom said, "the people..."

"I share your concern for the populace, Highness. But according to reports, many have already left the city. Besides, the lives of a few civilians must be weighed against the gains. A bombing attack would annihilate the Mooncrow's army."

"Still,"—the Emperor looked bewildered—"to bomb our own city..."

Altazar shrugged. "We can follow my plan, Highness, or we can wait here like women for the armies to rescue us. In my opinion we should use the fire. The provincial rulers will not forget it if we show any weakness now."

"The idea is monstrous," Gildaro whispered to the Emperor. "Altazar proposes it only to evade the proper issue. It's his bad judgment which has led to all this trouble."

"I don't know," the Emperor frowned. "If we can destroy the Mooncrow's army this way..."

The Council debated the Veglane's plan all day, but adjourned without reaching an accord. Pending a decision on the following day, Altazar received permission to make ready for the attack—to align the small catapults and order the bombs carried up from within the Pillars. He told the Council these preparations would take at least twenty hours to complete.

In the late afternoon, the Veglane and Count Bartuzzi mounted to the lofty bastion over the main gate of the imperial palace—from which vantage point most of the sprawling Citadel could be viewed. Poring over maps and inventory lists, the two officers plotted the details of the bombing, and sent couriers trotting off to relay orders and check on the progress of preparations.

Finally the planning was finished. The remaining couriers were dismissed and the two men left alone on the bastion. Bartuzzi rolled up his charts.

"Now, Luiz, perhaps you'll explain to me why you told the Council it would take a day and a night to prepare for this bombing, when obviously we'll be ready in a few hours."

Altazar's lips formed a faint smile. "Isn't it obvious,

Bartuzzi? I'm going to order the attack tonight."

"Without permission, Luiz?"

"There's no risk. The Council as usual is too divided to stand against me. And I shall simply tell the Emperor the truth: I had to keep the attack a secret even from him for fear of word leaking to the Mooncrow. Bortoom will be so grateful the slaves are scattered he won't much care how it was done. Afterward, to save face, he'll have to tell the Council he did give permission beforehand."

Bartuzzi considered, then laughed. "Luiz, you amaze me. Your gift for taking charge."

"Someone has to. This whole business dragged me away from Tann at a crucial time, Bartuzzi. It may well prove costly later. But at least I'll have the satisfaction of smashing this rebellion completely." Altazar gazed down at the lower city. "Who knows? Perhaps I'll have a chance to kill the Mooncrow too.'

Teron spent the whole evening in attendance to the Emperor—fixing drugs to numb his aches and relax his nerves, applying poultices to his swollen knees and ankles, laboriously massaging his pain-wracked thighs and calves.

Bortoom grunted and whimpered and poured out his troubles: his distrust of the Pallantines and the Guildsmen, of Altazar and the army, his dread of the Mooncrow, of impending death.

When the Emperor retired to his bedchamber Teron withdrew momentarily to his own apartments, saying he needed to replenish his supply of unguents and powders.

When the Mooncrow entered the Emperor's bedchamber he carried a black bundle under his arm. The oakwood door was shut behind him by the guards outside. Teron stepped quickly across the room, to the narrow iron-screened windows where two of the Emperor's guards stood at mute attention.

Before the guards had time to react Teron pierced their forearms with two small needles he'd concealed in his sleeves. The guardsmen stiffened and one tried to rub his arm. Then both dropped to the carpet.

Teron walked back toward the canopied bed where

Bortoom watched, his jaw hanging open.

"Bhendi, what did you—?"

"A non-lethal nerve poison. They'll be unconscious for several hours."

"But why?"

"So we could talk in private, Highness." Teron picked his bundle off the floor and tossed it open on the Emperor's bed—a cloak of black feathers and a red-eyed bird mask.

Bortoom sucked in his breath.

The psithe-sword gleamed in Teron's hand. "Don't cry out."

"I—I don't believe it."

Teron pulled off his turban with a quiet laugh. "Yes, Highness. I am the Mooncrow. The same Aurik Ib Bhendi who has tended your afflictions all these months. You see, I do have redeeming qualities."

Bortoom shuddered.

"Relax," Teron said. "I'm not going to hurt you. As I mentioned earlier, I want to make terms."

The Emperor answered in a tremulous whisper. "Your terms are hard. You ask me to give up my Empire."

"Only those parts conquered by unfair advantage, Highness. Not so bad a deal when you consider the alternative."

"My alternative is to trust Altazar to beat you and your slaves."

The sword point hovered near the Emperor's throat. "No, Highness. Your alternative is to die by my hand, sooner or later. Altazar may be able to stop my army, but he'll never keep me from getting to you. For that matter, why should he even try? He is second in line for your throne, after all. Have you thought of that, Highness? I'm sure you must have. Listen, this is what I came for: I know there's a hidden mechanism that controls the iron hatches. I want you to tell me where the mechanism is and how to work it."

Bortoom grimaced and held his belly. "You're mad. Your slaves would butcher us all."

"I'm a man of my word, Highness. I'll make sure you're protected."

"Why should I trust you?"

With a turn of his hand Teron changed the sword to a cup. He began to mix a potion for Bortoom's cramps.

"Who would you rather trust, Highness, your own physician who's nursed you all day and night, or the Veglane, who openly defies your orders, who tells you to drop bombs on your own city?"

Teron offered Bortoom the psithe-cup. The Emperor eyed it hesitantly despite his obvious discomfort. The Mooncrow laughed gently.

"I'm not going to poison you, Highness."

Hands shaking, Bortoom seized the potion and gulped it down. After a moment he sighed heavily and sank back on the pillows.

"The mechanism, Highness," Teron said.

"I need time to consider, to talk it over with Gildaro. Will you give me until tomorrow night?"

The Mooncrow stretched the cup into a sword again. "Don't stall me, Highness. If you wish to confer with Gildaro, summon him now. But be sure he comes alone."

The Emperor's stammered reply was cut off by a horn blasting in the night. Warning Bortoom to stay quiet the Mooncrow darted across the room to the windows. The horn was followed by a whistle of air and a tremendous barrage of explosions. Teron's stomach lurched as he gazed through the window screens. Across the Citadel, in the glow of numerous lanterns, Moldorn soldiers were dumping bombs over parapets and firing them from catapults. The shrill noise and the thunder continued.

Teron dashed back to the Emperor, who now sat on the edge of the bed.

"You hear that, Highness? Altazar has defied you again. He's bombing the city." Teron gestured threateningly with his blade. "I've no time to waste now. Where is the mechanism?"

"It's below in the Pillar," Bortoom whimpered. "Seventeen flights down the main stairs. But the combination—I don't know it."

"You're lying."

"No. I swear, Bhendi. I can never remember it. I have it written down, hidden in my antechamber downstairs."

The Mooncrow's knuckles whitened on the sword. Even with the combination, by the time he reached the mechanism half the lower city would be in flames. The one fast way for the army to escape was up the hill. Lothar would try to storm the old wall. But the battlements would be well-manned, the iron-bound gates bolted. Teron pictured the bolts in his mind, simple bars of iron. The wand could move them.

Teron flung off his outer robes, revealing the black-feathered garb beneath. "The attack has altered my plans, Highness. You'll have a day to consider my terms after all. Consider them well; it's the best bargain I'll offer you."

The Crow wrapped himself in the feathered cloak. He decided to leave the mask with Bortoom, as a reminder. He ran to the window and smashed the lock on the iron screen with a single blow of the psithe-sword. Then he yanked back the folding screen and pushed open the casement. With one leg over the sill he paused.

"And, Highness, don't think to betray me when I return for your answer. Be assured you'd regret it."

The Mooncrow leapt out from the window ledge, transforming the sword to a wand as he fell. It was a clear drop from the Emperor's tower to the burning streets five hundred feet below. Teron plunged quickly past the main levels of the Citadel, and only then began to slow himself—drifting down between the huge, dark Pillars. Smoke flowed up, stung his eyes and choked his breath. The bombs continued to shriek and explode. Hanging on the wand Teron cringed, but bent his Norrling-trained mind to the power's flow.

Avoiding forty-foot walls of flame the Mooncrow landed on the cobblestone street. Smoke swirled all around him, and the fire emitted a constant roar—pierced at times by the wail of human voices. In the gutter near his feet a crumpled body smoldered and writhed.

The magician set off running for the hill. The wooden buildings on both sides of the curving street blazed. People fled past him, mad with fear, some with clothes or hair or flesh burning—for the Moldorn fire burst from the bombs and clung to whatever it touched. Black corpses and fiery rubble lay everywhere. Teron forced himself to keep running.

At last he neared the marketplace and found the streets there jammed with people. A sea of flame raged a block behind, advancing quickly. The bombs had by now stopped falling.

Teron fought his way through the dense, terrified crowds. Whimpers, groans and curses filled his ears. Finally he despaired of reaching the marketplace this way, and tried to levitate up the side of a building. He made it halfway, but his concentration faltered and he slipped. He saved himself by grabbing a window ledge, then smashed through the window. Climbing inside, he found a stairway that led to the roof.

Aided by the wand the Mooncrow moved swiftly over the rooftops. He reached a building next to the marketplace and stared down. The surging mob half-filled the square, but stout lines of Lothar's men kept them from overrunning the other half. In the open space before the old wall a furious battle raged—imperial guardsmen holding off a desperate assault by the rebels.

The Crow circled to a rooftop on the other side of the rebel lines and dropped down, landing hard and awkwardly on the pavement.

Along the battlefront, rows of archers fired at the Meldorns atop the old wall. The imperial troops responded with stones, darts and arrows, repelling the foot soldiers who tried to scale the walls with ropes and ladders, or to batter down the iron-bound gates with wagons improvised to serve as rams.

Teron found Lothar stalking back and forth along the line, exhorting his troops to fight harder—and threatening to whack with his broadsword any man who panicked.

The Mooncrow ran to the general. "Lothar!"

"You! You overconfident puppy." The redbeard shook his sword and his bare fist. "You said you'd warn us."

"Altazar double-crossed the Council," Teron shouted back. "The Emperor himself did not know."

Lothar glanced in the direction of the fire, then pointed his sword at the wall. "We have to get those gates open."

"I know," Teron said. "Have some men ready to storm the middle one. And don't make it obvious."

The Mooncrow scrambled forward in a half-crouch to where a party of Lothar's men futilely battered a wagon that was too light against the tall middle gates. Teron ducked beneath the wagon and ordered the men to do likewise.

"When I give the word, be ready to push," he said.

Then the magician aimed the wand at the gate and closed his eyes. He pictured the massive iron bolt, the exact points of its location. Then he focused and cast the power. Three times he swiveled the wand sideways without resistance. The fourth time his aim was perfect. The psithic force echoed back, a tugging sensation. Wincing with the effort Teron swung the wand to the left—sliding the iron bolt as well. Two seconds, three. He felt the bolt slip free of the gates.

"Now push," he shouted, and leapt to the rear to help.

The wagon trundled forward, smashed into the gates and forced them partway open. In the rear, General Lothar gave a ferocious battle-cry and led a horde of men across the pavement. They shoved the gates wide open, pushing the wagon all the way through.

At once the dazed Mooncrow was engulfed in the frenzied chaos of battle. Moldorns swarmed in from all quarters and for several moments Teron was crushed against the wagon's side. Blades and spears flashed everywhere. There was screaming and splashes of blood. On reflex Teron changed the wand to a sword. A pike thrust narrowly missed him and he stabbed back before even looking.

Then strong hands clutched his shoulders and propelled him down under the wagon.

"Stay there, damn it," Lothar yelled. "I need you alive, magician."

Teron crouched on all fours and strained to clear his mind. The battle stormed all around him. Moldorn horns wailed and echoed above the clash of steel and the groans of men.

When the Mooncrow finally emerged from under the wagon, the imperial guard was in full retreat. Lothar's men pursued them up the first of the zigzagging streets. The three gates of the old wall stood open and streams of townspeople and rebel soldiers poured through. Beyond the wall an orange glow flickered, and clouds of black smoke rose against the Pillars.

Chapter 19.
THE CITADEL UNDER SIEGE

"AND WHAT do we do *now*, magician?" Lothar demanded, when he'd returned from the top of the hill.

They stood beside the bloodstained wagon, surrounded by rebel soldiers. Leaning on his wand Teron glanced up at the cliff and the Pillar-tops.

"They'll retreat into the Citadel now," he said. "March the army up the hill. The same mechanism that works the hatches will also open the drawbridge."

"But you never opened the hatches!"

"The Emperor was about to tell me the combination. The bombing interrupted us. I'll have to go back tonight and pay him another visit." Teron spoke in a nonchalant tone, but inwardly the prospect worried him.

Lothar frowned. "Meantime we're to wait like lambs for another bombing?"

The magician shook his head. "The catapults in the Citadel are too small to hurl bombs across the chasm. And I doubt the Moldorns would bomb the escarpment anyway. Let our men and the townspeople take whatever they need from the houses up there, and try to recruit as many townsmen as you can."

"Aye, they'll join us willingly enough now, I suppose. But I still don't like waiting another whole day."

"I'm not asking you to like it, Lothar," the Crow's gray eyes flared. "It'll be light soon. I'd never make it back to the Citadel unseen. We have to wait."

Through the first dim light of morning, the rebel hordes and the surviving people of the lower city trudged in long lines up the streets and the steps of the imperial hill. Lothar walked beside Teron, grumbling in a surly voice about the Moldorn's attack and the Mooncrow's failure to give warning.

Teron ignored him, searching the crowds before and behind. Eventually he spotted Adria, and dropped back a distance to talk with her.

Adria's face and clothing were smudged by smoke, her eyes dim and glazed.

"Are you hurt?" Teron asked.

"No. Not hurt. I escaped the fire."

"Have you seen Topiedeon and Mirabelle?"

Her head shook. "I was outside when the bombing started. I just ran. I don't know what became of the others."

"Will you be all right if I go look for them?" Teron asked.

Adria nodded and continued up the hill.

The magician stepped aside and let the throng move past him. Perhaps half the mine slaves had perished, but the fire had killed even more of the townspeople. Only about eight or nine thousand had reached the hill alive. Teron searched until the grim parade of survivors had all passed. He did not see Topiedeon or Mirabelle.

He climbed the long flights of silver-railed steps and traversed the top of the cliff, still searching. Throngs of townspeople maundered on the broad paved streets, or stretched out on the open lawns. Others joined the armored soldiers and broke into the grandiose mansions, looting them of food, clothing, medicines and wine.

Teron passed beneath a silver-worked arch into a granite square that sprawled before the cantilever bridge—which now stood closed. Across the chasm the black and gray Citadel loomed against a dingy sky. A few dozen soldiers were posted in the square. Teron found Topiedeon at the edge of the escarpment, leaning on a spear.

"Topiedeon, I've been looking for you. But why the spear? I thought you promised Mirabelle you'd take no part in the fighting."

"Mirabelle is dead. She died in the fire."

Teron stared at the minstrel, benumbed. He saw now that Topiedeon's hair and beard had been singed, his face partly scorched.

"The tavern was hit by the first round of bombs. Mirabelle was caught in the cellar. I heard her screaming. But the floor caved in before I could get to her."

Teron put a hand on his friend's shoulder.

Topiedeon's jaw trembled as he gazed at the Pillars. "Who would've believed they'd bomb their own people, Teron? Their own people. Such men should not live. That's why I've joined the army now. I can no longer abide their existence."

"I understand," Teron said. "I promise you, Topiedeon, they won't escape us. This time we'll finish them."

But as he turned to leave the minstrel, the magician wondered if he'd be able to keep his promise—without a wide swing of his luck to help.

In the family palace of House Altazar, in a wide, high-vaulted and silent dining hall, Count Bartuzzi sat alone at a long rectangular table. He sipped a bowl of pheasant soup, the first course of his luncheon.

Two slave girls in low-cut bodices flanked Bartuzzi's chair. A Gashoon with a scimitar guarded an oaken door at each end of the hall. Otherwise the dim and sparsely furnished chamber was empty.

Then the door at one end opened and Altazar strode through. He crossed the wide carpet and took the place at the head of the table, next to Bartuzzi.

"The Council's over so soon?" the count asked.

"The Emperor's not feeling well so we adjourned early." The Veglane looked at one of the slave girls and ordered his meal—venison, white bread, chilled Istrian wine.

"How did it go?" Bartuzzi inquired.

"About as expected." Altazar evinced minor irritation. "The Guildsmen waxed wrathful because their mansions are being plundered. Some of the Pallantines complained that the air stinks and the smoke has stained their linen. Harroman, of course, pointed out that the lower city rabble will probably join the slaves now."

"Was the Crown Prince sitting with Harroman again?"

Altazar nodded. "Did Yvonn manage to report to you while Ebbel was at the Council?"

"No. I expect she'll come this afternoon, though. Did the Emperor back you on the bombing attack?"

"Of course. He had no other choice." The Veglane frowned. "Yet when I talked with him about it prior to the

Council I sensed he was hiding something from me. Later I realized that the Indusian physician was absent. And the man didn't even appear later, when Bortoom felt so ill he had to leave the Hall of State."

Bartuzzi chuckled over his soup. "Come now, Luiz. You're not going to add the Indusian to your list of worries."

"I've always been wary of the man," Altazar said, as a gold platter was set before him.

The Veglane carved his meat into tiny peices, which he chewed thoroughly and rinsed down with sips of the pale Istrian wine. Bartuzzi was savoring his fourth course—wild boar cooked with pears and melons—when a distant door opened and Yvonn the Khesperian woman entered. She walked quickly to the table and bowed—red hair, scarlet gown, white-powdered face. Altazar ordered the two slave girls away before questioning the spy.

"Your master and Prince Harroman are sitting together in Council these days. What are they talking about, Yvonn?"

"My lord, I bring you information that is worth more than enough gold to buy my freedom," she said. "Harroman has been scheming against you for some time, but after your bombing of the lower city he's decided on drastic action. He plans to murder you, milord, tonight. He and Ebbel left the palace a short time ago, to try and gather more support from the Pallantines and Guildsmen."

Altazar and Bartuzzi exchanged alert, high-browed glances.

"Do you know how the murder will be attempted?" the count asked.

"They spoke of that only vaguely," Yvonn said. "They're dining together this evening in Ebbel's apartments. I think they'll make the final arrangements then."

"You've done well," the Veglane said. "I am deeply in your debt. But for now you'd best return to the palace, before you're missed."

Yvonn's white forehead wrinkled. "I hoped you would not send me back, milord. Ebbel looks at me suspiciously these days. I fear one of the women may have told him of my absences."

"All the more reason why you must return now," Altazar insisted. "If he finds you gone he's sure to know you've been spying. There are great prizes at stake, Yvonn. When the game is won you will be generously rewarded. But in the meantime you must play according to my commands."

The woman stared at him a moment, then bowed her head. "Very well, milord." She crossed the chamber, red slippers making no noise on the carpet.

"So Ebbel's finally taking an interest in politics," Bartuzzi observed, staring at his beer. "And Harroman has decided to go for blood."

"We might have expected it," the Veglane said.

"To gamble everything on an assassination attempt? Harroman's always seemed more cautious than that."

"The Pillars are under siege and a tottering coward sits on the throne," Altazar replied. "In times of instability, ambitious men take chances."

"I imagine they'll strike with blades," the count said. "How do you intend to meet them?"

"I'm not thinking in terms of defense. I too am ambitious."

"What do you have in mind, Luiz?"

Altazar picked up his table knife and traced its point on his platter. "The situation offers an excellent opportunity to be rid of the Crown Prince once and for all. We will catch Harroman and Ebbel at dinner tonight and slay them both."

Bartuzzi's pupils grew wide. "Assassinate the Emperor's son? And without even evidence against him other than the word of a bed-slave?"

The Veglane gestured with his knife. "We own the lieutenant of the guard in charge of Ebbel's chambers, do we not?"

"Yes."

"Then we will require the lieutenant and three of his men to help us. As for dealing with the Emperor afterward, there's a simple and flawless solution: We blame the murders on the Mooncrow."

The count nodded slowly. "I take it then there can be no witnesses."

"Including the lieutenant and his three men," Altazar said.

"Does it also include Yvonn, Luiz?"

"I'm afraid it must."

Bartuzzi sighed. "A pity. I would have liked to try her out at least once."

Teron awoke in an overstuffed featherbed. He lay motionless, nerves taut, sensing with sureness he was not alone.

The gilt and satin bedchamber, which belonged to an extremely wealthy merchant, was dark and silent like a lavish tomb. Heavy velvet drapes covered the tall windows. The scent of stale roses hung in the air.

A footstep sounded to the left, a rustle on the fur carpet.

The Mooncrow sprang from the bed, sword held high and glittering. He halted just as quickly. The bluish radiance of the psithe illuminated a blond head.

"Adria."

She let out her breath with a tremble. "I thought you were going to kill me."

"I always try to look first." Teron lit a candle with the gleaming saber point. "What are you doing here?"

"Lothar sent me to wake you. It's nearly nightfall." Adria glanced down at his unclothed body—gray-skinned and scarred from his battles with the Moldorns.

"Why did he send you?" Teron demanded.

She cast her eyes to the floor, then confronted him with a steady gaze. "He wanted me to tell you something. I've accepted his protection. He wanted me to tell you because he's afraid of your magic."

"I once warned him to leave you alone on pain of dismemberment," Teron said. "But if it's what you wish, Adria."

Her head tilted up. "He'll treat me well. And it's better than being passed among the common soldiers."

"Then you don't wish it?" Teron asked.

"Yes. I do. I've been without a man a long time, and Lothar desires me, thinks me beautiful. I do wish it."

"Then it's not my concern." The Mooncrow returned to the featherbed.

Adria followed him. "Teron, after you stole me from Ebbel's castle, I thought for a while that you and I might become lovers again. I don't think I would have minded. But you never tried."

"There were many things on my mind."

"Is that the only reason?"

The magician's eyes seemed to stare inward as he puzzled over the question. Abruptly the answer came to him: Rania was the one he wanted; Rania alone.

"There's someone else," he muttered. "I didn't even know it until now."

"I see." Adria gave a faint smile. "I'm glad, Teron. I thought perhaps you despised me."

"No." The Mooncrow frowned. "Of course not."

"I'm glad." She stared at him a moment longer, candlelight and shadow wavering on her face. Then, "Lothar's waiting for you," she said.

The Mooncrow slid lower on the pillows. "Tell him I'm not leaving until almost midnight. I must try to catch the Emperor in bed. Meantime I'll be in bed myself. Good night, Adria."

"I'll tell him," she said. She blew out the candle and departed from the chamber.

Teron stared at the dim glisten of gemstones inlaid in the ceiling and thought of Rania. An appreciable irony—that a Norrling adept who knew himself so well in most things, could in this be so ignorant. And that the feelings should surface now, when he was about to make a final assault against the Moldorns... Rania was promised to Altazar: one more reason why the Mooncrow could not bear to fail.

The Infanta was observing the moonrise when she heard the first distant screams of the women. She looked down from her observatory tower, and spotted a flurry of motion in an upper-story window of her brother's apartments. The first screams were echoed by others.

Rania swung the telescope around and stared intently—through a broad, open casement and into a luminous chamber. One of Ebbel's concubines was caught and stabbed through the breast by an armored man with a saber. Behind him another guardsman slashed the throat of a servant. Rania's hand shook on the telescope, but she steadied it and kept watching.

Three more armored men, spattered with blood, moved past the window. Rania recognized one of them—the Veglane Altazar. The clamor of screams and shouts continued. Then Rania glimpsed her brother as he fled shrieking past the window. But next moment the Veglane yanked Ebbel back with a handful of curly hair, and sliced off his head with a rapid sword stroke. Ebbel's body collapsed on the floor, gushing blood.

The Infanta shuddered and bent over, gagging. Bintah, the pet klurri, meowed with alarm at her feet.

By the time Rania could raise herself the shouting had ceased in the chamber. The telescope revealed only the still, gory bodies on the floor.

Rania stood up and for a moment gazed blankly at the telescope. The black klurri rubbed against her ankles and she glanced down. Then suddenly she whirled and ran from the balcony.

It had come to her all at once, through the fog of shock and sickness. She had to warn her mother and father.

Barefoot, Rania hurried down the winding steps of the tower. At the bottom she fled past the sentries—fearing they too might be Altazar's men, waiting to kill her. The corridors and marble stairways flashed in a blur through her mind.

Dazed and panting, she reached the Emperor's tower at last and entered his round antechamber. But gazing past the rows of silent guards and servants, she saw that the Veglane was already present.

Altazar stood before a velvet divan, his armor and clothing splashed with fresh blood. Upon the divan sat Rania's parents, staring aghast at the Veglane. Gildaro stood to the side, arms folded and face pale.

"I heard the screams of women," Altazar was saying,

"while touring the outer walls of the palace. I hastened at once to the Crown Prince's apartments. But the Mooncrow had already struck."

"He's lying," Rania declared in a loud, quavering voice. "He killed my brother, and all his women."

All the eyes in the chamber turned to her.

"Look!" she cried. "Isn't he covered with blood?"

The Veglane answered in a cool and level voice. "When I reached Ebbel's apartments, Highness, four guardsmen barred my way. The Mooncrow must have bewitched them. Together with Count Bartuzzi I slew the four guards. But by then the Mooncrow had escaped."

"He's lying," Rania wailed.

Unez came and embraced her daughter. "It's all right, child. Hush."

"But I saw him, through my telescope."

"The assassin left this note behind." Altazar took a bloodstained parchment from inside his baldric and read: "'Men and women, masters and servants, all in the Citadel soon will perish. The final hour draws near. Mooncrow.'"

He offered the note to Bortoom, who waved it away with a timorous gesture. Instead Gildaro took the parchment, and examined it closely.

"This note could be a forgery," he declared. "I suggest we compare it to the Mooncrow's earlier ones. Meantime, Highness, perhaps we ought to keep the Veglane under guard, just to make certain."

Altazar's black eyes narrowed. Slowly he drew his sword. "Have me arrested, Highness, and I will break this blade over my knee and resign my post. Subjected to such an indignity I would gladly return to the ranks of the Pallantines, and let you find another to save you from the Mooncrow."

Bortoom wiped his brow. "Please, Luiz, stay calm."

"Father, don't trust him," Rania pleaded. "He killed Ebbel. I saw him do it through my telescope. Why don't you believe me? Why should I lie?"

"I do not accuse the Infanta of lying," Altazar answered. "I've already said I was in the chamber, and that I fought with the guards. The scene was one of carnage and confusion. Her Highness was understandably upset."

"I know what I saw," Rania sobbed, trying to break from her mother's arms. "You killed my brother."

The Veglane shrugged. "Then, too, we must remember the Mooncrow's a master of illusions. It may be that the Infanta saw exactly what the assassin wished her to see."

The Emperor raised his head and nodded. "Yes. That could be it. That must be it."

Gildaro said, "Highness, I wouldn't be too hasty—"

"Silence, Gildaro!" The Emperor stood, his huge form quivering. "Should I trust the Veglane, who's served me loyally all these years, or the Mooncrow, who's murdered my son?"

"But Altazar murdered him," Rania moaned.

"Quiet, damned girl. You're bewitched. You don't know what you're saying. Unez, take her back to her rooms. And be sure she's well-guarded. The Mooncrow will butcher us all before he's through."

Bortoom approached the Veglane and gripped his arm. "Luiz, you must protect us. I never meant to arrest you. You *must* protect us."

Gildaro cast his eyes to the floor.

"Rest easy, Highness," Altazar said. "I recommend that you place the palace under my personal supervision."

"Don't trust him," Rania cried in despair, as Unez and a servant-woman tried to lead her away.

"Yes, Luiz. I'll do whatever you say," the Emperor declared. "But I must tell you, the Mooncrow, he is Bhendi, my former physician. He came to my tower last night, and he said he'd return."

As Rania was led weeping from the chamber, her father was telling Altazar about the secret mechanism that opened the hatches and the bridge.

Chapter 20.
FURY ON THE STAIRS

NEAR MIDNIGHT the Mooncrow departed from the rebel camp on the escarpment. Clad in the Norrling costume he descended the numerous flights of steps, the feathered cape rising in his wake. At the base of the hill he waved a hand to the rebel sentries at the old wall, and passed in silence through the open middle gate.

Teron marched alone down the wrecked, smoldering streets of the lower city. The dense air hissed and reeked of decay. Charred, twisted bodies littered the winding streets. With a twinge the magician recognized the ashy ruins of the Smiling Serpent, where Mirabelle lay entombed.

Two blocks farther Teron stood at the huge, smoke-stained base of the central Pillar. Staring upward, he observed the wink and glow of sentries' lamps across the Citadel. Reaching the Emperor's tower would not be easy.

The Mooncrow leaned on the wand and removed his boots. The iron hatches sealed the interiors of the Pillars to one man as well as to an army. Teron would have to climb the outer surface. He took a running leap, flung his mind-force into the wand and began—bare feet clambering over the blackened masonry.

The magician scaled the first hundred feet, then rested, perched on a narrow ledge that marked an air vent. He'd been prudent enough to rest fully, to practice meditations and chanting when he could no longer sleep. Now his mind was clear and alert, his whole being vibrant with that intensity and single-mindedness which the Norrlings considered the wizard's optimal state. Whatever the outcome of tonight's adventure, Teron would not fail for lack of a supreme effort.

Resting at every chance, the Mooncrow continued to climb, a silent and shadowy figure invisible against the

vaster darkness of the Pillar. At last he reached the iron
corbels beneath the Pillar's main level. Lightened by the
wand he scrambled up and over a dimly lit esplanade—
painfully aware that being spotted there meant quick
alarm horns, flare lights, arrows.

But two seconds later he dropped from the esplanade
to the dark corner of a palace garden. From there he
scaled the walls and lower roofs, reached at last the upper
roof, then the Emperor's stout tower.

Teron ascended to the window of Bortoom's bedchamber and crouched on the narrow ledge. Peering inside he
saw the Emperor lying in bed, eyes open and anxious. No
guards were posted in the room, and the lock Teron had
burned from the iron screen the previous night had not
been replaced. Either the Emperor was planning to
welcome the Mooncrow, or to trap him.

Wondering which, Teron pulled open the casement
and slid aside the folding screen. The Emperor drew in his
breath and stared as the Mooncrow slipped into the
chamber.

"Greetings, Highness," Teron said softly.

He was halfway across the room when a sudden noise
made him look up. A wide metal net was falling from the
high ceiling. The Mooncrow leapt aside as doors flew
open and flare lights blazed. He rolled free of the net, only
to be swarmed under by a rush of imperial guards.

Teron tried to fight free, but strong arms clutched his
limbs and held him down. His hand was twisted back and
the wand torn from his fingers. A spear butt struck him
hard in the head.

"Beat him soundly, but don't kill him," the Veglane's
voice commanded.

The magician writhed and clawed as fists and spear
shafts battered him. His hooded cloak was yanked away.
Then a hand grabbed his hair and smashed his head back
several times on the floor. Pain and insensible blackness
flashed back and forth in his brain.

The Mooncrow was hoisted up and dragged. He
blinked and through a haze saw Altazar standing above
the Emperor, who sat at the edge of his bed.

"We should kill him at once, Luiz," Bortoom declared.

"No." Altazar peered closely at Teron, his eyes kindling with triumph. "Just as I thought. Without the mysterious weapon he's an ordinary man—powerless. And I shall hold the weapon."

"But Luiz—"

"Don't be concerned, Highness. He'll die soon enough. He'll suffer the traditional fate of assassins—the condors."

Teron's wrists and ankles were bound with shackles. Face swollen, eyes narrow, he stared balefully at the Emperor.

"You've betrayed me, Highness. But you're not finished with me yet."

Bortoom's hands were on his belly. "Please, take him away."

"To the dungeonkeep," Altazar said.

Four guardsmen carried the unresisting Mooncrow from the chamber. At least a score of men made up the detachment which conveyed him from the Emperor's tower. Altazar led the way, both hands clasping the psithe-wand.

Teron relaxed his muscles, slowed his breathing, waited for his head to clear. Then he focused his mind and started reaching for the psithe. At this small distance he could change the psithe's shape by mental command. But changing the wand to disk or sword would do no good, since Altazar would still hold the physical manifestation. Only the fifth attribute, the intangible energy-shape which his mind could draw to itself—only the quinteer— offered a chance of escape. Though recollections of the manhead made Teron loath to take that chance, he wasted no time hesitating. Instead he poured his will across the few feet of space to where the wand traveled in the Veglane's hands.

The party was traversing a long clerestory hall when the wand began to shimmer and flash. Altazar jerked to a halt and whirled to look at Teron. In a silent burst of light the wand disappeared.

"Hold him," the Veglane roared.

Eyes shut, Teron perceived the psithic energy rushing at him in a wave of multicolored light. When the wave

engulfed him he was seized by a vast, awful shudder, a
crawling of the flesh. In that moment he felt the
loathsome, unmistakable presence of the manhead, felt
the entity tearing free of him—and vanishing. Next
moment the shudder had passed and Teron experienced
the familiar merging of life-force and psithe.

In the bird's body he wheeled and darted—past the
clutching arms of the guards who'd held him.

"Slay him," the Veglane yelled.

But the nimble bird avoided the swat of blades and the
thrust of spears. With a high-pitched cry he flew past the
Moldorns and through an open window.

Thrashing his wings furiously the Mooncrow soared
into the cool darkness. Alarm horns blasted below him
and soon echoed across the palace. Teron flew to a
pinnacle of the upper roof and perched himself there,
overlooking the entire Citadel.

The manhead had exerted no influence on the
bird-form. Nor could the magician sense the entity's
presence anywhere within his being. Apparently the
manhead had used the quinteer bond to cloak itself in
energy and then escape to the outer world. How long it
could exist without a physical form Teron did not know.
He would have to guard the psithe carefully in moments
of transformation, lest the entity seize it again. Beyond
that the Mooncrow did not think about the manhead.
Other problems claimed his attention.

No hope now that the Emperor would help him
willingly. And since the Mooncrow was loose, Bortoom
would be strongly guarded. Teron considered whether
anyone else in the palace might help him. Ebbel Therion
would surely know the master combination, and there
was a small chance that Rania might.

Teron flew from the pinnacle, glided over roofs and
courtyards, and drew near the Infanta's apartments. He
landed on the window ledge of her bedroom and gazed
past the iron screen.

Bright lamps glowed in the chamber. Rania sat on the
bed hugging her knees with a bleak, woeful expression.
Teron resumed his human shape. He made the psithe a
wand and tapped it on the windowpane.

In a moment Rania came to the window holding a lamp. Teron had opened the casement and he spoke to her through the screen.

"Don't be afraid, Rania."

"Bhendi!" She glanced at the door, then put a finger to her lips. "There're two guards just outside."

"May I come in?" Teron whispered.

"Yes. Altazar took the key, but I've another one hidden."

Rania set down the lamp and hastened from the window. Teron decided to wait for her, though he could have burned the screen open with his sword. In a few moments she returned with a small key, unlocked the iron screen and quietly pulled it aside. Teron slipped feet-first into the chamber.

"My father said you were the Mooncrow, Bhendi. I wasn't sure I believed it until now." Then Rania winced as the lamplight gave a clear view of his face. "You're hurt."

"More embarrassed," Teron replied. "Why should Altazar have the key to your window screen?"

"He's in charge of the palace now. Didn't you know?" Rania folded her bare arms. "He killed Ebbel this evening, and blamed it on you. My father believed him."

"So that's why the Emperor turned against me," Teron muttered. "Rania, I need your help."

"What can I do?"

"I know there's a hidden mechanism that opens the hatches and the drawbridge—"

"My father told Altazar about that too. It'll be heavily guarded."

The Mooncrow frowned. "It's still the only chance. I need to know exactly where it is and how to work it."

Uncertain, Rania glanced out the window. "You want me to help you open the bridge for your army. But how can I be sure they won't slaughter everyone in the Citadel?"

"No one who doesn't fight us will be harmed," Teron said. "Those are the orders I left the army."

Rania's head shook. "I'm not sure I can trust you. Bhendi I would have trusted, but now I learn he never really existed. I don't even know your name."

"Teron," he said. "And think about the alternative, Rania. Unless you help me Altazar wins. And who will stop him after this?"

For moments the Infanta searched his eyes with a dark, questioning gaze. Finally she nodded. "Very well, Teron, I'll trust you. I do know how the mechanism works. My father showed it to me a few years ago, at the same time he showed me the hidden passageways. He was angry at Ebbel and did it to mock him. I wrote down the combination among some notes."

She walked to a large desk and began to shuffle through the cluttered drawers. "The mechanism's complicated to explain. It'll be easier if I go with you."

The Mooncrow shook his head. "Too dangerous."

"I'm not afraid. And I may help you get past the guards."

"The guards don't worry me," Teron replied. "But there's another enemy I might meet."

"Who?"

"No time to explain. Or to argue. I'm going alone."

Rania shrugged. Presently she found the right parchment and tore off the piece on which the combination was written. "I'll explain as best I can. The mechanism is seventeen flights below the level of the palace, on the main Pillar steps. There's a jutting stone on the landing, with a hidden switch under it. The switch works a device that opens the wall and reveals a secret alcove. The mechanism is inside—nine levers attached to chains. Each lever must be pulled down until a certain number of links are exposed. The same combination opens both the hatches and the bridge:"—she read from the parchment—"four links, then three, then seven, then four three six, then five three eight."

Teron repeated the numbers and fixed them in his memory. Rania offered him the strip of parchment, but he took her hand instead.

"If I prevail tonight, I promise you won't regret helping me."

Her fingers tightened on his. "Good luck, Teron."

The Mooncrow started for the window, but Rania grabbed his wrist. "Wait. There's a passageway that will lead you down below the palace. I doubt it'll be guarded."

She led him to a corner of the room and slid open a narrow panel—revealing a low, dark corridor.

"At the end of the passage are stairs. Take the downward flight, then follow the corridor to the right. Take the third staircase all the way down. It ends on the main Pillar stairs six flights below the gate, so it's eleven flights more to the mechanism. I'll get you a candle."

"No need," the Mooncrow said. He glanced back across the room. "Be sure you lock the screen, in case they search for me here."

"Don't worry about me, Teron. Just go."

The Mooncrow looked at her a moment more, his gray face drawn and anxious. Then he turned, bent low and hastened down the passageway.

At last the manhead was free of the magician. It had been captive a long time, helplessly bound to the one it hated.

But the manhead was crafty. It had bided its time, waited for the opportunity. And when the chance came it did not hesitate.

The manhead had stolen an instant's worth of the psithe's energy—enough to break free of the magician. Now, a sentient energy-form, the manhead moved invisibly through space and matter—passing like a ghost through the palace walls and floors.

Each instant its energy diminished, wasted on the air. But soon this would no longer be a problem. Soon the manhead would possess a body.

There had been much time for planning. In their last encounter the magician had known victory, but only because his physical form was stronger. This time the manhead would possess a different body—one that none could match in size or power. The manhead had found an image of such a body in the magician's memory. Better still, the body was dormant; it contained no living will to resist the manhead's will. The manhead knew exactly where this perfect body was to be found.

The entity descended to a dark hall near the bottom of the central Pillar, where artifacts from ancient times lay encased in steel and glass. The manhead glided to the end of the hall and hovered above a case containing a blue-skinned body eight feet long. The entity passed through the case and settled into the artificial flesh.

The blue eyelids flicked open, red eyes gleaming with unnatural life. Arms stirred, moved up, testing the glass, then pushing through. Air rushed in. The manhead breathed. With a grunt it started to climb from the case, lost its balance and tumbled to the polished floor. Innumerable sense impressions streamed into its consciousness.

Time passed before the manhead could sort out the senses and control the movements of the body. First it stood falteringly, then walked about on unsteady legs. To test its strength it lifted the huge cases and smashed them on the floor. At last it felt ready.

The manhead crossed the hall in great loping strides and tore the door from its hinges. Soon the entity found the zigzagging stairs and began to climb them, five at a time.

At first the manhead sensed the magician's presence far above. Then it could feel that its enemy was moving closer—coming down the steps to meet it. The manhead was full of joy. This was as it should be. Tirelessly, the creature continued to climb.

Seventeen flights beneath the level of the palace the manhead encountered eight Gashoons, whom Altazar had set to guard the mechanism. The Gashoons were slow to draw their blades—fear and incomprehension slowed them.

The manhead waded into the guards with murderous fury, swiping them aside with its fists, flinging bodies down the stairs and against the walls, crushing others underfoot. Scimitars bit its limbs, but pain meant little to the artificial body. In less than a minute the Gashoons were all dead or maimed beyond fighting.

Towering above them the blue-skinned creature glanced about. Then its red eyes gazed up the stairs. The magician was drawing even closer. The manhead eagerly resumed its climb.

•   •   •

Rushing down the iron stairs, Teron heard screams and the tumult of a battle. He paused an instant, scowling doubtfully. Then, sword in hand, he plunged on down the steps.

Two flights lower the Mooncrow rounded a corner and abruptly flung himself back—barely escaping the grasp of sinewy blue arms. Teron's feet slid out from under him. His stomach cringed. He knew at once it was the manhead.

The creature roared and grabbed for the magician. Teron swung his blade wildly and tried to wriggle away. A huge hand closed on his ankle and dragged him back. Teron gave to the sword lethal heat and plunged it into the monster's belly. But the unliving flesh took the blade an inch and no more.

The Mooncrow made himself limp as the manhead caught him up in a bear hug. If his Norrling-trained body had not been abnormally pliant the creature's embrace would have snapped his spine at once. Instead the manhead snarled and tightened the pressure, bending Teron almost in half. In agony the Mooncrow stabbed at the creature's head and neck. The edges of his vision blinked with stars.

Suddenly Teron changed the sword to a wand and thrust the tip under the creature's jaw. His mind was near blacking out but he forced it to focus and feed the psithe power. The wand pushed the monster's head back.

The manhead yowled like a dog and staggered to the rear. Still it maintained its crushing hold. Teron pressed harder on the wand, grunting with exertion and pain. Locked together, the two bodies stumbled back to the edge of the landing.

Teron put his whole strength into a violent, wrenching twist. The manhead tottered on the edge and fell—losing its grip on Teron as its arms flew instinctively back. The huge body bounced and crashed down the steps. But the wand allowed the Mooncrow to turn in the air and land, unsteadily, on his feet.

Grimacing with pain, Teron looked to the manhead, which sprawled across the landing, momentarily stunned. The Mooncrow sprang on the creature before it could rise. He set the wand over the throat and pushed it down with all the strength of his arms and mind.

The manhead's eyes bulged. It lay hands on the wand and tried to lift it. But the psithe's power was stronger than artificial thews. The manhead gagged and spit, struck at Teron with its fists. The magician endured the weakening blows. Gray eyes blazing, he forced the wand deeper into the rubbery blue flesh.

A scream rattled in the creature's throat. The manhead cast itself out from the artificial body and sought to enter the magician's again.

But this time Teron expected the tactic and shielded his body with walls of energy flung from his mind. In a mental flash he perceived the manhead, caught in the open space between the two bodies. Teron's will reached out and seized the entity, surrounding the spark of energy it still retained.

The Mooncrow's face took on a fearsome look—teeth bared, eyes squeezed shut. Cordavius' words: "annihilate it with your mind." Teron tightened the pressure of his will, squeezed harder and harder and harder as the manhead shrank. At last he heard in his brain a faint, shrill cry, and felt the last motes of energy flicker into nothingness.

Then, slowly, the magician relaxed his mind and body. Dizzyness swarmed though his head and each breath brought jagged pain to his back. Leaning on the wand he climbed halfway to his feet. But then the darkness overtook him and his eyes rolled back and he was falling.

The Mooncrow collapsed on the landing and lay motionless. One flight higher a detachment of Moldorn soldiers stared down at him warily, steel-headed pikes leveled and ready.

Chapter 21.
RANIA SAVES THE MOONCROW

...for no bond, natural or mind-engendered, is stronger than that of a perfect empathy between two sentient beings.

> —The Humble Book of Exquisite
> Wisdom (The Emerald Book)
> *Norrling Year 1640*

FIRST TERON became aware of his breathing, soft and faraway.

So the manhead hadn't killed him after all. Spirit still resided in mortal shell.

But he could not feel through the channels of the body. It seemed his being had plunged into trance—to recuperate from the combat. Teron stirred himself, began the slow, blind ascent back to consciousness.

After an indeterminate time he heard voices, muffled and indistinct. He groped toward them in the darkness.

A pungent stench burned behind his nose.

The Mooncrow snorted and choked. A fit of coughing shook him awake with stabbing pains.

"He's coming around." The voice was Count Bartuzzi's.

"Excellent," the Veglane said.

Teron's eyes blinked open. Foul yellow smoke curled into his face. He twisted aside, gasping.

"Enough," Altazar said. The smoke went away.

Teron looked overhead. He was chained, shoulder and thigh, to a low-arched ceiling, tilted forward to the floor. His feathered shirt was torn to shreds, his torso splotched with dark bruises.

A yard below stood Altazar and Bartuzzi, and a gray-cloaked old man—a leech—holding a bowl that emitted the yellow smoke. Behind them towered four Gashoons with torches. A wooden stair descended from

191

the ceiling: the chamber was an oubliette.

"I'm happy to see you're still alive," Altazar said.

Teron's eyes settled dully on the Veglane.

"I feared the giant might have slain you—as you apparently slew it. I hear it was quite a battle. All of us are perplexed as to how the artificial man suddenly came to life."

Teron answered hoarsely, "These are restless times."

Bartuzzi gave an uneasy laugh. Altazar said:

"In any case, I'm glad you survived, Mooncrow. Now you can be fed to the condors at dawn, in full view of your mutinous slaves. A living, screaming victim is always more impressive."

"I shall try to be as unentertaining as possible," Teron said.

"No matter," Altazar rejoined. "You'll be ripped to pieces just the same. I'm afraid your slaves will be demoralized. The more so when they notice the *Basilisk* has returned. The legions from Ponn-Dorqual and Istria and Tuvar are on the march. The Pillars will be relieved in two days. The rebellion is finished, like its leader."

Teron grimaced at a spasm in his neck. "All of us finish sooner or later, Veglane. Even you."

"I'll take my lot over yours," Altazar said. "By the way, Mooncrow, we've also discovered your accomplice, the Infanta."

Teron was quiet an instant too long before answering with a feeble laugh. "If only she had been, I could have beaten you in a week."

Altazar shook his head. "It wasn't hard to guess. Since you were heading for the mechanism you must have known the combination, and she was the only one who could have given it to you. I've just come from her chambers, Mooncrow. She's admitted helping you."

"You're lying," Teron said. "Why should she help me?"

"Why indeed?" The Veglane said. "Of course she did claim that I slew her brother last evening. That might be a reason. Then too I recall certain rumors of Rania's eh...fondness for the Emperor's physician. It seems you've tried to pilfer more than one of my prizes, Mooncrow. But don't be alarmed for the Infanta's sake. I doubt I'll formally charge her with treason. More likely I'll punish her as befits a disobedient child—after our wedding."

Teron's features remained expressionless, but his eyes brightened with venom.

Bartuzzi frowned. "Perhaps we should loose the Gashoons on him now, Luiz. Just to make certain."

"No. He'll not be spared the condors, Bartuzzi."

"He's escaped us before."

"Not this time. Look at him. He's half-dead already from the beatings he's had tonight. Besides, there'll be three men here. Even if he did become a bird, how long could he avoid their scimitars in a chamber without doors or windows?" He eyed Teron. "You have less than three hours to live, Mooncrow, that is certain. I shall return at dawn to conduct you personally to the outer wall."

Proceeded by the silent leech the Veglane and the count climbed the steps, posting three Gashoons to watch Teron and taking the fourth—the Mooncrow gathered—to guard the upper chamber. Behind them the wooden stairway rose on whining chains and rumbled as it joined the ceiling.

For a moment Teron stared at the Gashoons, their faces watchful and malevolent in the torchlight. Then the magician's eyes closed and his head sank forward.

The numbness of trance returned and Teron welcomed the deadening of pain. But his mind remained awake, the awareness of his defeat all too plain and prominent.

If he could only reach the psithe with his mind, work the quinteer from a distance. No, it was hopeless. Only high masters could control their psithes from more than a few yards away. Teron tried nonetheless—concentrated, cast his mind-force into the ether. It vanished without echo.

Finally he gave up. No chance of reaching the psithe. Perhaps he could find a way to escape without it. If he could entrance the guards by the force of his will alone . . .

The magician opened his eyes and stared sharply at the three Gashoons, reaching out to grasp their minds. The guards glowered back, muttered to one another. Presently one of them stepped forward menacingly, touched his blade-edge to Teron's nose and warned him to stop staring. The other guards laughed harshly. The Mooncrow murmured apologies and hung his head when the blade was removed.

Beaten. The Manhead had beaten him. The irony stung: to have come so close only to be defeated by an inverted image of himself, an entity without substance. Pictures of the Moldorns' trained condors sprang to mind and Teron recoiled. He wondered how much time was left till sunrise.

His failure meant the defeat of the rebels as well. Lothar, Topiedeon, Adria: death, or slavery again. And Rania left to Altazar's whims. A chill rippled Teron's spine. He hated the Veglane most of all for Rania's sake. He recalled the night she'd been flogged by the Emperor's guards, the empathy he'd felt between their two souls.

The magician's eyes opened, stared intently at the floor. Empathy. Norrlings of adept class or better commonly practiced a telepathy independent of the psithe. The key was to establish a mental bond based on perfect empathy of mind and soul.

Since the basic empathy already existed, perhaps Teron could make mental contact with Rania. And if so, maybe together they could retrieve the psithe. A miniscule hope, the Mooncrow admitted, but like the others worth trying.

Teron had no training in the telepathic technique, but he knew the basic method: to build a mental picture of the other person, an image of both appearance and felt essence; then to focus all faculties upon that image, bringing one's own energies into alignment. Norrling scripture used the analogy of two harps playing one song in unison.

Teron combined his whole sense and knowledge of Rania into a mental picture and focused, chanting her name with each even breath.

Rania: softly, an urgent, whispered summons.

Rania.

Time passed, perhaps an hour. Teron gave up hoping it would work. Still he continued—eyes shut, senses drifting. The image and chanting eased his mind.

Rania.

"Teron?"—an answer, low and distant. The Mooncrow's heart leapt to his throat.

Rania, do you hear me?

"Teron?... Where are you?" The words were clear, but with a strange resonance—thought echoed by speech.

In the dungeons below the palace. I'm sending my thoughts to you.

A flash of telepathic detail: she sank back on her pillows. "I'm dreaming."

No Rania. It's hard to believe, I know. But it's true. Do you know what became of my wand?

"Altazar has it." The echo disappeared, *Can you hear my thoughts as well?*

Yes. Where might the Veglane have put the wand?

Rania paused. *He's sleeping tonight in my father's private guest chamber. He boasted of it when he came here a while ago.* Teron felt her emotions, hatred and fright, as she recalled the Veglane's visit. *He accused me of helping you. He said it must have been I who gave you the combination, or else someone I've told it to. He threatened to accuse my uncle and my mother of treason unless I confessed. I did. But I don't trust him, Teron. He wants to kill my whole family ...*

Listen, Rania. There might still be a way to beat him.

How? Teron, I'll try anything.

Can you steal back the wand?

Perhaps. But then what?

It's a magical device with more than one property, Teron answered. *Perhaps we can work it together, use it to get you to the mechanism so you can open the bridge.*

No. Altazar had the mechanism destroyed after you were recaptured. He didn't want to take any more chances with it.

The Mooncrow's spirits plunged. But then another thought occurred: *The main bridge mechanism at the Citadel gate, it works to the same combination, doesn't it?*

My father said so. But I'd never make it out of the palace.

I might, Teron replied. *It's a thin chance, Rania, and risky, but you might be able to set me free.*

I told you, Teron. I'll try anything.

Good. First we'll need the wand.

He dimly sensed her rising from the bed. Then, in the darkness, tactile sensations: fur, and the ivory hilt of a dagger. The Mooncrow remembered her white ermine robe.

A moment later: *Teron, are you still there?*

Yes.

I'm taking the secret passageways. Altazar knows they exist now, but it's still our best chance of reaching him.

Be careful, Teron bade her.

Time elapsed and the telepathic bond grew stronger. Teron had momentary visual flashes: a candle in a silver holder moving along a narrow passage, Rania's bare feet on the stones. He clearly perceived her emotional state—fear and nervous excitement held in check by an icy determination.

We're in my father's tower now. I've set the candle down. Altazar's chamber is just beyond this wall. There should be a spyhole ... Here.

Image: an elegant bedchamber illuminated faintly by two lamps. Altazar lay in bed, eyes shut. The psithe-wand leaned against a nightstand near his head. No guards were visible, but neither was the chamber door.

Rania sighed, *Here goes.*

Fearful, Teron wanted to warn her again to be careful. Foolish idea. How careful could she be?

Image: the sliding panel into the chamber was ajar. A Gashoon stood at the threshold drawing his scimitar. From Rania: a pang of dread, fingers groping for the dagger.

Darkness.

Rania!

It's all right. I threw my knife and hit him in the neck. We were very lucky, Teron. He didn't scream, only grunted. And he slumped against the wall without much noise. Altazar turned in his sleep, but the two guards at the chamber door didn't hear.

I thought you'd been killed.

He could feel her smile. *You underestimated me again, Master Mooncrow. The guards are still facing the other*

*way. I'm going to creep around the divan and slip under
the bed*...

Teron listened to the loud thumping of her heart, felt
keenly the rough carpet under her fingers and toes, then at
last the smooth, solid touch of the wand.

I have it.

Teron sensed her crawling back the length of the bed,
and through her eyes caught a glimpse of the two
Gashoons standing outside the door. Then she was
crawling again, then running.

I'm back in the passage now. Which way?

*Down, quickly. Don't stop till you're well away from
that chamber.*

You don't need to tell me that.

Fleeting images and sounds: Rania pausing to retrieve
the candle, the rustle of her garments as she ran, the wand
seen in flickering light, flights of steps winding down.

At last she stopped, panting. *Now what?*

Sit down. You're doing fine.

*There's no time to rest, Teron. Altazar might awake at
any moment.*

*I know. But if this is to work at all your mind must be
calm.*

Very well, I'm sitting.

*Then listen. We have to see if our minds, working
together, can change the wand into a disk. I can help
shape the thoughts, but the mental energy must come
mainly from you.*

I don't understand.

*You don't have to. Just clear your mind and
concentrate on the wand. Let no other thoughts
obtrude*... *Good. Now try to imagine it not as a wand any
more, but a smooth golden disk the size of your palm.*
Teron sent to her mind the exact image. *Do you see it?*

Yes. I'll try.

Minutes flew by, Teron's mind focused, Rania's
straining to keep in focus.

It's not working, Teron.

*Keep trying. Our minds are in concert. In theory it
should work.*

But after several minutes more the Mooncrow's hopes

were dwindling close to nothing.

Then: a tingling felt through Rania's hands. *"It's working,"* she whispered. *"Fantastic!"* For an instant Teron saw through her eyes the golden form of the disk.

"Now what?" she asked, and he perceived her mouth was dry.

How long till dawn, do you think?

Not long. An hour or a little more.

We'll have to work fast.

Yes, but at what?

Invoking magic, Rania. Enough to disguise you perfectly as the Veglane.

When Rania entered the dungeon chamber, holding the psithe-disk in her hand, the Gashoon guardsman jerked to attention—perceiving her as his master, Altazar. Rania gave a brusque command that the stairs be lowered. The guard hastened to obey.

It's working, she told Teron.

They had prepared the illusion together, carefully selecting details, repeatedly projecting them into the glimmering substance of the psithe. Now their minds were focused in unison to cast the illusion. Both could feel the invisible energy emanating from the disk.

On the heels of the Gashoon Rania descended the stairs. She glanced at the three guards below and ordered them to unchain the prisoner. They bowed their heads and moved to obey.

Eyes shut, Teron felt the chains moving, hands supporting his weight.

Rania stood at the base of the steps and gazed up at his body—battered and gashed. Teron saw it through her eyes, and felt her tremble in response. Her concentration wavered and for an instant the illusion faltered.

Teron—

I know. Concentrate. Order them to lay me on the ground.

The Infanta gave the order to the three Gashoons.

Opening his eyes Teron saw the fourth guard, standing to the side, glowering at Rania with puzzlement and suspicion.

The Mooncrow felt the cold stone floor against his

back. He strained to move his limbs, deadened from the trance and the chains.

All four Gashoons looked at Rania. Her control of the psithe faltered again. So did Teron's, his mind invaded by the prickling pain of muscles returning to life.

I can't hold on.—Rania's thought, heard in his mind.

The guard farthest from Teron muttered something in the Gashoon tongue. Standing over the magician, the other three grunted and nodded. Scimitars hissed from their scabbards. The illusion had come undone.

The three guards started toward Rania, then one thought better of it and turned back to watch the Mooncrow.

"I can't hold them," Rania cried.

Teron reared his head and cast a thought to her mind. *Throw me the disk.*

An orange hand grabbed her wrist as she flung the disk away. It skimmed across the stone floor, past the two advancing Gashoons. Teron rolled over and lunged. His long fingers grasped the disk as a guardsman loomed over him, raising a scimitar.

"Halt!" the magician ordered, thrusting the disk toward the Gashoon's face.

The man snarled, but his sword arm froze in the air. Teron scrambled to his feet and knocked the blade away. Two more Gashoons rushed him now, and the fourth one struggled with Rania. Teron held the disk aloft.

"Don't move," he commanded, voice deep and wrathful.

The Gashoons fought his will, growling and straining to move. Teeth bared, the Mooncrow flung more power into the disk—and felt the guards go under, one by one.

Arms shaking, Teron moved past them, keeping the now-brilliant psithe-disk high. He removed the Gashoon's hands from Rania and gestured for her to climb the steps.

The Infanta was half-entranced herself, but the effect wore off by the time she and Teron reached the upper chamber. She pulled the lever to raise the stairs, then came and knelt beside the magician, who sat against the wall clutching his forehead.

"Are you all right?" she asked.

"Mostly dizzy. It'll pass."

"Poor Teron." She caressed the side of his face. "But we did it. You and I."

The Mooncrow smiled and touched her hair.

An alarm horn blasted overhead.

"Altazar's awake," Rania said.

Teron nodded, climbing to his feet. "And this is the first place he'll look."

"Then you must hurry."

Teron glanced at the chamber's one small window— cut in the six-foot wall and covered by grating at both ends.

"I can escape that way," he said. "But what about you? They'll find the Gashoon you killed and search the passageways. You'll be caught."

"It doesn't matter. I'm still Altazar's only link to the throne. He won't harm me."

"But you can't be sure of that, Rania." He gripped her shoulders tightly.

"You care for me, don't you, Teron?"

"Yes."

Rania smiled. "I care for you too. But this is no time to act like a lovesick idiot. You must go and open the bridge."

Another horn sounded, closer.

Eyes fixed on hers, Teron nodded.

"Hurry now," Rania said, and kissed him on the lips. "For luck."

The Mooncrow changed the psithe to its energy-form and uttered the invocation. With a silent burst of radiance the psithe expanded around him.

Chapter 22.
THE STORMING OF THE PILLARS

OUT FROM the central Pillar flew the Mooncrow, over the roofs and battlements and spires of PonnTherion—all faintly visible in the earliest predawn light.

He reached the outer fortifications of the Citadel: parapets lined with Moldorn spearmen and archers, men who'd been on duty now two days and nights. Across the abyss Teron glimpsed the rebel army, seated in ranks along the escarpment and upon the cantilever—ready to attack the moment the bridge should open. Lothar had maintained order through the long hours of waiting.

The Mooncrow swooped down toward the gatehouse, a wide bastion set above the main doors of the Citadel. Four imperial guards stood watch on the roof. The bird plunged past them, toward a line of narrow windows one story lower.

He landed on a window ledge, glanced into the chamber and gave an inward wince. At least fifteen men guarded the control mechanism. Some noticed the Crow at once, started moving for their weapons.

Teron hopped from the window ledge and snapped the quinteer bond. He materialized in human shape, holding the psithe-disk overhead.

"Behold!" he commanded, and cast his mind-force into the psithe.

A few of the Moldorns relaxed at once, eyes blanking out, shoulders slackening. The others resisted, edged forward raising spears and blades. Teron wrung out his will, forcing the dimness into their minds. The guards kept moving. Some tried to shield their eyes. In the rear two men lifted alarm horns toward quivering, taut lips.

"Be still," Teron ordered, leaning on the wall to keep his balance. More power coursed from his mind. The disk pulsed and glittered.

One by one the guards fell under. The horns dropped

unblown from the buglers' mouths. Pikeheads and swords sank to the floor.

When all the Moldorns were still, the Mooncrow dragged himself toward the controls, clutching the wall with one hand and holding the disk high with the other. Part of his mind continued to feed the psithe power. With the other part he studied the mechanism.

It was similar to the one Rania had described—nine levers attached to iron chains. Teron began pulling down the levers—4 links, 3, 7. Then 4, 3, 6...

Counting distracted his attention. Two of the Moldorns shook themselves awake and haltingly lifted their weapons.

"Look!" Teron yelled, and the psithe in his hand emitted sparks.

The Moldorns slipped back into trance. Teron counted out the last three numbers.

The master combination clicked and the huge machinery rumbled into motion. Chains rattled in the gatehouse and thicker ones down within the Pillar. Worked by a system of pulleys and weights, the spiked steel doors beneath the gatehouse swung open. The long steel slab of the bridge rolled forward and with a thunderous crash joined the cantilever.

Glancing through a window Teron spied the rebel horde—on their feet and charging. Within the Citadel, alarm horns blared.

The four spearmen from the gatehouse roof descended a curving stair into the chamber. They stared at the motionless ranks of guards and then at the Mooncrow. Teron ordered them to be still, holding the disk aloft with both gray hands. One of the men threw a spear, but missed him.

"Don't move!" Teron shouted, straining his mind against barriers of torment.

Gradually the four men succumbed.

Moments later an officer and two more soldiers entered the chamber, from below. Teron succeeded in placing these three also under trance, though his arms trembled violently and his skull felt ready to split.

The magician expected his will to buckle at any

moment, and the roomful of men to rush him all at once. His vision grew blurry. The roar and clamor of battle seemed distant to his ears.

But it slowly drew nearer, and the Mooncrow held on.

Then more armored men poured into the chamber, shouting. Teron squinted at the mass of blurry shapes—Lothar's men, striking down the Moldorns.

With a moan of relief the Mooncrow lowered his arms. But then the floor reared up and knocked him senseless.

In a steady stream the rebel army—former citizens and slaves—poured across the drawbridge and through the wide gates of the Pillars. On the battlements around the gates some three thousand imperial guardsmen met the attack. Outnumbered seven to one these Moldorn veterans fought a dogged delaying action, and sold their lives dearly, to the last man.

A mile away the Emperor of Moldorn stared down at the battle from a window of his lofty tower.

"The guard are being slaughtered," he murmured. "Soon only the Pallantines will stand between us and the slaves. We're doomed, Gildaro."

Clad in a silken nightshirt, Bortoom turned bewilderedly and moved across the round antechamber, through a throng of guards and attendants.

Prince Gildaro moved at his side. "Highness, I suggest that you order a white flag be raised above the palace. The Mooncrow might be merciful if—"

"Not after I betrayed him, Gildaro." The Emperor slumped wild-eyed into his iron and ruby throne. "We're doomed."

"Bhendi always comported himself with honor," said the Empress, who stood at Bortoom's shoulder. "I'm sure he will spare us."

"You don't understand, Unez," the Emperor cried. "Bhendi was only a role, a mask. We're speaking of the Mooncrow now, the assassin."

The voice of an attendant announced the Veglane Altazar, and the wall of spearmen to one side parted. Altazar stalked through, dragging the Infanta by the hair.

Count Bartuzzi and some twelve Gashoons followed.

"Veglane," the Empress cried. "Release my daughter at once!"

Altazar flung Rania at her mother's feet. "She deserves to be punished, woman. It was she who freed the Mooncrow and told him the combination to open the bridge."

The statement roused Bortoom from his stupor. "What? Is this true, Rania?"

The Infanta swayed on her feet, one arm supported by her mother. "The Mooncrow will spare us, father. He promised me."

"Promised you? *Promised you?!*" Enraged, the Emperor grabbed his daughter's collar and began slapping her head.

Unez and Gildaro struggled with the Emperor's arms and begged him to cease.

"I won't," he cried. "The traitorous brat's thrown away all our lives."

"There's no cause for hysterics, Highness," Altazar intervened. "The Mooncrow has won a battle, not the war."

"What do you mean, Luiz?" Bortoom let go of Rania, who fell back whimpering into her uncle's arms.

"My airship," the Veglane whispered so that only those close by could hear. "The *Basilisk* will carry us all to safety."

Bortoom's eyes brightened and he took a huge breath. "Yes. Yes, Luiz. We shall join our legions in the north and march back and retake the city."

"Precisely," Altazar said. "At the moment the crewmen are preparing the ship for flight. I suggest, Highness, that you take your family and go at once to the port-tower. Meantime Bartuzzi and I will round up the guards and deploy them for a final defense of the palace—which will give us ample time to disembark..."

"Just as you say, Luiz," the Emperor replied. "We will leave at once."

Altazar and Bartuzzi hurried off, emptying the chamber of guards. The Emperor commanded two servants to fetch him an outer robe, and ordered the rest from his presence.

"Stop frowning, Gildaro," Bortoom grunted. "If you'd rather stay and make terms with the Mooncrow, you have my permission."

The prince shook his head. "I've devoted myself too long to you, Highness, and to my sister. I will meet my fate as your servant—whatever that fate might be."

"Well, I'm not going." Rania stared defiantly at her father, hair tangled, face red and swollen.

"Quiet, you vicious brat," Bortoom growled. "Yes, I'd be glad to leave you behind to be raped by the slaves. It would serve you right. But I've promised you to Altazar and he will have you. You're coming if I have to drag you by the hair myself."

As the rebels stormed inward toward the central Pillar, Altazar and Count Bartuzzi strode the battlements of the imperial palace, stationing the guards and exhorting them to fight to the death. The gates of the palace were locked and bolted—not only against the oncoming rebels, but against the Pallantines. Many of the Moldorn lords had fled to the central Pillar with their servants and women and guards. A gathering mob, they filled the open spaces before the locked gates and cried out for asylum.

From a high parapet Altazar taunted them. "We're all to die anyway. Why not behave like men and stand where you are?"

The guards on the palace battlements laughed and jeered. The Pallantines screeched and roared curses, blaming Altazar for the Citadel's fall.

The Veglane and Bartuzzi hurried back into the palace, followed now only by the Gashoons. When they passed into the base of the port-tower, the Veglane suddenly wheeled about, slammed the door shut against the Gashoons, and bolted it.

"I was expecting that, Luiz," Bartuzzi said. "It would look ill if you saved your personal guard when so many others had perished."

"Exactly," Altazar said.

The Veglane and the count climbed the winding steps of the tower—to the upper platform, where the imperial family waited. The moveable parapets were open and the *Basilisk* sat ready to depart—the silvery curve of its gas-filled shell rising overhead.

"Finally you're here," the Emperor said. "The crewmen refused to let us board."

"I know." The Veglane drew his saber. "They had their orders from me, Highness."

At that moment Bartuzzi scooped up Rania and slung her over his shoulders. The Infanta shrieked, struck at his head with her fists, kicked at his groin, but all to no avail. Bartuzzi laughed and started up the gangplank.

"Luiz, what's happening?" the Emperor cried.

The Veglane leveled his sword. "I'm afraid, Highness, that I've decided to leave you behind."

Bortoom stammered, "But—don't be absurd, Luiz. You told me to come here."

"To separate you from your bodyguard. I feared you might order them to stop me."

"But why? Why betray *me*?"

"Because I no longer need you, and the moment is convenient. The Pallantines will all be dead. I shall return with the army and establish a whole new government. Why should I keep you alive to stand in my way?"

"But you're taking Rania!"

Altazar shrugged. "This defeat will taint my reputation as it is. But if I save one member of the imperial family, then saving myself won't be deemed so dishonorable."

"Rania will tell the truth," Unez declared.

The Veglane smiled. "I hope to convince her otherwise during our voyage to Tann. If not, I shall exhibit her to the army as one whom the Mooncrow has bewitched. Either way she'll help keep the legions loyal to me."

The ship's propellers began to whirl. Altazar saluted Bortoom with his sword, turned on his heels and strode up the gangplank.

"Don't leave us, Luiz," the Emperor pleaded. "What shall I do?"

Altazar replied from the ship's rail. "Your choice,

Highness. Take your own life like a soldier, or wait and beg mercy from the Mooncrow."

Propellers spinning, the *Basilisk* slipped from its moorings and rose into the sky.

Cold water splashed Teron awake. He wiped his eyes and forehead, glared up through one eye into a youthful, redbearded face—one of Lothar's Khesperian lieutenants.

The man lifted the Mooncrow to his feet. Teron groaned, brain and body aching.

"Sorry to wake you like this, but Lothar said to rouse you quickly. I'm to tell you at once that the Veglane's airship has escaped from the Citadel."

Teron's gray face turned ashen. Clutching his sides he staggered across the chamber. A narrow window faced the central Pillar, but the towers and walls of the Citadel jutted up and blocked his view.

"You can't see it from here," the Khesperian said. "It departed a few minutes ago, bearing north. Lothar assumes Altazar's on board."

"Of course he's on board." The Mooncrow turned back into the chamber. "I planned on all his options. But I didn't expect the airship to be back before we took the Pillars."

"Lothar said that if the Veglane escapes—"

"I know."

Teron spied the disk lying on the floor. He bent over for it, lost his balance and had to prop himself with both arms.

The Khesperian helped him up again. "Are you ill?"

"I'm fine. How's the battle going?"

"Most of the Pallantines surrendered without a fight. When I left, the outer defenses of the Emperor's palace were beginning to crumble."

"Then get back and remind Lothar that no one who doesn't resist is to be harmed. Do you understand?"

"Aye."

"Tell him I'm going after the airship."

"But you can hardly stand."

"The flight will clear my head. Go!"

The Khesperian gave a curt salute and trotted from the chamber.

The Mooncrow looked down at the disk in his palm and it bloomed into a sparkling globe. He uttered the invocation. The power stung as it passed through his brain. But the sting vanished—with all human senses—as his life-force joined the psithe.

Teron flew from a window of the gatehouse. The bird's body rose above the roofs and towers of the Citadel. Beating his wings rapidly, the Mooncrow set off in pursuit of the *Basilisk*, which dwindled in the northern sky—a black dot among the jagged blue mountains.

Chapter 23.
ON BOARD THE BASILISK

ON LEAVING the Citadel, the Veglane had proceeded first to the rear of his airship. There he checked the course and speed, and stationed aeronauts to guard the pilot house and engine compartments.

Next, Altazar traversed the uppermost of the three tiers, beneath the overhanging shell. The deck was deserted now, with the entire crew on duty. Altazar climbed two flights of steep wooden steps into the tall forecastle.

He entered his own cabin—a spacious single chamber tapering to a point at the extreme front of the ship. That narrow point was flanked by two broad casements, both open now and offering a startling view of the mountains.

Ten aeronauts stood in the cabin, armed with sabers and pikes. Count Bartuzzi leaned on a writing table and kept an eye on the Infanta, who sat upon the lacquered floor next to the Veglane's bunk. Rania still wore the white ermine robe, though her dagger had long since been seized.

Altazar acknowledged the salutes of the aeronauts. "I'll take over here," he told his cousin. "You go aft and keep watch in the pilot house. And be alert for the Mooncrow. If he's not on board yet I expect he will be."

"You may count on it, Veglane," Rania said.

"I do, Highness," Altazar replied.

Bartuzzi grinned. "Remember to treat her gently, Luiz. You're not married quite yet."

"Go," Altazar told him.

With a light-hearted laugh the count marched past the aeronauts and out of the cabin. He descended the wooden steps, rounded the curved corner and strode along the upper tier. Past the ship's rail lay the fallen Citadel, shrinking away now in the distance.

Suddenly a black bird swooped down—a strident cry

and a flash of scintillating light. Bartuzzi's saber leapt from his belt. . The Mooncrow stood before him, glimmering sword in hand.

"I've been told to watch for you," the count said.

"Where's Altazar?"

Bartuzzi was on his toes, blade circling. "Forward in his cabin. But first you'll have to pass me."

The count feinted and lunged. As Teron parried he gambled and stepped in close. Before Bartuzzi could strike again the Mooncrow leapt and with a shout kicked him high in the chest. Bartuzzi stumbled backward into the railing. Landing low, Teron darted in and shoved the Moldorn over the side.

The count's long scream faded in Teron's ears as he hurried forward along the deck. He chose to avoid the forecastle steps and instead clambered out upon the airship's prow. The huge basilisk carved there provided an adequate surface for climbing. Still, Teron slipped more than once from dizzyness, and needed the wand to save himself from falling.

At last he edged along the top of the basilisk's wing, reached a broad rectangular window and peeked into the Veglane's cabin.

The ten aeronauts stood along the far wall, two of them holding Rania's arms. Altazar sat upon the writing table, bare-chested, a dueling saber in his hand.

"Come in, Mooncrow. I've been waiting for you."

The magician gripped the windowsill and stepped deliberately into the chamber.

"Teron," Rania said. "I was sure you would come."

"As was I," the Veglane said. "You promised one day we would fence again, Mooncrow. I'm calling in that promise now."

He hopped from the table, pointing his weapon.

The wand in Teron's hand became a blade. He'd been a fool to enter the chamber at the narrow end. Altazar had expected it, had him cornered now before the fight even began.

The Crow gave a sudden yell and dashed to the left, hoping to escape the corner. The Veglane blocked him, and a blinding thrust cut Teron's shoulder. The magician lurched back, deflecting the slower second thrust.

Altazar smiled fiercely, made two quick passes and drew blood again, this time from the arm.

"In our first duel you came close to beating me," he said. "A pity you're too battered now to put up a decent fight."

"Yes. Go easy on me, Veglane."

The Mooncrow parried the next blow and riposted swiftly. Then he sprang in the air, slashed, landed in a crouch, thrust, sprang up again. For moments the practiced Norrling attack kept Altazar at bay and forced him to retreat.

But just when Teron thought he'd won free of the corner, the Veglane matched the attack, and better. His saber lanced forward in a series of murderous thrusts that cut the Mooncrow twice more and sent him reeling against the window frame.

Eyes ablaze, the Veglane gave a double feint and lunged. Baffled, the Crow did the one thing Altazar did not anticipate: pitched his body head-first out the window.

Changing sword to wand Teron twisted in the air and landed crouching on the basilisk's wing. With a curse Altazar stepped to the window and looked about. Teron aimed his blow and struck hard, thrusting the psithe-wand into the Veglane's solar plexus.

Groaning, Altazar staggered back into the narrow corner of the cabin. Teron vaulted through the window, saber flashing in his hand. Before the Veglane could raise his guard the Mooncrow lunged and ran him through.

Altazar gazed down at his spitted belly with a look of shock and disbelief. The sword slipped from his hand and rang on the wooden floor. Teron held his blade in place until he felt the life-spirit pass from the Veglane's body. Then he withdrew it and let the dead man fall.

The Mooncrow turned and stared at the line of aeronauts, who gaped at him mutely, amazed that Altazar had been beaten. Rania broke free of them, crossed the chamber and embraced Teron—gently because of his cuts.

"I knew you would win," she said.

"You knew more than me."

Trembling, Teron propped his back against the wall for support. His eyes remained fixed on the aeronauts, who'd yet to move. Rania confronted them.

"What are you standing there for? The traitor has been slain. Remove his body at once. Then find Count Bartuzzi and put him in chains."

"Bartuzzi's dead," Teron told her.

"Then go and turn the ship around," Rania commanded. "We must return to PonnTherion at once."

The airmen looked at each other, unsure and frowning.

Rania glowered at them. "I think you have two choices. You can return us to the capital and be proclaimed heroes, or fly on to Tann and explain to the imperial armies why you kidnapped the Emperor's daughter."

After another pause one man found his voice. "Highness, we're at your service."

Two aeronauts came forward, cautiously moving past the Mooncrow, and carried off the Veglane's body. When they'd gone the other eight men bowed in unison to Rania, then filed from the chamber.

The door shut and Teron lowered his saber. With a rush of numbness his overstrained mind blacked out. Next moment he found himself on the floor. Rania was kneeling beside him, cradling his head against her breast.

"Are you badly hurt, Teron?"

The Mooncrow sighed. "Just tired. The past few days have been . . . strenuous."

Laughing, Rania kissed him on the forehead, then found his lips.

A short time later the airship turned in the wind.

Chapter 24.
THE AIRSHIPS COME TO PTOLLODEN

*There can be no question that this wave of
scientific preeminence will eventually wane. Human
history continuously reflects the cosmic principle
that all things are in flux. It seems safe to predict
that in time even our own Norrling order will pass
away.*

> —The Terrestrial Histories of
> Fystus the Grackle, *Epilogue*
> *Norrling Year, 6256.*

*What became of this highly advanced culture? The
answer is shrouded in time. For reasons we'll
probably never know their technical skills declined.
The age of the airships flourished perhaps one
hundred years, perhaps five hundred. But finally
darkness and barbarism returned to northern Ibor,
and the wonderful technology vanished as
mysteriously as it appeared.*

> —Ivann Demmering,
> Anomalies of History.

ARRIVING BACK in PonnTherion, Teron and Rania were
conducted by a jubilant troop of rebels to the great hall of
the palace. There the Emperor sat in a narrow wooden
chair, surrounded by about threescore of his nobles—and
some fivescore of Lothar's men.

Rania ran and embraced her mother and uncle, who
stood to either side of the Emperor.

In front of Bortoom's chair General Lothar leaned on
his broadsword. Adria stood beside him, bright-eyed and
beaming. The redbeard greeted the Mooncrow:

"The Citadel is ours, magician. Did you take care of
that other matter?"

Teron nodded. "The Veglane is dead. Also Bartuzzi."

Lothar grinned wolfishly. "Tidings to make us all

213

rejoice. What shall we do with the Lord of the Earth
then?"

Several former mine slaves offered baleful suggestions.

Meek and trembling, Bortoom glanced at Teron. "I'll
do whatever you say, Bhendi. But you won't torture me,
or feed me to the condors?"

The Mooncrow laughed. "No, Highness, I think your
life can be spared. I'd even let you keep your throne if you
hadn't proved untrustworthy. Instead, I'm afraid you'll
have to abdicate."

The Emperor nodded. "Bring pen and paper. I'll write
whatever you say."

"Good," Teron said. "You shall name as your
successor the rightful heir to your throne, the Infanta.
And you will make it clear that whatever her future choice
as to marriage may be, the sovereign power will remain in
her hands alone."

All eyes turned to Rania.

"Is that what you wish, daughter?" Unez demanded in
a puzzled voice.

"Why shouldn't I rule?" Rania said. "Do you honestly
think I could do worse than my father?"

Gildaro chuckled. "I, for one, think it's a splendid idea."

Bortoom was already writing. "I'll put down whatever
you say, Bhendi. But a female to rule Moldorn? The
Pallantines won't like it."

The Mooncrow glanced archly about the hall. "They'll
learn to live with it, Highness. If they wish to live at all."

Topiedeon the minstrel would accept no rewards from
Teron or the new Empress. With only his mandolin and a
small purse of silver he left Ponn Therion soon after
Rania's coronation—saying the city had brought him too
much evil for him to stay. It was afterward believed he had
changed his name and resumed the life of a wandering
entertainer.

Adria stayed with General Lothar for about three
months. They parted on friendly terms. Adria was going
home to Telyrra at the head of her gathered people. In late
autumn she ascended the island's throne—taking the title
of Grand Duchess—and began the slow work of
rebuilding what the Moldorns had destroyed.

General Lothar meantime was serving in the post of Veglane under the new Empress. Lothar's first crucial duty was to deal with what remained of the expeditionary force sent to Tann. As the Mooncrow had predicted, the huge imperial army splintered after the Veglane's death—for lack of a strong leader. Altazar had always made certain that no potential rival existed among his officers. Many of the Moldorn units fell prey to vengeful Tannite armies. The rest straggled back to Ibor by land or sea or air. Lothar took charge of those legions which pledged loyalty to the new Empress, and conquered those which raised dispute.

Besides Lothar, the new imperial order included Gildaro, who remained chief minister to the throne, and also Teron, who filled the newly created post of imperial magician.

In its first eighteen months the new government made a number of profound changes. The Empire's borders shrank back to the old, pre-airship limits. Innumerable slaves were freed and returned to their homelands. Laws were rewritten, war damages paid, the military reorganized on a smaller scale.

And, by imperial command, the giant Pillars of PonnTherion were torn to the ground. The steel and building stones were used to rebuild the lower city, and to raise a new palace atop the escarpment. Of the old Citadel nothing remained but the steel cantilever jutting out from the cliff—half a bridge leading nowhere.

Nineteen months after the storming of the Pillars a squad of ten Moldorn airships sailed across the tundras of Ombernorr, and landed on the frigid plain before the High Sanctuary of Ptolloden. Fourteen hundred wizards gathered on the craggy hill, garbed in feathers and masks, holding wands and swords—ready to confront whoever emerged from the ships.

But the aircraft had come on a mission of friendship and peace. The Empress of Moldorn herself had journeyed north to pay her respects to the wizards.

Inside Ptolloden, in a huge crystal-domed chamber, Teron the Mooncrow reported the successful completion of his Deputation. Further, he asked the permission of the masters to return with his psithe to Ibor—a sort of permanent ambassador from the wizards of Ombernorr to the peoples of the Warmlands. Pleased beyond all expectations by Teron's accomplishments, the assembled masters and high masters gave their consent—though not without vigorous debate from certain factions, wizards who still objected to any interraction between Ombernorr and the other nations of the world.

Fystus the Grackle expressed different concerns when Teron and Rania paid him a visit that afternoon in the library.

"You've managed to change the political course of things for the moment, Teron. But you haven't extracted the roots of the trouble. Science still flourishes in Ibor."

The Mooncrow sighed. "It's not a weed that can be torn up and burned, Brother Fystus. If we tried to repress all the knowledge and curiosity in Ibor we'd become worse tyrants than those we've replaced."

"Maybe so. But it still troubles me, Teron. So long as science thrives there's danger."

"I know," Teron said. "But I've learned, too, that science has its worthy aspects, Fystus. It's the men in power who must be watched."

"That's why we asked your masters to establish the ambassadorship," Rania added. "So Teron and his successors can keep watch."

"A prudent idea," the Grackle agreed. "Of course in time the wave of science will run its course and the threat will fade. But in the meantime, Mooncrow, I hope you and those who follow will be wary."

Late that night, while Teron was preparing for bed, a toucan flew into his chamber. The bird changed to the human shape of Cordavius, seated with folded legs in midair, a long beaming wand across his knees.

"Pardon my visiting so late, Mooncrow. But there's something I wanted to ask you in private."

"Of course, good master," Teron said. "What is it?"

"Frankly, Mooncrow, you continue to baffle me. I had thought that by the time you'd mastered the psithe of an adept, and had lived for so long among the Warmlanders, that your fondness for the world would have faded. But you seem happier now than I ever remember. Are your sensual appetites still unsatiated? Doesn't your spirit yearn for release? Or do you find the duties of a minister of state fully satisfying?"

Teron sat down on the fur-covered bed. "I do find the duties satisfying, master. There are challenges: dissident nobles and neighboring kings to be outwitted, occasionally an assassin to frustrate. Then I have other interests: I practice with the psithe, I study and read. I'm gathering whole volumes of information which I'll eventually send to Fystus the Grackle." Teron shrugged. "Then there's the warm climate of the south, which I've always found delightful. The oceans and mountains..."

A door swung open and Rania appeared. Her black hair was unbound and she wore a flowing robe of golden fur, with a nightgown of silk and lace beneath. Seeing Cordavius she paused, uncertain. But Teron held out his hand and she came to him smiling.

"Oh, yes," the Mooncrow said. "There's one other thing that keeps me interested in the world..."

ABOUT THE AUTHOR

JACK MASSA grew up in New Jersey and graduated from New College in Sarasota, Florida in 1975. He wrote MOONCROW while attending the graduate program in creative writing at the University of Massachusetts, where he studied under novelist George Cuomo. He taught English and creative writing in a special program at the University, and received his master's degree in 1978. He is married and living now in Atlanta, Georgia—working as an editor and painstakingly assembling another novel.